Also by Carolyn Brown

What Happens in Texas
A Heap of Texas Trouble
Christmas at Home
Holidays on the Ranch
The Honeymoon Inn
The Shop on Main Street
The Sisters Café
Secrets in the Sand
Red River Deep
Bride for a Day
A Chance Inheritance
The Wedding Gift
On the Way to Us

LUCKY COWBOYS
Lucky in Love
One Lucky Cowboy
Getting Lucky
Talk Cowboy to Me

HONKY TONK
I Love This Bar
Hell, Yeah
My Give a Damn's Busted
Honky Tonk Christmas

SISTERS IN PARADISE
Paradise for Christmas
Sisters in Paradise

SPIKES & SPURS
Love Drunk Cowboy
Red's Hot Cowboy
Dark Good Cowboy Christmas
One Hot Cowboy Wedding
Mistletoe Cowboy
Just a Cowboy and His Baby
Cowboy Seeks Bride

COWBOYS & BRIDES
Billion Dollar Cowboy
The Cowboy's Christmas Baby
The Cowboy's Mail Order Bride
How to Marry a Cowboy

BURNT BOOT, TEXAS
Cowboy Boots for Christmas
The Trouble with Texas Cowboys
One Texas Cowboy Too Many
A Cowboy Christmas Miracle

Dear Readers,

There is always a bit of sadness when I end a series. By the time I finish three books, the characters have become my friends and neighbors. The seven sisters of Paradise have been with me for many years. In my mind, I've watched them grow from little girls to amazing women, but now their stories have been told, and it's time to move on. However, there is a surprise in store for all my readers that involves a spin-off series, and the sisters will be making appearances in those stories. I won't ruin the surprise now, but you get a little clue at the end of *Coming Home to Paradise*.

Until next time,

Carolyn Brown

Coming Home to Paradise

CAROLYN BROWN

sourcebooks
casablanca

Copyright © 2024 by Carolyn Brown
Cover and internal design © 2024 by Sourcebooks
Cover design by Stephanie Gafron/Sourcebooks
Cover images © Anjelika Gretskaia/Getty Images, AHS
Photography-Alex Schregardus/Getty Images

Published by Sourcebooks Casablanca, an imprint of Sourcebooks
P.O. Box 4410, Naperville, Illinois 60567-4410
(630) 961-3900
sourcebooks.com

Cataloging-in-Publication Data is on file with the Library of Congress.

Printed and bound in Canada.
MBP 10 9 8 7 6 5 4 3 2 1

In memory of Mr. B,
who was my biggest supporter for
more than fifty-seven years

Chapter 1

Nine whole days of freedom.

Bo kept repeating five beautiful words to herself—*nine whole days of freedom*—when she awoke to the smell of bacon and coffee floating up the stairs and into her bedroom. Tomorrow morning it would be the aroma of cinnamon that wafted up to her bedroom. Lots of things changed with time, but not her mother's special Thanksgiving and Christmas Day breakfast sweet rolls.

People changed. She thought of her youngest sister, Endora, and her messy breakup a couple of years before. She had always been such an outgoing person, and after she found out her fiancé and best friend were sleeping together, she went into a deep depression. Now she was engaged to the local preacher and had turned her life right back around.

Dreams change. That brought on a sigh when Bo remembered the dream she chased for ten years, and finally gave up a few months ago. She had gone to Nashville right out of high school and thought she would be the next big country star. She found out really quickly that she wasn't the only young girl in Tennessee who wanted to sing for a living. A decade later, she finally gave up and came back to Spanish

Fort and now helped her great-aunt out with her advice blog and speed-dating events business.

"What are you thinking about?" Her twin sister, Rae, peeked into her bedroom. She was wearing an oversized T-shirt from the police department, where she'd worked in Boise City, Oklahoma, for several years.

Bo sat up and inhaled deeply. "I was thinking about how things change. We can always depend on Mama's cinnamon rolls on Thanksgiving Day. That never changes."

Rae sat down on the edge of the bed. "What has changed?"

"All seven of us sisters," Bo answered.

"Amen to all of that," Rae said, "but it seems strange to have just three of us living here. Every time I've been home for the holidays, all the bedrooms were full."

"You've only been here a week," Bo told her. "It took me at least a month to get used to not having Ursula, Tertia, Ophelia, and Luna in their bedrooms."

"But we do have Aunt Bernie!" Rae giggled.

"Don't remind me," Bo groaned. "Don't get me wrong. I love our great-aunt, and she was quick to give me a job when I came home, dragging my tail behind me."

"Don't say that!" Rae scolded.

"It's the truth," Bo said with a long sigh as she threw back the covers and stood up. "All six of my sisters fulfilled their dreams. If I'd been fishing for my supper, I would have gone hungry. I didn't even get a nibble of a singing contract the whole ten years I was in Nashville."

"Crap on a cracker!" Rae fussed.

Bo whipped around and stared at her sister. "What brought on that Sunday school cussin'?"

"What you said," Rae answered. "Think about the dream we each had and look where we are now. We all couldn't wait to get away from the Paradise. Now, one by one—well, Luna and Endora came back at the same time, so that was two—we are coming home to Spanish Fort. Seems to me like we just made a big old circle."

Bo slipped a hot-pink robe over her red pajama pants and matching shirt. "Kind of like that Rascal Flatts song about God blessing the broken road."

"Yep, only this isn't a boy-comes-home-to-girl song," Rae said with a nod. "It's a girl..." She paused.

"It's seven girls coming home to find happiness," Bo finished for her. "And the last two—that's me and you..."

Rae laid a hand on her sister's shoulder. "Are going to have to run from Aunt Bernie's matchmaking."

"You got that right." Bo nodded. "I hate to say it, but I'm glad she's going to be gone for a few days. Freedom from her trying to hook me up with every eligible bachelor in Montague County sounds like heaven right now. You might as well wipe that smile off your face. As soon as she gets back, she will start her campaign to find you a husband."

"I figure I've got a few weeks." Rae gave her sister a gentle push toward the door. "She's still scrounging up every available male in a forty-mile radius for *you* right now."

Bo stepped out into the hallway and got an even stronger

whiff of cinnamon. "Not every single one. She's already warned me that I cannot even look crossways at the bartender at Whiskey Bent. She found out that he doesn't stay in one spot more than a few months or a year at the most."

"Isn't his name Maverick?" Rae asked.

"Yep," Bo answered. "What kind of guy comes to mind when you say *Maverick Gibson*?"

"Bibbed overalls, a dip of tobacco and gray hair," Rae said with a giggle. "How about you?"

"Not what you said." Bo started down the stairs. "That sounds a lot like Henry Marshall, who has that orchard and truck farm south of town. I imagine him being middle-aged, round-faced, and with a three-day-old beard. I used to wonder how some men were always somewhere in between a clean shave and a real beard."

"Then you had a relationship with a guy who put a guard thing on his electric razor that gave him that sexy look, right?" Rae followed her to the bottom of the stairs.

"I don't kiss and tell"—Bo stopped in the middle of the foyer—"but a one-night stand does not a relationship make. Tell me all about how you found out how men could do that."

Rae's crystal-blue eyes twinkled. "I read it in a magazine."

"Yeah, right," Bo said. "And FYI, I'm going to steer Aunt Bernie toward you. I'll tell her that I always wanted to be the last one to get married so I could have the biggest wedding of all seven of us."

"You are a rat from hell," Rae snapped.

"Yep, and I will own it," Bo giggled and took a step

forward. "Since I work for Aunt Bernie, I can always tell her what kind of man you prefer. Do you want tall, dark, and handsome? Policeman or rancher? Cowboy or combat boots? Sensitive or alpha male?"

Rae pushed her into the kitchen. "Mama, Bo is picking on me."

Their mother, Mary Jane, and stepfather, Joe Clay, both looked up from the table at the same time. A little bit of salt had sprouted in their dark hair for both of them, and crow's-feet had showed up around their eyes, but they would always be young to Bo—even if they were in their late fifties.

"Do you both want to have dry toast for breakfast instead of the spread over there on the bar?" Mary Jane teased.

"Or worse yet, have to go stand in the corner?" Joe Clay's grin left no doubt that he was joking.

"We'll be nice," Bo answered, "but for the record, Rae started it."

The hour hand on the old alarm clock that had sat on Rae's bedside table since she was a little girl moved slowly to the eleven o'clock position. Two weeks ago, she was getting into her squad car and making her first rounds for her shift. Before she left, her partner had warned that leaving the graveyard shift and going back to a normal sleep pattern would take a severe adjustment. He had been right. She was still wide-awake at this time of the night and got sleepy sometime around eight in the morning.

She wandered out onto the balcony that was wrapped around three sides of the house and figured out quickly that it was too cold to sit out there in nothing but a thin nightshirt. She went inside and wrapped a quilt around her shoulders, then went back outside, closing the French doors behind her, and sat down in the ladder-back chair. Three more were lined up down the length of the balcony, and there were four on the other side of the house.

A brisk wind made eerie music when it rattled the bare limbs in the pecan trees around the house. Rae scooted her chair back against the wall of the balcony just off her bedroom. She had thought the balcony was the best thing about the Paradise when Mary Jane moved the girls to Spanish Fort.

The old brothel must have been built on a solid foundation because it had stood like the last silent sentinel of the cattle-run days for a century and a half now. Twenty years ago, it had been put up for sale, and Mary Jane learned about it from a friend. The house and the location were exactly what she wanted, so she moved her girls without even taking them to see the place first.

"And the older sisters threw a pure old southern hissy fit because there was only one electrical plug-in their bedrooms." She giggled at the memory.

That vision in her mind faded and another image appeared. Mary Jane had hired Joe Clay to remodel the whole place—room and board included and a bonus if he finished the job by Christmas. He moved in before he knew he would be living in a house with seven bickering and conniving little girls.

The sound of a door opening next to her brought her back to reality, but only for a few seconds when a visual popped into her head of all seven of the sisters spending time on the balcony in times past.

Bo came out of her room and dragged her chair over close to Rae's. "This is a whole new ball game for us. It's our first holiday to be home and not leave at the end of the weekend. Think we'll have to fight the urge to pack our suitcases and get ready for the long trip home after church on Sunday?"

Rae shook her head. "Not me. I'm glad to be here, to have time with family and figure out what I want to do with my life from here on out."

"You've got more options than I have. You can always go back to working for a police force or maybe for the sheriff's department in Montague," Bo suggested. "Or maybe you can put in your own private investigative business. Or even teach since you have that double degree. You covered your bases better than I did when it comes to getting a job."

"Hey, now! You are still singing," Rae argued.

"Playing the piano and singing in church doesn't bring in money," Bo said in a grumbling tone.

"But it makes Endora and Mama happy, so that counts for something," Rae reminded her. "Aunt Bernie keeps you busy with her advice blog and the matchmaking events she's getting into. At least you aren't bored while you are trying to figure out your place in life."

Bo slapped her on the arm. "Don't say the word *bored* out loud. Mama can hear it from a mile away on a day when there's not even a breeze to blow it to her ears."

"I forgot," Rae whispered.

Bo shivered. "I'll never forget washing all the downstairs woodwork and washing down the entire porch."

"Floor and walls both, and there were spiders in the corners," Rae remembered.

"Took the two of us all weekend," Bo said.

"We never said we were bored again," Rae said with a chuckle. "And the others learned from our mistake."

"What's going on out here?" Endora asked. "Are y'all having a preholiday party without me?"

"We were just reminiscing. Come on out and join us," Rae answered. "It's late for you to be working on your next children's book, isn't it?"

Endora brought her chair over to join them. "I wasn't working on that. I still have time before the deadline, and right now I'm concentrating on the Christmas program at the church. Seems like the holidays always bring out memories. What you thinking about?"

"The day when we first saw this place, and when Daddy first met us," Rae answered.

The wind seemed to carry Bo's and Endora's giggles out across the land.

"I remember Mama promising us that our bedrooms would look different by Christmas," Endora said. "Luna and I had always shared a room, and it took a long time for me to be able to sleep in my own room, even after it was remodeled and ready for me."

"I loved the balcony," Rae said. "I used to sneak out here late at night and look at the stars."

"You always were the night owl," Bo reminded her.

"Yep, and the graveyard shift these past few years has suited me well," Rae admitted.

"How are you adjusting?" Endora asked.

"Slowly, but then—on a different level, and a very different situation—it took you more than a year to get your sea legs back under you and figure out things," Rae reminded her.

"Yes, it did, and I have to admit when I found out my fiancé and my best friend were having an affair right under my nose, it knocked me for a loop and shattered my heart." Endora pulled the hood of her jacket up over her head. "But Parker Martin has put all the pieces back together, and we are going to have a wonderful life together. I just wish March wasn't so far away."

"It will be a beautiful wedding"—Bo reached across the distance and patted her baby sister on the knee—"and we're all here to help you plan it."

"You've made new memories," Rae said.

"Yes, I have, and Parker gets the credit," Endora said. "I'm going inside. I'm freezing."

"Me too," Bo said. "Good night to y'all. Tomorrow is going to be crazy with all of us here, so we should get some sleep."

"Thanksgiving is always crazy and so much fun," Endora said and disappeared down the balcony.

"Think she's really all right?" Rae asked.

"I believe she is," Bo answered and closed the door to her room.

Rae wondered if she and her twin sister would be able to say that they were all right with their decisions to move back to Texas. Would another year bring happiness, or in her case, would she finally be able to adjust to a normal sleep pattern?

"Will Aunt Bernie succeed in her attempts to marry us off, so we'll settle down somewhere in this county?" Rae muttered to herself.

Chapter 2

THE FAMILY TRADITION WAS that each person around the table on Thanksgiving would tell something they were thankful for. Bo listened to others saying what they were grateful for that Thanksgiving Day, and the only thing she could think of was the fact that Aunt Bernie would be gone for more than a week. She rolled her eyes toward the ceiling and said a quick prayer begging God, the Universe, and even Fate not to let anything go wrong with her great-aunt's plans to go on a senior Caribbean cruise. Bo loved her aunt, and most of the time, working with her was a hoot, but being with Bernie every single day for the past six months had begun to wear on her.

When it was Aunt Bernie's turn to tell what she had been thankful for the past year, she glanced across the table at Bo and smiled so big that the multitude of wrinkles around her mouth smoothed out. "I'm grateful that Bo came home to the Paradise to help run my new dating service business and help me with my advice column. That way I can leave and not worry about a thing."

Bo felt a slight pang of guilt, but not enough to change her mind about being relieved that Aunt Bernie would be out of her hair for a little while. If she didn't have a vacation from the old girl, she swore she would go back to Nashville and give her dream of being a country star another shot.

"I'm thankful for two things," Endora, the youngest of the seven girls, said. "Parker"—she leaned over and kissed her fiancé on the cheek—"and that my last two sisters are home."

That brought about a little more guilt for Bo's thoughts of going back to Nashville. Her youngest sister needed her, not only to be there for her wedding in the spring, but to help with all that she had going on at the church. Poor Endora was in love with her preacher fiancé, but she bit off a big chunk when it came to all the responsibilities of being the First Lady of the Spanish Fort Community Church.

Bo nudged Endora on the shoulder. "You're just thankful for me and Rae being home because you need help with the Christmas program at the church."

"Well, there is that…" Endora said with a giggle.

Keep up the bantering so I can think of something other than Aunt Bernie being away, which means that for a few days she won't be trying to fix me up with every single man in the state of Texas, Bo thought.

"Bo?" Mary Jane asked.

"I'm sorry." Bo shot a smile across the table at her mother. "I was woolgathering. I'm thankful for every single one of the folks around this table today."

"Even Aunt Bernie?" Rae whispered out the side of her mouth.

"Some days," Bo mouthed to her twin sister—who

looked nothing like her. Rae had crystal-clear blue eyes and straight black hair that flowed down her back like a river's still waters at midnight. Bo's ultra-curly hair was what Aunt Bernie called strawberry blond, but these days, most folks just referred to her as a ginger. Her eyes were pale aqua—not blue, not green.

"I'm grateful for Clayton and hope to have a whole yard full of kids someday," Ursula said, and kissed the baby boy in her arms on the top of his black hair.

"Me too," her husband, Remy, agreed.

Bo's two other sisters, Tertia and Ophelia, said something and so did their husbands, but Bo was only listening with one ear.

"Family," Joe Clay said.

After several years in Nashville, away from family, Bo could add a hearty, silent *amen* to her stepfather's one-word comment. Her dream was to be a country music star, and she had given it her best shot for nearly ten years. Last fall, she had given up and moved back to north Texas, and she didn't have a single regret.

"That my family is all home again." Mary Jane glanced around the table at all her daughters and her four sons-in-law. "I love all your thankfulness, and since I'm the last one, we'll bring in the dessert. Bo, will you help me?"

"Yes, ma'am," Bo said with a brief nod. "I can't wait to cut into that pecan pie."

"Don't you dare take half the pie before it even gets to the table," Rae said.

"I'm the one doing the cutting," Bo teased.

Rae pushed back her chair and stood up. "I'll help y'all. I haven't had pecan pie since last Christmas. I have to protect my interests."

"Y'all can do taste testing on the pecan pie, but the pumpkin pie better not have a slice missing when it makes it to the table," Aunt Bernie called out. "I won't get any more until Christmas."

"So, you're planning to be back by Christmas?" Ophelia teased. "I thought you might love cruising so much that you would just get off that ship and book another one for a different port that very same day."

"Oh, no!" Bernie disagreed. "I'm coming home for Christmas. I wouldn't miss the church program or the Paradise holiday party for anything. Besides, if I leave Rae and Bo alone for more than two weeks, God only knows what kind of men they'll drag in for husbands. I've helped all five of you other sisters find the right match. You think I'm going to turn these last two out on their own? No, siree!"

And there is the reason why I'm grateful that Aunt Bernie is going to give me some breathing space for a few days, Bo thought and quickly glanced over her shoulder to be sure that she hadn't said the words out loud.

"You are as jumpy as a rabbit hiding from a coyote," Mary Jane said in a low voice on the way to the kitchen.

"I don't want anything to go wrong with Aunt Bernie's vacation. I love her, Mama," Bo answered and pushed the button on the coffeepot to start it, "and I appreciate her giving me a job, but I need a break from her trying to fix me up with a husband."

"Me too," Rae said as she took two pumpkin pies from the refrigerator, "and I don't even work with her eight hours a day."

"I don't mind the work," Bo said, "and like I said, I love Aunt Bernie, but…"

"But…" Mary Jane butted in before she could finish. "I understand. Do you think you can handle the Senior Meet and Greet all by yourself? Rae could help out if you need her."

"Glad to," Rae said. "Sitting in a bar with however many sixty-and-older folks that show up will be boring, but I can bite the bullet and be there for you. After all, what are twin sisters for?"

"I've got everything organized, and the bartender, Maverick, came with the package deal when we rented the place," Bo said. "He says that the bar will probably make more money on drinks in those two hours than it does in a week. All of those older folks will be trying to be young and full of spit and vinegar that evening. That means lots of liquor being mixed in red disposable cups."

"I'm surprised that Aunt Bernie isn't already trying to fix you up with Maverick," Rae said with half a giggle.

"Oh, no!" Bo shook her head. "According to her, he's just a vagabond."

"Why would she think that?" Mary Jane asked.

Before Bo could answer, Bernie marched into the room. "What's taking so long?"

"We were waiting on the coffee to finish so we can bring it to the table, too," Rae answered.

"Sounds to me like it's done," Bernie said as she rolled a cart over to the cabinet and put the full coffeepot plus some mugs on it. "I ate way too much, but I still want pumpkin pie and coffee. Don't forget the whipped cream."

Bo rolled her eyes.

"Back to the vagabond," Mary Jane whispered when Bernie had left the kitchen.

"He doesn't stay in one place very long, and he's already been in Nocona for six months," Bo answered. "We had better get the pies delivered, or Aunt Bernie will be back in here fussing at us."

"Yep," Rae agreed with a nod. "Mama, what's she going to do after—and that's more of an *if* than a *when*—me and Bo get married? She won't have anyone else to find husbands for."

"She's always got her internet advice column to fall back on," Mary Jane answered. "Life has never been dull when Aunt Bernie's around."

"And never will be," Bo added as she looked at all the people around the Thanksgiving table—four sisters with husbands beside them, her mother and dad, Endora with her fiancé, Rae, and Aunt Bernie. Then she focused on the new baby, Clayton. The next generation would be coming on. Someday in the distant future she might be ready to add a couple of children to that list, but not anytime soon.

Thanksgiving was over for another year, but that didn't mean all the family fun ended after the feast. Tomorrow morning bright and early, Christmas decorating would begin, and at the Paradise, that involved a lot more than a few lights strung around the windows of the big two-story house. Rae peeked in each of the four empty bedrooms of her married sisters on the way down the hallway that night. Years ago, there would be equal amounts of giggling and arguing about which girl had the prettiest tree in their room. Now nothing but silence and memories met her.

She was glad to hear a loud sigh, proving that there was still life in the upstairs rooms, when she passed by Endora's door. She peeked inside to see her baby sister standing in front of the balcony doors. Endora was one of those petite blonds with baby-blue eyes—and a perfect match to her twin, Luna. On one hand, Rae envied the youngest of the seven sisters. Unlike her and Bo, they actually looked alike, and like a lot of twins, they were super close. Maybe if she and Bo had been identical or had the same dreams for the future, things would have been different.

But they were like the North and South Poles—so far apart that believing they were twins at all was difficult. Bo had gone off to Nashville right after they graduated high school, hoping to become a famous country music star. Rae went to college and got a degree in forensics and criminology, with a minor in early childhood development, then became a police officer in the Oklahoma Panhandle. Bo questioned why Rae would study two very diverse courses. Rae told her that she liked both and couldn't make up her mind which way to go until she got the job offer to be a police officer. She never could wrap her mind around why her sister would wait on tables or clean motel rooms in hopes of being discovered in the country music field.

"Everything all right in here?" Rae asked.

Endora turned around slowly and almost smiled. "Come on in. I was pretending that I was looking out the window of the parsonage and that Parker and I were already married."

"That's sweet." Rae sat down on the edge of the bed.

"I wonder if I can make a preacher's wife. There's so much to do, especially with the Christmas program, and I'm trying to get ready for the wedding in March. Most of the time I'm completely overwhelmed and in a state of acute stress," Endora whispered.

Rae crossed the room and wrapped her sister up in a hug. "Darlin', you are already a preacher's wife in every sense of the word except moving into the parsonage with him." She lowered her voice. "And to tell the truth, I'm surprised that hasn't happened. Y'all are in love, and you've been dating for months."

"Appearances," Endora said with another long sigh. "Preachers and their wives are held to a pretty high standard. I wish we hadn't decided to get married in the spring and that we could just go to the courthouse tomorrow."

Rae took a step back but kept an arm around Endora's shoulders. "Just do it!"

Endora shook free of her sister and sat down in a rocking

chair at the end of her bed. "Too many people would be disappointed if we did that. The church ladies are planning a wedding shower"—she paused—"and if we eloped, there would be rumors that I'm pregnant."

"Who cares about rumors? They would know pretty quickly that you didn't 'have'"—Rae air quoted the last word—"to get married, as Aunt Bernie would say."

Endora pulled her knees up and wrapped her arms around them. "I want everything to be perfect."

"There's no such thing." A smile tickled the corners of Rae's mouth. "Not even a perfect relationship. If you don't have an argument with Parker every now and then, how are you ever going to have makeup sex?"

"Leave it to you to tease me when I'm trying to be serious," Endora snapped.

"Brought you out of the doldrums, didn't I?" Rae asked. "Anything more I can do to help?"

"You're already helping Daddy with the props for the Christmas program," Endora answered.

"I've still got time for one more job if you'll let go and delegate," Rae assured her sister.

"Think you could teach my Sunday school class?" Endora asked. "It's the kindergarten and first grade group, and there's only eight of them—four girls and four boys."

"Duh!" Rae slapped her forehead with her palm. "I'm not just a policewoman. I do have a minor in early childhood development," Rae reminded her. "That's only an hour on Sunday morning. I paint props for Daddy through the week, and if it will help you plan your wedding rather than having you stress about everything else, I'll be happy to take care of your class."

"Thank you," Endora said as she stood up. She opened her closet door and brought out a box. "Here you go. You'll find a folder for each month of the year. You'll need to start with December since this coming Sunday is the first day of the month. You'll be teaching the lesson for the first part of the hour, and then Bo will pop in for a few minutes to help with the songs they'll be singing at the Christmas program."

Rae had faced off with rattlesnakes, bobcats, and a couple of mountain lions in her police career, not to mention the two-legged wild critters. "After you get settled in the parsonage, you'll take over again?"

"By then Christmas will be over, so you won't be helping Daddy," Endora answered. "The Christmas cookbook will be finished and the quilt. Both will be auctioned off for the missionary fund. Things will settle down, and I can probably take the class back."

"There's no way you would ever give up those kids permanently," Rae said with half a giggle.

Endora frowned. "Why would you say that?"

"You love little kids, and they flock to you like bees to spring flowers," Rae reminded her as she stood up.

"I do love children." Endora's smile lit up her eyes.

"You and Parker planning on having a big family?" Rae asked.

"Yes, we want at least four," Endora answered. "I loved having all you sisters, and I'm so glad y'all are all back home."

"But there's only you, Bo, and me in the house now," Rae reminded her.

"Tertia and Noah live across the road," Endora said. "Ophelia and Jake are only a few miles south of us at the winery. Luna and Shane are right around the corner."

"And all we have to do is jump the fence between us and Ursula and Remy's place." Rae nodded and headed out to the hallway. "Everyone but me and Bo are settled. Tertia has a café. Ophelia, the winery, and"—she smiled—"Luna has a beer, bait, and bologna store."

"Give Aunt Bernie some time." Endora followed her to the door. "She'll get you all fixed up."

"I'd just as soon do my own picking when I'm good and ready," Rae said.

Endora shook her finger at her sister. "Doesn't matter. Aunt Bernie will take credit for it anyway."

"I have no doubt that she will," Rae agreed with a nod.

———————

Bo opened the door to the bathroom, stepped out into the hallway, and almost collided with Rae. The ends of her terry-cloth robe brushed against the floor, and a towel was wrapped turban-style around her head.

"What is in the box?" she asked.

"Sunday school stuff for five- to seven-year-olds," Rae answered.

"You are a brave woman." Bo flipped the towel off and used it to dry her hair.

Rae frowned. "Why would you say that?"

"Last month, Endora had a fever, and I taught that class," Bo explained. "After services that morning, I told her that she had to be well by the next week or talk someone else into going into that rattlesnake den."

Rae shivered all the way to her toes. "Why would you call a bunch of little kids such a thing?"

Bo patted her twin sister on the back. "Honey, not all of them will give you fits. Just Daisy and Heather. Those are Gunner Watson's daughters."

"I think I can handle twin girls." Rae tried to laugh away the bad feeling that had made her uneasy, but it came out more like a cough than a giggle. "After all, we grew up right here in this house with two sets of twins, didn't we?"

"Yes, we did, but think Luna and Endora with tiny little horns coming out of their identical hair," Bo whispered. "I don't know how anyone can tell them apart, and to make matters worse, they are always dressed just alike. Their aunt Rosie thinks it's cute, and I would guess it makes it easy for Gunner to just buy two of everything."

"Why? Mama didn't make either set of us dress the same," Rae frowned.

"Stacey, their mama, died when they were three years old. I heard it was cancer, but someone else said it was a blood clot. Anyway, Rosie is Stacey's great-aunt, and she stepped up to help with the girls," Bo explained.

"Identical like Endora and Luna?" Rae remembered back when her two sisters changed places—even in high school.

"Kind of, only these two little terrors have black hair and big blue eyes," Bo answered. "Just be prepared for chaos. Getting them to be still and sing when I go into the class-room for a few minutes is a total chore."

"Why didn't you or Endora warn me about these girls before I took on the job?" Rae groaned.

"Hey, you were on the police force." Bo chuckled. "You'll do fine. Just start off tough the first Sunday, and don't let up. And it might be a good idea to separate them."

"Why's that?" Rae asked.

Bo raised both eyebrows. "Think, Sister! Endora and Luna were identical. Remember all the shenanigans they pulled when they switched places, or when a teacher at school couldn't pinpoint which of them it was that did something ornery. And *they* weren't even dressed alike most of the time."

"I'll remember that," Rae said. "Got any more tips?"

"Nope," Bo said and headed toward the office that Aunt Bernie had set up in Ursula's old bedroom. "I'm going to go over all the details for the meet and greet on Saturday evening."

"Going to be a busy day," Rae said.

"Yep," Bo agreed. "By Sunday night, we'll be ready to drop."

Rae nodded and went into her room. She assured herself that she had been on the police force for years and had dealt with some hardened criminals during that time. A set of five-year-old little girls was not going to intimidate her, not one bit.

Chapter 3

ENDORA AWOKE THE MORNING after Thanksgiving to find her two cats, Poppy and Misty, curled up on the pillow beside her. Sassy, the older cat, who had been at the Paradise for several years, was sleeping at the foot of the bed. Thank goodness Parker wasn't allergic to animals because she couldn't imagine rehoming her cats when she moved to the parsonage. She buried her hand in Poppy's thick orange fur and smiled at the way her diamond engagement ring sparkled in the sunlight that flowed in from the balcony doors.

"It's less than four months until I get the wedding and honeymoon to go with this," she whispered as she removed her hand from the cat's fur, pushed back the covers, and sat up. "I wish we were already married."

Misty opened one eye and purred a couple of times before she wrapped her fluffy tail around her nose and went back to sleep. Poppy moved away from her sister and claimed Endora's pillow.

Endora glanced at her phone and bounded out of the bed so fast that both cats' eyes flew open for a few seconds.

"My alarm didn't go off!" she said, jerking on jeans and a sweatshirt. She brushed her long blond hair out and braided it so that the thick rope hung down over her shoulder. When she opened her bedroom door, she could hear the buzz of several conversations going on both outside and in the kitchen. Most of what she heard was just noise, but when she reached the foyer, she could separate Parker's voice from two of her brothers-in-law with no trouble. She watched them drag a big cedar tree up onto the porch and was amazed, once again, at how well Parker and all four of her sisters' husbands had been accepted into the family.

"So, where do we put this thing?" he asked. "I've never known anyone to cut down a tree and put it on the porch."

"I forget that you weren't here at Christmas last year," Remy said. "You'll be surprised at how many decorations will go up around here today. Folks drive from all over this part of the state to see the Paradise at Christmas."

"And there's a big party where everyone is invited," Shane added. "Hundreds of folks come out here to take pictures in front of the sleigh. Sometimes it's family photos and Joe Clay says that engagement pictures have been shot right here in the yard."

"Okay, let's get this beauty set up and bolted down in the stand," Remy said.

Parker held on to the trunk of the tree with his right hand and waved his left one toward the front yard, where Noah and Jake were helping Joe Clay take a sleigh from a flatbed trailer. "That is a full-sized Santa sleigh! Where did that come from?"

"Joe Clay made that years ago. Mary Jane has a picture of

the whole family with it in her picture albums," Remy said. "You'll have to ask to see them sometime."

Parker's smile sent warmth right into Endora's heart. "I'd love to see pictures of Endora when she was a little girl."

"What are you thinking about, and why are you hiding in the shadows?" Aunt Bernie asked, breaking into Endora's thoughts about her family, and especially Parker.

Endora whipped around. "You scared me."

"You must've been deep in thought about that handsome fiancé of yours," Bernie said with a chuckle. "You and four of your sisters are welcome."

"Thank you." Endora had learned in the past year just to go with the flow where Bernie was concerned. "I'll repay part of my debt by helping Bo take care of Pepper while you are away."

Bernie shook her head, but her dyed red hair stayed in place—the benefit of good hair spray. "No, darlin'. You have enough on your plate, even with what help your sisters are giving you. Bo is going to look after Pepper," she said with a long sigh. "I'm going to miss him. We haven't been apart since I got him, but time away from me might make him appreciate me more. He's gotten to where he thinks he's entitled, and besides, even if I could take him on the cruise, I'd be afraid someone would recognize him in Mexico and say that I stole him."

"I didn't think you'd ever been to Mexico," Endora said.

"I haven't, but a 'good friend,'"—she put air quotes around the last two words—"gave him to me, and he'd been there. I've spoiled Pepper ever since. He's a lot like those two cats that sleep with you. What are your fur babies going to do when you move into the parsonage?"

"They'll have the run of the whole house, but at night, we'll shut our bedroom door," Endora answered.

"Smart girl," Bernie said. "Go on out there and give Parker a kiss, then get back in here and help unpack all the decorations. Your sisters are all in the living room, grumbling because you overslept. Before you get started with all that, grab a cup of coffee and one of Tertia's muffins for breakfast. I'll help out for a while, but I've got to finish packing. Gladys and I are leaving early in the morning. It will be damn…dang…good to get into warmer weather for a few days."

"You almost cussed," Endora said with a broad smile.

"I know," Bernie sighed. "Mary Jane's rules about not cussin' or having liquor before breakfast haven't been easy to live with. Sometimes I just stand in the middle of my living room and cuss the walls to get all the words out of my system." She glanced around the foyer and up the stairs, then lowered her voice. "And sometimes I add a drop or two of Jameson to my first cup of coffee in the morning. Now you go kiss that good-looking feller out there. I might find a sexy middle-aged man"—she slid a sly wink at Endora—"on the cruise and let him warm me up a little."

"Aunt Bernie!" Endora gasped.

"Honey, I'm old, but my memory is excellent. I don't need a how-to book to remember what to do between the sheets, or even naked out on a balcony, either one." She gave Endora a gentle push.

As if on cue, when Endora stepped outside into the icy-cold wind, Parker turned around and hurried across the porch to wrap her up in a hug. "Good mornin', darlin'."

She brushed a kiss across his lips. "Good morning to you. Your alarm must have gone off. Mine didn't."

"I wish mine wouldn't have," Parker said. "I was having a wonderful dream about us when we are so old that we have gray hair. We were cutting a cake with a big gold fifty on the top."

"I hope that's an omen," she whispered and brushed a second kiss across his lips.

"I have faith that it's a sign from heaven," Parker told her. "But right now, Shane tells me that our next job is to climb the pecan trees that line the lane and put lights on them. I should help him load them in the back of Joe Clay's work truck. I'd rather stay here and make out with you, though."

"Save that thought for later. I love you, Parker," Endora whispered.

"I love you more," he said and picked up a box marked Lights for Trees.

Endora watched him load the lights into the bed of the truck. When she was a little girl, the truck had been bright red, but now it had faded somewhere closer to orange or maybe a dirty pink. So much had happened since that vehicle first drove up in the yard more than twenty years ago.

Joe Clay had turned out to be an amazing father to the seven little girls who had just moved into the Paradise.

She had thought her life was blessed right up until two years ago when the bottom fell completely out of everything. She'd been engaged to someone she thought was a great guy. She and her sister both had good jobs at an elementary school in the southern part of the state. Then it had all fallen apart—including *her* heart, soul, and mind—in a split second. She discovered that her fiancé was having an affair with her best friend, and the whole bunch of them worked at the same school.

When the cold wind sent a shiver down her spine, she left the chill behind and rushed inside to the warmth of the house.

"What are you thinking about?" Rae asked, carrying a box marked ORNAMENTS down the stairs. "You look like you are about to cry."

"Just looking back over the last two years and thinking about how grateful I am for my sisters, who helped get me through that difficult, depressing time." She took a deep breath and smiled. "And for Parker, who has healed my heart and helped me believe in love again."

Rae set the box down on the bottom step, bent slightly, and gave her sister a sideways hug. "I'm glad your heart is all better, and we all love Parker. But honey, if that son of a..."

Endora held up a hand. "If Aunt Bernie can't cuss, then you can't either."

"He is a son of a bitch, and that's not cussing," Rae declared. "It's just stating facts, and if he ever shows his face in these parts again, no matter how far or how well anyone hunts, his body will never be found. What he did to you was unforgivable."

"We *have* to forgive him," Endora said. "But that's the past—done and finished. This is the present, and it's already better than what we had back then."

Rae tucked a strand of dark hair back into her messy bun. "Why do we have to forgive such a sorry sucker?"

"Because hatred makes it hard to have a whole heart," Endora answered.

Rae picked up the box of ornaments. "I'm not in a hurry to give my heart to anyone, so I don't have to forgive that sumbitch."

"Tell that to Aunt Bernie," Endora said. "She's already making lists of guys who might make suitable husbands for you and Bo. But she says it can't be that bartender at Whiskey Bent because she heard that he's not one to put down roots. So, neither one of you can date him."

Ursula came through the back door at the same time Endora made it to the kitchen. "Hey, sleepyhead! Or have you been awake since dawn and spent half the morning working on the Christmas program?"

Endora poured herself a cup of coffee. "Nope, I just overslept. With all y'all's help, I'm not nearly as stressed over that right now as I am about my wedding."

"You can't decide on the dress, and you haven't even started looking at cakes or flowers," Ursula reminded her. "Ever think that maybe those are signs that you don't want a big wedding? Maybe you should do what me and Remy did. Go to the courthouse and get it over with."

Endora put three muffins on a plate and carried it and her coffee to the table. "I would in a heartbeat, but you know small towns. Gossip would have it that I was pregnant, and that would be bad for a preacher's reputation." She frowned and took a sip of her coffee. "Wouldn't it?"

"Are you pregnant?" Ursula asked.

Endora shook her head.

"Then when no baby appears in less than nine months, they'll realize that it was just a rumor," Ursula told her. "I should be getting to the living room. Since I'm the tallest of all us girls, I'm on duty for stringing garland and lights."

Endora finished off a muffin and took a sip of coffee. "Since Luna and I are the shortest, we get to sit on the floor and tie ribbons around the sprigs of mistletoe and hang ornaments on the lower half of the tree. Who's got Clayton?"

"Mama and Daddy are taking turns spoiling him," Ursula answered. "Mama gets him when Daddy is outside, but when Daddy comes in the house, then he belongs to Daddy. When he cries or needs a diaper changed, he belongs to me or Remy."

"Naming him after Daddy was pretty special," Endora said.

Ursula headed out of the kitchen. "It was the only name Remy and I could agree on. Don't take too long with your breakfast, or our other sisters will be in here fussing at you."

Endora waved over her shoulder. "Don't I know it."

Ursula had barely gotten out of the room when Parker came in by the back door. He opened his arms and crossed the big country kitchen in a few strides. Endora pushed back her chair, stood up, and met him halfway. She barely had time to moisten her lips before he kissed her, and like always, she wanted to forget about holidays, church programs, and even her wedding and drag him up to her bedroom. But they had agreed to wait for that step until they were married.

When the kiss ended, Parker cupped her face in his hands. "I wanted a real kiss, not just a peck on the lips. From where I'm standing now, three months seems like eternity."

"I know." Endora laid her head on his shoulder. "Want to move the date up to Valentine's Day?"

"Or maybe New Year's Eve?" Parker said with a twinkle in his eyes. "How about next week?"

"We've got too much going with all the events around here to do that, but all our families and friends will be at the Christmas program, including our old preacher," she suggested.

Parker touched her on the cheek and buried his face in her hair. "Are we crazy to even think about that?"

"Maybe so, but I could borrow Luna's dress, and you'll be dressed in your best suit," she told him.

"What about the honeymoon?" Parker kissed that soft spot right below her ear.

Desire shot through her whole body. "Program is on Sunday morning," she panted. "We have to be here at the Paradise on Christmas Day, which is Wednesday. That's the only time we'd have to leave the parsonage until the next Sunday. Darlin', every day we are together after we are married will be part of our honeymoon. But you are right, this is just a fairy tale."

"It's a beautiful fairy tale, though," he whispered.

"Hey, Endora." Luna's voice floated from the foyer to the kitchen. "You've played hooky long enough. It's time to come help us."

"On my way," Endora yelled and took a reluctant step back.

Parker drew her back to his chest and gave her a quick kiss on the forehead. "See you later."

She watched him leave and then tried to sneak past the archway leading from the wide foyer into the living room. Luck was not hiding in her pocket. Her twin sister caught her as she was tiptoeing toward the stairs.

"Hey, get on in here," Luna called out. "Mama has twice as much mistletoe as usual, and you tie the mistletoe bows prettier than I do."

"Will do, as soon as I make a trip to the bathroom," Endora replied and raced up the stairs. To keep from having told a lie, she checked her hair in the mirror. Then she hurried into Luna's old bedroom and slung open the closet door. Luna's wedding dress was still hanging there, and her silk bouquet was lying on the shelf.

"Getting married after the Christmas program would be doable," she muttered. A visual popped into her head of how gorgeous the church had been when it was decorated for

Luna's wedding. The same place would already be all decked out for Christmas if she and Parker got married then.

All the wedding planning that was supposed to get into full swing right after Christmas could be eliminated—no worrying about picking out a dress, no working for hours on floral centerpieces, bouquets, and corsages, or even deciding whether to have the reception at Paradise or in the church fellowship hall.

But right now, you have to go tie bows, the pesky voice in her head reminded her.

Endora patted the clear garment bag that held the dress. "You hang right there and don't go anywhere. I may need to borrow you in a few weeks."

———

"The prodigal daughter has finally arrived," Rae teased when Endora made it to the living room.

"I don't see a fatted calf roasting in the backyard, and Mama didn't give me her ring," Endora shot back.

"Bravo!" Rae gave her younger sister a thumbs-up. "The smart-ass that we all used to know has kicked the moody Endora to the curb."

Endora did a perfect head wiggle. "That's right, and it took a good man like Parker to do the job."

"Whoa!" Rae shook her head. "I believe you've got half a dozen sisters who helped with that."

"And a mama who was happy to let all of you move back into the Paradise," Mary Jane reminded them.

Endora took a deep bow. "To all of you, I am grateful, and I love you more than words can say. Now, let's get on with this decorating. We need to get as much as we can done today, because we're all going to the parade in Saint Jo tomorrow."

"And we have to get up early to wave goodbye to Aunt Bernie and Gladys," Rae said. "I'm still not comfortable with Aunt Bernie driving all the way to Galveston."

Endora plopped down on the floor and picked up a roll of red ribbon. "That woman could drive to Alaska and still have the energy to do battle with a grizzly bear. She's got the stamina of a teenager, but I'm glad Gladys is going with her. If either of them needs help, the other one can call us. Too bad her whole crew couldn't go with them."

"Vera and Dolly said they didn't want to leave their husbands for that long," Rae told her. "But truth is that Vera probably can't bear to be away from baby Clayton that long. Dolly and Walter have family coming in and out all during this month."

Endora whipped up a red bow to tie to the first bunch of fresh mistletoe that Joe Clay had brought in the previous week. "What do you want to bet that she gets into matchmaking on the ship?"

Rae raised her dark brows. "I'm not losing my money on a bet like that. How about the rest of you?"

"Not me," they all chorused together.

"Whatever got her into that business anyway?" Endora asked.

Ursula raised her hand. "That would be me. Since she couldn't bring Endora out of her funk, she zeroed in on me and Remy. And that gave her the matchmaking bug. Luna was already seeing Shane when I came home, but Bernie still takes credit for that too."

"Shame on you," Rae said with a giggle.

"Hey, it doesn't matter to me if it was Aunt Bernie or Fate, I'm glad that Remy and I are together," Ursula declared.

Mary Jane handed baby Clayton to Ursula. "This baby is hungry. You'll have to take care of that. And back to Aunt Bernie, I understand that she did help Luna get past a pretty big argument she had with Shane."

"Yes, she did, and I'm very grateful for her advice," Luna said.

Tertia and Ophelia finished hanging lights around the picture window and then headed out of the room.

"Where are y'all going?" Rae asked.

"We're on food duty," Tertia answered.

"Can't expect us or all those big strong men out there to get this place ready for Christmas on an empty stomach," Ophelia added.

"What are we having?" Rae asked.

"Chili for dinner with crackers, or else folks can make a Fritos chili pie. Hot rolls stuffed with ham for break time at around three o'clock, and lasagna for supper," Tertia answered.

"I'm going to gain ten pounds over the holidays, but I don't even care." Rae groaned and thought about all the years that she had worked nights on the police force. Breakfast was usually at a small diner on the way home from her shift at seven thirty or eight in the morning. Lunch was when she woke up, usually around midafternoon. Dinner—or supper, as it was called in Texas and Oklahoma—was a quick burger or sandwich, sometime in the middle of the night. Adjusting to sleeping at night and having what she called a normal schedule was still a work in progress, but she loved it.

By the time the guys came in from outside at noon and her two sisters yelled that dinner was buffet-style on the bar, Rae was starving. They had gotten a lot done that morning— lights and garland were on the tallest artificial tree that could still fit in the living room, and there were bows on every single sprig of mistletoe.

"Our jobs after we eat are decorating the tree on the front porch, putting garland up the staircase banister..." Mary Jane said as she led the way to the dining room.

"I'm here," Aunt Bernie butted in from the front door. "I'm ready for the cruise, and Pepper is pouting, so I left him at home. I can help decorate all afternoon, or I can help in the kitchen. Just put me wherever you need me."

Rae threw her arm around Bernie's shoulders. "We never turn down help. Did you remember to pack a bathing suit and an outfit for fancy night?"

"Yep, I did, and a cute little red lace teddy"—Bernie's wide grin deepened every wrinkle in her cheeks—"just in case I might need it."

"Aunt Bernie!" Endora scolded.

"That's at least twice today that you've talked to me in that tone," Bernie snapped at her. "One more and I'm going to refuse to be in your wedding party."

"You wouldn't do that, would you?" Rae asked.

"Yes, I would," Bernie declared. "I might need a little excitement to hold me over until I get home and get busy finding you and Bo each a boyfriend. No, that's not right. I need to find you each a decent husband." She cocked her head to one side. "I can hear your biological clock ticking away. Baby boy Clayton needs cousins to play with as he gets older."

"Ophelia, Tertia, and Luna can take care of that," Rae told her.

Bernie narrowed her eyes and shook her finger under Rae's nose. "Yep, but you can contribute to the next generation when I find the right man for you. The Paradise needs lots of children to fill it with laughter, like it had back when you girls were little."

"Okay, if you find the right man—one that I can fall in love with, and who loves me just the way I am—we'll have that conversation," Rae assured her. "But until then, let's focus on planning Endora's spring wedding, and all this holiday stuff."

"Deal!" Bernie smiled so big that the wrinkles around her mouth disappeared. "But after Endora's wedding, all bets and deals are off."

"Joe Clay will say grace, and then we'll start serving," Mary Jane was saying when Rae and Bernie made it to the kitchen.

Rae stopped at the door and bowed her head, but she didn't close her eyes. Four of her sisters were married and holding hands with their husbands. She wanted what they had—like she had just told Aunt Bernie, a man to love her without wanting to change a single thing about her. She was independent, headstrong, and could take care of herself. She didn't need a man to do any of those things or to complete her. She just wanted someone to love with her whole heart, and who would return that love in equal amounts.

"Amen," Joe Clay said.

All four of her brothers-in-law gave their wives a quick kiss on the cheek before they lined up at the bar to fill bowls with chili. Yep, that's exactly what she wanted, and no matter what Aunt Bernie said, she would have it, or she would simply be the old maid aunt that all the nieces and nephews loved the most.

And every now and then you can take a lacy teddy and go on a cruise, the voice inside her head whispered. *After all, what happens on a ship stays on the ship.*

Endora nudged her with an elbow. "What are you thinking about? I could almost hear a giggle behind your smile. Do you think Aunt Bernie really has a red teddy?"

"Without a doubt," Rae answered, "and I was thinking about life. Want to share what was on your mind right then?"

"Wedding dresses," Endora whispered. "I think I have one picked out, but can we keep it a secret between us until after the holidays?"

"My lips are sealed," Rae replied in a low voice.

Chapter 4

"SOME THINGS NEVER CHANGE," Bo muttered as she glanced around the Saint Jo square that Saturday morning.

"Except that some of the time we didn't even need a jacket, and this year, we should have worn thermal long underwear under our jeans. This cold wind hasn't let up in days and days," Rae said.

"But the atmosphere is still the same as when we were kids," Bo answered. "The vendors might be different, but there's cotton candy and hot dogs. Those were the two most important things back then."

"Along with all the excitement when Santa came riding into town on the fire truck." Rae nodded. "Do you realize that twenty years ago, we thought the folks that are our age were just plumb old?"

"And the ones over sixty were downright ancient," Bo said.

Rae patted her sister on the shoulder. "You got that right, but time sure changed that attitude, didn't it?"

Endora and Parker waved from a few feet away and weaved their way through the crowd toward Bo and Rae. "Hey, what are y'all going to do first?" Endora asked when they reached Rae and Bo.

"I only have a couple of hours," Bo answered. "I'm going to get two hot dogs and sit on a bench and eat them."

"I thought that thing tonight wasn't until seven," Rae said.

"It's not, but Aunt Bernie rented the bar from noon to give me time to get the place decorated. Believe me, when I get it all done, Whiskey Bent will run the Paradise some competition. The event is over at nine, but the bar is open to the public until sometime after midnight," Bo explained.

Rae's mouth set in a firm line, and her brow furrowed in a frown. "*You* have gotten old if it's going to take you seven hours to get ready for a meet and greet. What do you have to do? Throw a few tablecloths on and set a few centerpieces out. I could plan Endora's entire wedding in that length of time."

"Okay then, smarty-pants, I'll stick around until the parade at one o'clock, and maybe all of us girls can gather around Santa for a picture. But I'll only do that if you go with me and help all afternoon and evening," Bo smarted off.

"You'll have to leave before noon then because I'm not going to help decorate," Rae declared.

Before Bo could argue, two little girls ran up to Endora and wrapped their arms around her waist. Dressed alike in jeans and red sweatshirts with Rudolph printed on the fronts, they even had identical backpacks slung over their left shoulders.

"Miz Dora," one of them stepped back and frowned.

"And Preacher Parker," the other finished, and also took a step back.

"What are y'all doing here?" the first one asked.

"We're waiting on Santa, just like you are," Parker answered.

"I'm glad you are here," Endora said. "I want you to meet your new Sunday school teacher. This is my sister Rae, and she'll be taking over your class for the next few weeks."

Both little girls turned their frowns and gazes toward Rae. Bo bit back a giggle when she noticed the look on her twin sister's face.

"I'm Heather," the one with a freckle in front of her left ear said.

The other one popped her hands on her hips. "I'm Daisy, and Rae is a boy's name."

"Daisy, that is rude." The crowd parted and a tall man stood behind the girls. His hair was as dark as the girls', but his eyes were mossy green.

"Sorry." Daisy kicked at the dirt and then whispered, "But it's the truth."

"I'm Gunner Watson, and these are my daughters." The man stuck out his hand toward Rae. "I understand you worked on the police force up in Oklahoma. I have a position open in the Nocona Police Department and would be glad to send you an application."

She shook hands with him. "Thanks, but no thanks. I'm taking some time off to decide what I want to do next, but I know it's not police work."

"Well, if you change your mind..." Gunner said. "And it's good to meet you. If these girls give you any trouble in Sunday school, just..."

"Daddy!" the girls both said in unison.

Gunner looked down at them. "You two might fool some folks, but I know both of you and guessing what you might do does not tax my imagination one bit."

"Can we go get a pretzel with cheese?" Heather asked in a sweet voice.

"And a hot chocolate?" Daisy smiled innocently at her father.

"They seem like two sweet little girls," Rae said when they were out of hearing distance.

Bo giggled aloud. "Don't let those blue eyes fool you."

"Bo is right," Endora added. "And remember, a tornado just looks like a black funnel until it hits. Parker and I are on our way to the hotel for a cup of hot chocolate. Y'all want to join us?"

"We're going for hot dogs," Bo said. "But thanks for asking."

"See y'all tomorrow in Sunday school," Rae called out before the twins were completely swallowed up in the crowd.

Both girls turned back and smiled.

"They don't look so bad to me," Rae said.

"Darlin' sister, those were let's-see-what-you've-got smiles, not sweet ones," Bo said with a giggle. "We'll agree to disagree."

"I can live with that," Rae said.

———

A picture of the bar chased through Bo's mind as she drove from Saint Jo to Nocona. Set on the east side of town, the place was only two years old. She had only been there one time, when she had gone with Bernie to make arrangements.

"I won't be here that evening," Dave, the owner, had told them when they signed the contract that day. "I'm taking my wife on a cruise for our twenty-fifth wedding anniversary. But I've hired a new manager, and he will take good care of you. His name is Maverick Gibson. You will need to be out by nine. I don't expect a lot of traffic since it's a holiday weekend, but I'd hate to close up on a Saturday night. That would be bad business for my regulars."

"And there might be a few stragglers who are tired of so much family being around for the Thanksgiving holiday. I owned a bar up in Ratliff City, Oklahoma, for many years. I know how folks are," Bernie said.

"Fish and visitors…" Dave grinned.

"Stink after three days," she said, finishing the old adage for him.

Bo had made flyers to advertise the Sixty-and-Over meet and greet event, and she and her aunt had put them up all over the county. Bernie had had Bo create a graphic to put on the Aunt Bernie's Advice to the Lovelorn blog that she ran on the internet.

"I'm glad that she figured out there was too much competition for her to make it in the online matchmaking business," Bo muttered as she pulled into the gravel parking lot of the bar, with a neon sign above the door that read WHISKEY BENT BAR. Painted deep green, the building seemed to blend right in with all the huge trees surrounding it.

She parked as close to the front door as she could, got out of her SUV, popped the back hatch open, and groaned at all the boxes she had to carry inside. Thank goodness Dave had agreed—and even seemed happy—to let her leave all the decorations up. That would save hours and hours of taking them all down.

"Hey, I've been looking out for you," a deep voice called out. "I'll help unload all that stuff."

"Thanks," she said before she turned around.

The guy stepped around her and stuck out his hand. "You must be Bo. I'm Maverick."

Bo had pictured Maverick as an older man, maybe with a bald head like the bartender in the last movie she had watched. She couldn't have been more wrong. The man gripping her hand was well over six feet tall and had light-brown hair that hung to his shoulders and dark-green eyes with gold flecks in them. The combination was totally breathtaking. Especially when added to his snug-fitting blue jeans, his scuffed-up cowboy boots, and the plaid shirt showing from under his denim duster. All in all, he looked like he should be on the cover of a romance novel—one that came with a free handheld fan—or maybe one of the country singers in Nashville. He had the whole package for either one.

"Pleased to meet you," she said and dropped his hand.

"Likewise," he said, picked up two boxes and headed toward the bar.

"Wow!" Bo mumbled under her breath.

No, no, no! Aunt Bernie's voice yelled inside her head.

Dave said that Maverick is not the kind to put down roots. He's not for you.

"Shhh," Bo shushed her and carried a box toward the bar. "Let me enjoy the moment, and you go on and have a good time on your cruise. Find someone who will appreciate that red lace teddy."

The inside of the place was bigger than Bo would have thought. She set her box on one of the tables for four that were set up all around the floor. Maverick followed her lead and then headed back outside.

He stopped halfway across the floor and turned back. "How many folks are you expecting tonight?"

She took a couple of steps toward him. "One hundred people paid for tickets. About seventy-five women, and the rest were men."

Maverick chuckled. "I have twenty tables on the floor, and five up on the stage, so we should be good."

Bo glanced over her shoulder at the stage area where an old upright piano had been pushed back against the wall. A desire to hear the tinkle of a piano, the whine of a fiddle, and the beat of the drums swept over her. She'd left the dream behind—or so she thought—but even after six months, she still yearned for the feeling that she got every time she picked up a microphone. "Do you ever have live bands?"

"Not very often, but we do have piano music sometimes," Maverick answered and continued to take long strides toward the door.

Bo followed him and mentally tallied up the profit

Bernie would make at the event. The tickets to get through the door were fifty dollars each. All of the decorations came from holiday leftovers that had been stored in the barn, and Bernie had talked Dave into giving her a healthy discount on the free beer that would be served in exchange for leaving the decorations up for the season. Considering all that, Bernie was making a nice little profit on this venture.

"I've never been a part of an event like this." Maverick hefted two more boxes up on his shoulders. "My first gig as a bartender was several years ago in Deadwood, South Dakota. I was worried that I wouldn't know how to mix all those fancy cocktails, but the guys mostly ordered whiskey, neat or on the rocks, and the ladies wanted wine."

"Have you learned to make the cocktails since then?" Bo asked.

He chuckled. "No, but I've got a really good app on my phone that tells me exactly how to fix them. What did you do before you became an event planner with your aunt? Dave says she is quite a character."

"I spent ten years in Nashville chasing the dream of becoming a country music singer," Bo answered and opened the door for him.

"What made you give up on your dream?" Maverick asked.

"Disappointment, boredom, missing family—any one or all of the above," she answered. "What made you leave Deadwood?"

Maverick set the two heavy boxes on a table and pulled

out a chair. "I get antsy after a few months in one place. Might as well sit down and catch your breath before we start unloading all this stuff. Want a drink or a bottle of water?"

"I'd love a beer," Bo said. "I'm not particular about what kind as long as it's cold."

"Coming right up," Maverick said, and brought two longneck bottles to the table. "I'm judging from all these boxes that you intend to do some serious decorating this afternoon."

"Aunt Bernie left all kinds of orders about what to use and where to put it, so it will take a few hours," she answered and then turned up the bottle and had a couple of long drinks.

Maverick took a sip and set his bottle on the table. "Well, darlin', I'm all yours until after the party is over, but I've got a question."

"Shoot," Bo said.

"You're going to shut down the party at nine, and I'm opening the place up to the public at that time. What do you intend to do with all the decorations?" he asked. "Taking them all down and packing them with people all around will be even more trouble than putting them up in an empty room."

Bo took another drink of her beer. "Didn't Dave tell you about the deal that he and Aunt Bernie made?"

Maverick shook his head. "No, he was in such a hurry to get out of here that he must have forgotten."

"Instead of Aunt Bernie paying full price for the beer, the decorations all stay. That way you've got everything all fancy through the holidays," she told him.

"That's a pretty good deal," Maverick said.

"Aunt Bernie is a wheeler-dealer," Bo said with half a giggle. "After she made that deal, she asked my mama for all her leftover decorations. Mama never throws out a single thing, and there's always too much for the families and the Paradise."

"Families? Paradise?" Maverick's brow furrowed in a frown.

"I have six sisters. Four of them are married, hence *families*. One is engaged to the preacher in the only church in Spanish Fort—another family plus the church. The Paradise is the name of the house where all of us girls grew up. It was a brothel back in the cattle-run days," she explained as she stood up and ripped the tape from a box marked GARLAND.

"Seven girls?" Maverick shook his head again. "I can't imagine having that many siblings, much less sisters. What are their names?"

"Ursula, Ophelia, Tertia, Luna, and Endora, and then there's me and Rae. There are two sets of twins in the mix. Rae is my twin, but we are not identical. Luna and Endora are the youngest in the family, and not many folks can tell them apart."

"Where did your mama find such unusual names?"

"She named us from characters in whatever book she was writing at the time. She is a famous romance author. My character was a lady spy slash singer in an old-time honky-tonk. Rae's was a policewoman in a romantic suspense story. We're the only two that grew up to follow our namesakes."

She brought out a piece of paper with instructions on where everything was to be hung or placed. "We start with garland and put it up there." She pointed toward the area between the shelves of liquor and the ceiling. "I'm supposed to weave three strands together—two red and one gold—and once it's up, we string twinkle lights all through them. I hope you have a ladder, but can I ask you a question? Where did you get your name?"

"My grandmother liked the movie *Top Gun*, and Mama let her name me since I was a surprise baby," he answered. "I'll get the ladder from the storage room."

Bo fanned her face with her hand. Aunt Bernie was right about not getting involved with a bartender who never stayed in one place for long, but her hormones were sure enough ignoring the warnings. "But…" she muttered, "just because Aunt Bernie says I can't have that particular piece of man candy doesn't mean I can't look through the window of the store."

Just keep the glass between you and the displays so you aren't tempted to reach out and have only one tiny little sample. Aunt Bernie was back in her head.

"I promise," Bo whispered with a long sigh.

"Did you say something to me?" Maverick asked as he carried an old wooden ladder with green paint spatter all over the rungs into the room.

"No, I was just mumbling about getting all this done." She crossed her fingers behind her back the way she had done when she was a child and had told a white lie.

"We've got more than three hours," Maverick reminded her. "We could decorate your Paradise place in that length of time."

Bo laughed out loud.

"What's so funny? I used to help my mama get the Christmas tree ready and put the lights up outside in a couple of hours."

"It takes at least three days to get the Paradise ready for the holidays," she answered. "You should drive up to Spanish Fort sometime between now and New Year's and see the place."

"Just how big is this house?" Maverick asked as he set the ladder up.

"I have no idea." Bo took out the garland and began to weave it together. "It has seven bedrooms upstairs—one for each of the original ladies who lived there—and one downstairs for Madam Raven, who owned the place. The size is why Mama bought it and then had it remodeled for us girls. We all had our own space that way, and the downstairs room and office belong to her. She's a pretty famous novelist."

Maverick unplugged the neon sign hanging up near the ceiling, took it down, and laid it on the bar. "We'll have to be super careful with this. It's been here since Dave opened the bar. A beer company gave it to him at his grand opening. He hung it up there because a plug-in wasn't far away."

"Then you take it somewhere. If it gets broken, it won't be my fault." Bo glanced down at the piece of paper Bernie left for her as she worked on the garland. The next job was to hang fake cedar around the edge of the bar and string more twinkling lights in it. She peeled the tape off the right box and brought out greenery that had been wrapped around squares of cardboard.

"Do you like working as a bartender?" she asked.

"Bartender slash manager," he corrected her, "and yes, right now I do enjoy it. I like this area, and the folks here in Nocona are friendly. Plus, I get a free apartment at the back of the bar, so I can save a lot of money."

"For your next journey?" she asked.

Maverick picked up the neon sign. "That's right. I'll take this to the storage room." He left with the sign and returned in a few minutes. "I never know where I'm going until something either comes up or, like you said, boredom or disappointment sets in."

"Or homesickness?" she asked.

"Don't have a home. My father and his fourth wife live in Thailand, or maybe it's Japan this month. I can't keep up with them any more than they can me. My mother left us when I was too young to remember her. My grandmother is in a nursing home in Houston and doesn't even know me anymore," Maverick said.

She heard a note of sadness mixed with a little yearning in his voice. She couldn't imagine not having a big family, especially with the holidays coming up. "I'm sorry. I was prying, and I shouldn't have asked so many questions."

His smile could have put the sun to shame on a bright day in July. "You weren't being nosy. That's just the way folks get to know each other, and if we're going to work together, even just for today, it's called conversation. So, you and your twin aren't identical?"

"Nope, and our personalities are different. Mama always said Rae was the introverted twin, and I was the extroverted one. That might not seem strange to you, but Rae worked for the police force, so you'd think she was the outgoing one. But I don't have a problem speaking my mind."

"I like a woman who isn't afraid to speak up, and I like your southern accent," Maverick said. "Did you pick that up in Nashville?"

"Thanks again, but I probably got most of it from being raised here in Texas and then living in Nashville for ten years," Bo answered. "I've got this part ready to hang up there. You want to climb the ladder or feed it up to me?"

"How are we going to get it to stay up?" he asked.

She held up a whole card of thumbtacks. "With these. It's not very heavy, so they should work, and they are green, so they'll be hidden in the garland." She would rather learn more about him than talk about decorations.

Chapter 5

AUNT BERNIE SURE HAD an eye for using leftover decorations, Bo thought as she stood in the doorway and took one final look at the place. "We got it done with fifteen minutes to spare, but I couldn't have done it without you." She picked up a Santa hat and handed it to him. "This is the last note on the list—we have to wear the hats."

Maverick shoved it down over his hair and then turned around slowly. "Place looks fantastic. Dave got the better end of that deal."

Bo put on the matching hat and was glad that her aunt hadn't made them wear jingle bell necklaces. "I'm not telling Bernie you said that. She thinks she pulled the wool over his eyes."

A hard knock on the front door was followed by a woman's loud voice. "Hey, are y'all open yet?"

"Looks like we've got an early bird," Maverick said.

Bo crossed the entry way. "Nope, that would be my twin sister, Rae." She slung the door open and gasped at a full parking lot.

"I'm not a stranger, and I realize the wind blew my hair a bit, but do I really look that bad?" Rae asked.

Bo grabbed her sister by the arm, pulled her inside, and quickly locked the door. "No, you look great, especially if you've come to help. I thought you were going to be busy with the Sunday school lesson for tomorrow."

Maverick took a couple of steps forward and extended his hand. "I'm Maverick Gibson, and Bo was right. You don't look anything alike."

"Nope, we don't," Rae shook with him and then dropped his hand. "We were Mama's trial run. She got the identical thing right on the next set of twin girls. Pleased to meet you, and, Bo, I'll take care of the Sunday school thing later. What can I do to help?"

"You're a day late and a dollar short, as Aunt Bernie says," Bo grumbled.

"I'm here now." Rae removed her coat to reveal a sweater the color of her blue eyes and skinny jeans that hugged every one of her curves. She sat down at the table near the door, pulled a brush from her purse, and straightened up her long dark hair. "Put me to work."

"You want to play hostess or sit right where you are and check tickets?" Bo asked.

"I'll check tickets and then mingle with the guests," Rae said. "You are better with a microphone in your hands or else singing to the crowd. Will there be dancing?"

"Maybe," Maverick answered and headed across the foyer toward the door. "I've got orders to keep the jukebox going. I'll let in the herd in two minutes. Y'all ready?"

"Give me just a split second to go to the restroom and…"

Rae stood up and then stopped at the archway into the bar. "This looks amazing, and so do you, Sister. You always did look good in green velvet. I love the little lit-up Christmas trees in the middle of the tables. I remember when Mama used those for the Paradise party when we were teenagers." She glanced over at Maverick, fanned her face with her hand, and mouthed a single word. "*Wow!*"

Bo shook her head. "*No way*," she mouthed back.

"I borrowed the dress from Ophelia," Bo said, "and thank you. You don't look so shabby yourself, but we could have used your help all afternoon."

"Ain't my job." Rae waved and did a fast walk across the room.

Maverick waited to open the door until Rae was back and seated. Bo took a few more pictures of the room to send to Bernie, then took her place on the stage in front of the microphone. When the room was full, she said, "Welcome to our first ever meet-and-greet event. I am Bo Simmons. My sister Rae gave you your name tags when you came inside. If anyone doesn't have a name tag, please go back out and tell Rae. You ladies all look beautiful, and you guys are really handsome. Y'all mingle and get to know each other," Bo said. "Maverick Gibson is behind the bar. Beer is free tonight. We take cash or credit cards for anything else." Bo stepped off the stage and headed through the crowd toward the bar.

Rae met her halfway across the room and looped her arm into Bo's. "Aunt Bernie didn't tell us how sexy Maverick was, did she?"

"I'm not sure she ever saw him," Bo said. "I believe she only met with Dave O'Connell, the man who owns the place. Maverick is the manager and bartender. "

"Honey, we don't have to buy the candy store to try all the samples that they're giving away for free," Rae said with a chuckle.

"I just felt a chill," Bo smiled.

Rae removed her arm and sat down on a barstool. "Why's that?"

"Aunt Bernie's spirit just swept through the room and heard what you said," Bo whispered.

"I don't believe in ghosts," Rae said.

"Well, hello, darlin'," an older man with silver hair and a cute little mustache said and turned his charm on both Rae and Bo. "Neither of you look like you are sixty or older."

"Thank you," Bo said. "That's so sweet of you. But we are the two women, along with Maverick, who are managing this event."

"And he could sure use some help," Maverick said from the other end of the bar.

Bo nudged Rae. "You go start pushing buttons on the juke-box and remember how old this crowd is. I'll draw up beers."

"I guess you did see him first," Rae grinned. "But honey, this bunch of people wasn't raised on Waylon and Willie. I'll try Blake Shelton, Alan Jackson, and Travis Tritt."

Bo shot her a dose of stink eye and then made her way behind the bar. She removed an apron from a hook on the wall and slipped it around her waist.

Rae just giggled and slid off the stool. In minutes, Waylon Jennings's voice filled the room with "I'm a Ramblin' Man." Bo jerked her head around in time to see Rae give her a long wink.

"That's my theme song." Maverick chuckled as he set four red Solo cups of beer on the bar and watched them disappear. "The lyrics warn a woman not to give her heart to a rambling man. Would you throw caution to the wind and ignore that?"

"Probably not," Bo answered. "I might think about a rambling man, but down deep, I would know that I was better off without him when he was gone," Bo said.

"If you thought about me, would it be with a smile?" Maverick asked with a twinkle in his eyes.

"Hun...nee." She dragged out the word and batted her long lashes at him. "I've been told to lock up my heart and throw away the keys where you are concerned," Bo told him. "But then what if there's a woman in this area who isn't afraid to stand close to the flame?"

One side of Maverick's mouth turned up in a grin. "I'd like to meet such a woman."

"Ramblin' Man" ended and Linda Ronstadt's "Blue Bayou" started. A few men must've gotten enough liquid courage by then to ask women to dance because the floor in front of the stage filled up pretty quick.

Bo worked her way down the bar until she came to the place where Rae was still sitting. "I would have never thought there were this many single men and women in the area. I figured you'd be out there mingling with the folks who are sitting at tables," Bo told her. "And from the information that each person gave when they bought their tickets, they came from as far north as Duncan, Oklahoma, and as far south as Rainbow, Texas."

"Are you serious? Is there really a town named Rainbow?" Rae asked.

"Yep, and just to be sure, I looked it up, and it's down around Granbury," Bo answered. "Now, what are you doing sitting at the bar when you should be out there talking to people?"

"I was, and I learned something valuable. They like the songs that are playing on the jukebox, but they want something with some spirit to it, and they wouldn't mind listening to the newer country music. One lady with kinky blue hair…"—she raised a palm—"I swear I'm not kidding"— she lowered her hand—"said that she wanted to hear some Chris Stapleton or Morgan Wallen. According to her and the three women at her table, over sixty doesn't mean over sex. Made me think of Aunt Bernie's lacy teddy, and if she will get to wear it."

"Maybe rather than peanuts and candy canes, we should have little blue pills in the bowls on the bar," Bo said.

"Bo!" Rae scolded, but she couldn't keep the giggle at bay.

Her sister held up two fingers. "If I'm lyin', I'm flyin', and my feet ain't left the ground."

"That sounded just like Aunt Bernie," Rae said.

"Yep, it did," Bo nodded.

Rae finished the last of her beer and slid off the stool.

"I'm off to give the folks some different music. The song playing now is the last one that I punched into the machine."

As soon as her sister vacated the barstool, a lady with big hair, lots of bling, and a T-shirt that fit like a glove, claimed it. "Dawlin', I would like a double shot of Jim Beam on the rocks."

Bo glanced down at the name tag plastered just three inches to the left of the woman's cleavage. "I will get right on that, Miz Dixie." She poured two shots of whiskey into one of the red plastic cups and added a couple of ice cubes. She set it on the bar in front of the lady, took her money, and made change.

"Fancy glasses you got here," Dixie said.

Bo agreed with a nod. "Red for Christmas."

"And for the cute little teddy I've got ready if I get lucky tonight." Dixie winked and carried her drink back to a table where the gray-haired guy who had hit on Rae was sitting.

"Good luck, Miz Dixie," Bo whispered, and made a mental note to tell Aunt Bernie that she wasn't the only one who had a teddy and hopes of wearing it to entice a fellow.

Fiddle music filled the room, and the folks sitting at the tables headed for the dance floor to do the twist to Mary Chapin Carpenter's "Down on Twist and Shout."

"Well, that sure livened them up. I guess sixty and above isn't so old after all," Maverick said.

Bo wiped sweat from her brow with the tail of her apron. "Gives us a little breather."

Maverick agreed with a nod. "Yep, but after a couple

or three songs like that they'll be thirsty, and we'll have a rush."

Bo took a longneck bottle of beer from the cooler, twisted the top off, and took a long swig. "Or else some of them like Dixie will talk someone like Hank into leaving this place and going to her room or apartment. How do you keep up when it's just you working the bar?"

Maverick drew up a beer in one of the cups. "It's not usually this busy. Are you aware that when the party is over, if half of these people stick around, the fine print on the contract that you and your aunt signed says you have to stay and help me until closing?"

She almost choked on the mouthful of beer she'd just taken. "You're sh…kiddin' me, right?"

He reached under the counter and brought out a folder. "Got it right here."

"Aunt Bernie didn't tell me anything about that," Bo said.

Maverick shrugged and turned up his cup. "Guess she wasn't expecting a crowd like this."

"Okay, then, if half of them stay, I guess I'll be here until closing," she said with a sigh. "At least, they'll be paying for drinks then and things might slow down."

"Maybe," Maverick nodded.

Luke Bryan's "One Margarita" started playing, and several other women joined Dixie on the dance floor. Bo was less than half their age, and there was no way she could move like they did.

"What are you thinking?" Maverick asked.

"Why do you ask?" Bo fired back.

"You were shaking your head, and your eyes had the deer-in-the-headlights look," Maverick answered.

"Honestly, I was wondering how they could move like that at their age," she answered.

"Determination," Maverick said.

"For what?"

"Love, companionship, feeling young again—any or all of the above. Some of them are single by lifestyle choice. Some have lost a loved one and crave companionship. But most"—he smiled—"are just feeling good and having as much fun as they can while they can."

"How'd you get to be so smart?" Bo asked.

"I've had lots of different jobs and plenty of time to study people," Maverick answered. "Wait for it. Wait for it."

"What?" Bo looked around the whole room.

"Here it comes," Maverick grinned. "Song is ending. There's been two fast dances in a row, and now they'll be lining up for more free beers."

Chris Stapleton's slow song "Tennessee Whiskey" filled the room, and Rae claimed the barstool at the end of the row. Bo set a beer in front of her.

"Every third song is slow," Rae explained. "I figured they could strut their stuff for a couple, and then two-step or waltz to one. That way the poor guys might not use up all their energy and need a fistful of those pills you were talking about earlier."

"Good idea," Bo agreed, and then went back to helping

Maverick set cups on the bar. For a few minutes, Dixie was the only one on the dance floor, and then the gray-haired man brought her a beer. She took a long drink, then wrapped her free arm around his neck and snuggled in close.

"With all that she's got going on, that guy might be primed and ready when the party is over," Bo whispered to her sister.

"Honey, I would bet dollars to cow patties that a lot of those men are carrying little blue pills," Rae said with a laugh. "They've only got an hour left to figure out who's getting lucky and who's going home alone. I wonder how many long-term matches will come out of this event."

"Count the couples that leave," Bo said and then went back to helping Maverick set filled cups on the bar for the folks to grab.

For the next hour the pattern was set: two fast songs, and a slow one. Five minutes before nine, "I Always Get Lucky with You" by George Jones played on the jukebox.

"Smart idea," Bo told Rae when the song started. "Do you think any of the folks have found someone to get lucky with tonight?"

"Maybe, but even if they all go home alone, it looks like they've had a good time," Rae answered and nodded toward the clock. "It's been fun. It's been real, but now I'm going home. See you there, Bo. Drive safe."

"You too," Bo said with a nod, and hoped that the whole crowd would leave. Her feet hurt after working two hours in high-heeled shoes. She wanted to go home, too, take a long hot bath and go to sleep.

If they didn't, she would definitely trade in her fancy dress and high heels for the jeans, T-shirt, and running shoes she had worn that morning to the parade. She removed her apron, went to the stage, and turned on the microphone.

"We hope all y'all had a good time. The event is now closed, but all are welcome to stay as long as you like. Just a reminder that beer and music is no longer free," she said.

That got a few laughs, and then Dixie raised her red cup. "Let's hear a big *yee-haw* for the folks that put on this event. Make it loud enough that they'll consider doing another one soon. I don't know about the rest of you, but I'm going to close down this bar tonight. So, one, two, three." She led the whole crowd in a *yee-haw* that came close to raising the roof.

"Thank you," Bo breathed into the microphone, and then heard piano music behind her. She recognized the song as "The Party's Over." She looked over her shoulder to see Maverick playing.

"Seems appropriate," he said. "But I need a singer."

Maverick started the introduction all over again, and she came in at the right time with the lyrics. The folks raised their lighted cell phones and waved them in the air. Bo looked out over the crowd and enjoyed the moment. For the next three minutes, she was onstage, living her dream—even if it was in Nocona, Texas, and not Nashville, Tennessee.

She had no regrets about turning out the lights and leaving the party when she moved from Nashville. But she had not realized how much she would miss the excitement of having a microphone in her hand—even with just a piano behind her and not a whole band.

Bo took a bow when the song ended, and the crowd exploded with a round of applause and whistles. Couples began to leave, some walking beside each other, and some holding hands like teenagers. If Aunt Bernie had been there, she would have been walking on air and declaring that she wasn't just good at advice; she was a true matchmaker.

Maverick left the piano. Bo turned off the microphone and put it back on the stand. The two of them headed back to the bar where folks had already lined up and were waiting to get drinks.

"You really are good," he said.

"So are you," she told him. "Where did you learn to play a honky-tonk piano?"

"Just something I picked up," he answered with half a shrug. "It looks to me like less than half the crowd left, and a few more are drifting in. Can you manage things for me to take a five-minute bathroom break?"

"When you are finished, I'm taking a few to go change into more comfortable clothes and shoes. If I've got to work until closing, I'm not doing it in high heels," she said.

"Sounds good to me, but darlin', the outfit you've got on might draw more customers to the bar."

She gave him her best dose of stink eye, and he laughed out loud. He didn't go out into the foyer where the bathrooms were located but went through the door to the storage room.

She knew what to charge for shots of Jim Beam, but she had no idea how much mugs or bottles of beer went for. Thank goodness, he returned before his five minutes were up and got busy filling orders, taking money, and making change.

"Go get a break before things get to really hopping," he told her as he stacked empty plastic cups together and tossed them in the trash.

"Be back as soon as I can," Bo told him.

She grabbed her tote bag from under the bar and raced off to the bathroom, only to find a long line of women waiting.

Dixie waved at her from the front of the line. "Hey, that was some party. Just flat out gave me the Christmas spirit and made me feel like I'd shed twenty years. The only thing missing was Santa Claus. I would have liked to sit on his lap and tell him I wanted to find my next true love." She shot a dramatic wink across the distance.

Bo removed her Santa hat and handed it to Dixie. "Wear this. Maybe it will make your Santa wish come true, even if he's not here."

Dixie pulled the hat down over her big hair and smiled. "Can I keep it to remember this night by?"

"It's yours," Bo said.

"I wanted to come, but I didn't hear about it until today and it was too late," the woman behind her said.

Dixie shook a finger at her. "You are married, Ilene!"

"Would you come if we have a couples' event in the near

future?" Bo asked. "It might be a fall-in-love-all-over-again event."

"I'll be there," the woman said. "And Dixie, darlin', you will have to get married to be able to attend."

"Never underestimate me," Dixie snapped and then turned back to Bo. "Honey, you come on up here and cut in line in front of me. Looks like you are here to change clothes. I hope you've got some comfortable shoes in that bag. I don't know how you worked for two hours in high heels."

"My feet *are* hurting," Bo admitted. "But…"

Dixie shook her head. "No *but*s to it. If any of these gals have a problem, I'll take care of it. Consider it payment for the evening and the lucky hat. You just scoot right on in there and change so you can help your handsome bartender until closing."

He is a handsome bartender, but he's not mine, Bo thought.

She changed as fast as she could and found the line outside to be even longer when she opened the door. "Thank all of you for letting me cut in line," she said.

"No problem, darlin'," Dixie said with a smile.

"Y'all enjoy the rest of the night," Bo said and then made her way back to the bar.

"Looks like the rest of the night could be busier than we were during the event," she said as she tied her apron around her waist.

"Yep," Maverick agreed as he shook a cocktail container and poured the contents into a stemmed glass. "Would you please gather up all the dirty red plastic cups from the tables?"

Bo had worked as a barmaid and as a waitress at different times during the past ten years, so she was no stranger to cleaning tables or taking care of empty bottles and glasses. She picked up a tray and two wet bar rags and headed for the back corner where several cups were lined up on a table.

An older man wearing coveralls and work boots sat down at the table. "Looks like y'all had quite the party. If you have another one, I might buy a ticket."

Bo gathered up more than a dozen cups and then wiped down the table before moving on. "I'm sure we'll schedule another one sometime. Just keep a watch out for flyers."

"Don't have it on Saturday night," the guy said. "I work the two-to-ten shift then. By the way, I'm Harold Anderson. You are one of Bernie's nieces, aren't you?"

"Yes, sir," Bo answered and introduced herself.

"I used to live up around Ratliff City. She talked about all y'all a lot," Harold said with a chuckle. "Bernie ran a tight ship, but I sure loved her bar. Tell her that I said hello next time you see her."

"I sure will, and it's nice to meet you," Bo said.

"Back at you, kiddo," Harold said with a big smile.

Three trips to the trash can later, the tables had been cleared of all the leftovers from the event and were being covered with beer mugs and highball, shot, and wineglasses.

"Thank you for the first cleanup round," Maverick said.

Bo dropped the bar rags into the bin and loaded what glassware she had collected into the dishwasher. "You are welcome. Do you have plenty of mugs left or should I start this?"

"Wait until it's full." Maverick set two beers on the bar for a couple of cowboys.

When he laid their change on the table, one of them tossed it into the tip jar.

"Thank you." Maverick nodded and went on to the next customer. "Hey, Bo, why don't you read what's in the folder with the contract before you do anything else?"

"Why would I do that?" Bo asked. "If Aunt Bernie signed an agreement, I will honor it."

"Just read it," Maverick said. "Dave would fire me if I was dishonest."

Bo wiped down the end of the long bar before she picked up the folder and opened it. "You rat! This is not a contract. It's a liquor and beer order form."

Maverick pointed his forefinger at her. "Gotcha! But thanks for cleaning up before you go. And darlin', if you ever need a job, there's one waiting right here at Whiskey Bent."

"That was a mean trick, and I've got a full-time job," she snapped at him.

"If you'll stay a couple of hours until the crowd thins out, you can have whatever is in the tip jar," he said.

She leaned back to get a better view of the quart jar at the other end of the bar. She could see at least two five-dollar bills and lots of ones. "Deal, but only until midnight. I've got to be in church tomorrow morning."

"Are you the sister that is dating the preacher?" Maverick asked.

Bo shook her head. "Nope. That would be Endora, my younger sister. I play the piano and help with the musical part of the Christmas program."

"Well, honey, anytime you want to play and sing for this bar, the stage is yours for as long as you want," Maverick told her.

"I appreciate that, but the answer is no, thanks," Bo said. "I devoted enough of my time to 'the dream.'" She air quoted the last two words.

"My offer of a job here or even an occasional gig has no expiration date," Maverick said as he drew up a couple of beers.

"I'll keep it in mind," Bo said and picked up a tray. "Looks like I need to make the rounds for orders and pick up another load of dirty dishes."

"How many bars have you worked in?" Maverick asked.

"Too many to count," she answered.

━━━━━━━━

Rae weaved her way through the ladies' room waiting line, zipped up her coat, and left the noisy bar behind. Black clouds covered the southern half of the sky, most likely bringing in more cold wind and possibly rain or sleet. But right over her head, she caught sight of a falling star as it streaked from the heavens toward earth. She closed her eyes, made a wish, and headed for her truck. A noise off to her left made her stop before she unlocked her vehicle. A couple was standing beside a brand-new bright-red sports car. Their coats covered up their name tags, but Rae was sure she had seen both of them at the party. Aunt Bernie would be so tickled to know that her event had netted at least one match.

She was wide-awake when she unlocked her truck door and slid in under the steering wheel. Her internal clock was still set from working night shifts for the past several years, and this was the time that she was usually getting ready to go to work. A little bit of guilt washed over her when she thought of leaving her twin behind to work until the bar closed down. Bo was probably ready for bed and sleep.

"But not guilty enough to stick around and help," she mumbled.

Before she could put the truck in reverse, her phone rang, and Bernie's face popped up.

"Speak of the devil." Rae chuckled and hit the accept button for FaceTime. "Hello. Are y'all getting excited to get onboard tomorrow morning?"

"We're giddy as teenagers getting ready for their first dates," Bernie answered. "I called Bo several times, but it went right to voicemail. Do you know how the event went?"

"Yep," Rae answered. "I decided to come help out for a couple of hours, and the place was packed. Over ninety folks showed up. That's pretty good since you capped the ticket sales at a hundred."

Bernie smiled, but her eyes looked tired. "That was

sweet of you. Did you girls follow the directions I left for decorating?"

"I didn't help with that," Rae said, "but they were great. I took a bunch of pictures. I'll send them to your phone soon as I get home. I helped scan the tickets. That way you'll be able to see who actually showed up. And I kept the jukebox going."

"Is Bo with you?" Bernie asked.

Rae set the phone on the dashboard stand and turned it so her aunt could see her. "No, she's not. According to the contract you signed, she has to stay and help Maverick until closing."

"That is a bunch of bullshit!" Bernie's face went from smiling to anger in a fraction of a second. "I liked that guy. Why would he lie to Bo like that? You go right back in there and tell her that she doesn't have to work one minute past nine o'clock." Her voice got higher with each word, and her face more pinched. "I paid extra money for cleanup, and nobody takes advantage of me. I'll have a come-to-Jesus talk with Dave over this when I get home."

"Yes, ma'am." Rae said with a nod.

"Hanging up now, and when you get back to your truck, you call me," Bernie said. "And hurry up!"

The screen went dark. Rae drew in a long breath and let it out in a whoosh. She got out of the truck, noticed that the couple had progressed beyond talking and were now making out like a couple of teenagers.

"It's cold out here. Go find a room somewhere," she whispered.

The song that was playing on the jukebox had brought the line dancers out in force, so she had to practically plaster herself to the wall to get back to where Bo was wiping down a table.

Her sister looked up and cocked her head to one side. "Hey, what are you doing back in here?" Bo yelled over the loud music.

"You need to call Aunt Bernie. She said to tell you that she did not sign a contract that said you had to stay and work until closing time, and believe me, she's fightin' mad right now," Rae told her.

"I'm staying until midnight, and getting paid for it," Bo yelled just as the song ended.

A couple of guys turned around and gave Maverick the thumbs-up.

"Getting paid to do what?" Rae teased.

"Waitress, bartend, the normal stuff," Bo snapped.

"Just call Bernie before she has a cardiac arrest and doesn't even go on her cruise. If she even survived the heart attack, we would never hear the end of it. And if she didn't, she would haunt us," Rae said and turned to walk away.

"Amen to that," Bo agreed. "Now, you need to go home and get ready to teach a Sunday school class in the morning."

Rae groaned. "Don't remind me."

Bo removed her phone from her hip pocket, turned it on, and waved at her sister. Rae glanced over her shoulder a couple of times to make sure that Bo had called their aunt. She sure didn't want to have to deal with her on her drive from Nocona back to Spanish Fort. When Bernie got on a high horse, she couldn't be budged with a block of C-4.

Rae got into the truck for a second time and was relieved that her phone didn't ring. She drove out of the parking lot and turned right. Christmas lights twinkled in a few houses on the way into the town, where lights were strung from one side of Main Street to the other. Several stores had decorations in their windows and holiday wreaths hanging on the doors.

"It's beginning to look a lot like Christmas," Rae sang off-key and out of tune. She had always been jealous of her sister's ability to play any instrument she picked up and sing like an angel. But she did love to listen to music, and chills ran down her spine when Bo made the fiddle whine in true Charlie Daniels style.

In another week, the town would have their ceremonies to celebrate the holiday—a parade with floats and area high school bands, the lighting of the huge Christmas tree, and all kinds of fun in the park. When she and all her sisters were young, they had looked forward to the event. Rae liked the face-painting booth and always loved the funnel cakes. Bo and the younger twins couldn't wait for their turn to sit on Santa's lap and tell him what they wanted to find under the tree on Christmas morning.

Rae was driving through the middle of town when she heard a pop, and her truck began to pull to the right. "Dammit!" she swore and brought the vehicle to a stop on the side of the street. That's when she noticed a low-tire signal flashing on the dashboard. She slapped the steering wheel. "A flat tire is not what I need at this time of night. And to top it all off, it looks like it could rain cats and dogs and baby elephants any minute now."

She slung the door open, put her feet on the ground, and stomped around to the back of the truck to get out the spare and jack. She inhaled deeply, and sure enough, she could practically smell the rain on the way. She had just made it to the tailgate when lightning zigzagged through the air and thunder rumbled.

"Less than ten seconds. Daddy would say that means the storm is less than ten miles away and moving fast," Rae muttered and then saw the familiar lights of a police car pulling in behind her.

"Hey, is that you, Rae?" Gunner Watson yelled as he got out of the Nocona Police Department truck.

"It's me, all right, and I've got a flat tire," she answered.

"You just stand back and watch this pro at work," Gunner said. "We've got a helluva storm coming in from the southwest, so I'll hurry."

"Hey, now!" Rae protested and flipped the hood of her coat up over her hair. "I appreciate your help, and I may not be a pro, but I've changed my fair share of tires."

"I don't doubt that one bit"—Gunner chuckled—"but I don't want my girls' Sunday school teacher to get wet. You might get sick, and Aunt Rosie has plans for tomorrow that do not include watching the twins after church services. That means you have to stay healthy to teach them, and I have to be able to take care of them tomorrow afternoon."

"Then thank you, and I'll do my best to be there for…" She tried to remember their names.

"Heather and Daisy." Gunner jacked the truck up. "They are so much alike that everyone has trouble telling them apart. Most folks just call them the Watson twins."

"Heather has a freckle in front of her left ear," Rae told him.

"You are very observant." Gunner chuckled again as he removed the flat tire and tossed it in the back of her truck. "Looks like you ran over a nail. It can probably be fixed, so you won't have to buy a new one. Now, let's get the spare on."

"Thank you, again." Her words came out a little breathless, but holy smoke, Gunner had hefted the old tire like it was nothing more than a package of marshmallows. She would bet that a ripped abdomen and thick biceps were hiding under that uniform shirt.

Gunner set the new tire into place, tightened the lug bolts, and removed the jack. "No problem. My one prisoner tonight has been in so many jail cells that they probably all look alike to him." He held out his hand. "Just in time. There's the first raindrop. See you around, Miz Rae."

She waved another thank-you and got into her truck seconds before the downpour. The police vehicle behind her pulled slowly out onto the street, and Gunner flashed the lights once to let her know he was gone. For a moment, she missed making the rounds in her police car up in the Oklahoma Panhandle, the camaraderie between her and her partner who retired the week before Rae left, and the independence she had.

Visibility was only two center yellow lines in front of her. Water ran over the roads so fast that using cruise control wasn't even an option. The twenty-minute trip to the Paradise took twice that long. When she turned down the lane to go to the house, the hard rain seemed to put a halo around every single twinkling light in the trees and on the top of the fence. She started to stop and take a picture, but a mere photograph wouldn't do justice to the sight.

Rae's phone rang, and she removed it from the holder and checked the time. 11:55. "Hello, Bo. Are you on the way home?"

"Yep, we lost electricity about ten minutes ago and had to close up the bar early, but I still got a jar full of tips for payment. I consider the power outage an act of God. Therefore, I do not have to prorate my two hours and give back part of the tips," she answered.

"I'm home but the rain is coming down so hard the ground can't soak it up, so the roads are slicker than…"

"Vaseline on a toilet seat?" Bo giggled.

"I wasn't thinking along that line, but yes," Rae answered. "Drive slow and don't use the cruise control."

"Yes, Sister Policeman," Bo said. "I'm coming through Nocona now. The Christmas lights look weird through the rain. I'm jealous that you are home, dry and in your room already."

"Woman, you haven't got any reason to be envious. I had a flat tire on the way home, and I'm sitting outside the house hoping this deluge lets up so I can make a mad dash between raindrops without getting too wet." Rae shivered at the thought of the bitter cold rain soaking her to the bone. "I may still be in my truck when you get here."

"Thank goodness Daddy taught us girls how to change a tire, check the oil, and pay attention to the gas gauge," Bo said. "I think I just ran a red light. I thought it was a Christmas decoration."

"Is there a cop car behind you?" Rae asked. "Maybe he'll let you off with a warning if you explain…"

"Stop worrying," Bo said. "No flashing lights in my rear-view, and I'm driving so slow that a snail could pass me. I can't see but one yellow line in the center of the road."

Another shiver ran from Rae's backbone down to her toes in spite of the fact she was sitting in a warm truck. "You stay on the phone with me until you get home. I'm worried about you. It is sitting on the dash, and you are not driving with one hand, are you?"

"I told you how fast I'm going, but I will keep talking until I get home. Besides, I'm not the one who slipped and slid all over the road last Christmas." Bo reminded her sister of what had happened the last holiday season when all seven girls went shopping.

"I got us to Wichita Falls, and all in one piece, didn't I?" Rae shot back. "But that was scary. Rain and slick roads can be just as dangerous as ice and snow. I'll feel better when you are home."

"Me too," Bo said.

"You must have talked to Aunt Bernie because she didn't call me back," Rae said.

"Yes, I did, and she was pleased with the outcome, but angry that Maverick pulled that trick on me. I told her that I considered him a good man since he owned up to the joke," Bo answered. "I just turned onto Highway one-oh-three, and the rain is coming down even harder. The weather report says it's not going to let up for another three hours. You and I should've gotten a hotel room in Nocona and driven home in the morning."

Rae turned off the engine and zipped up her jacket. "It's too late for *should have* now, and besides, I bet every room in town is filled with folks from the event tonight."

Bo giggled with her sister. "Aunt Bernie told me that she wasn't going to book another event at the bar because she didn't want me falling for Maverick."

"Think you could?" Rae asked.

"He probably makes a lot of women have trouble keeping their underwear from falling down around their ankles," Bo answered. "But I don't believe in love at first sight."

"Don't lie to me," Rae scolded. "I could feel the sparks dancing all around the bar."

"Don't tell Aunt Bernie that, or she'll have a conniption. I'm passing the winery, so it won't be long until I'm home. I'm wrong. That wasn't the turnoff to the winery. I'm seeing the lights at Remy and Ursula's place. And now I'm turning down the lane to the Paradise."

Rae breathed a sigh of relief and then noticed the lights of a vehicle coming down the lane. "You are home. We're safe."

"Yep, but it looks like we're both going to be drenched by the time we get into the house," Bo told her.

"Better wet than in a ditch," Rae said. "I'm going to make a mad dash for the house, and we can talk more about the event tomorrow after church. I'm so tense that I just want some warm pajamas and a bed."

"See you there."

Chapter 6

ENDORA GLANCED OVER AT the children's book she had been working on and sighed. She hadn't had time in weeks to get back to the Easter story about the dog Pepper and the three cats. Luck would have to come into play if she could meet the February deadline. She left her bedroom and stopped at Rae's door, knocked, and then peeked inside to see Rae and Bo sitting cross-legged on the bed, each holding a steaming coffee mug.

"What's going on in here?" Endora asked and opened the door wider. "I miss the twin mornings when Luna came to my room for a visit."

"Come on in and have a seat." Rae patted the bed beside her. "Getting home last night was a chore with all the rain."

"It rained?" Endora frowned.

"You didn't hear the storm?" Bo asked.

Endora shook her head. "I was exhausted and went to bed before ten. This wedding stuff has got me stressed out."

"No wonder," Rae said. "You're juggling too much with all you're trying to get done at the church. You need to delegate some more."

"I can't," Endora said with another long sigh. "But when Christmas is over…"

Bo threw up both hands. "We know! Then we can start planning a wedding as big as Luna's was. I still think you and Parker should go to Vegas or…"

"To the courthouse," Rae finished the sentence for her sister.

"I'm…well…worried…" Endora stammered.

"Spit it out," Rae said.

"Worried about what?" Bo asked.

Endora frowned and tears filled her eyes. "I love Parker, and I can't wait to be with him all the time, but I'm afraid I'll make a horrible preacher's wife and disappoint him and…" She stopped for a breath, and then went on. "What if I can't handle all the responsibility, and he winds up wishing he had never married me?"

Rae wrapped her sister up in her arms, and Bo joined them for a three-way hug.

"Parker is marrying you because he loves *you*." Rae patted Endora on the back.

Bo pulled a tissue from the bedside table and dried her sister's tears. "That's right. This is just a small community, but you've got a lot of help. You don't have to do everything, or even show up at every little thing. You could lose what's left of Endora if you stretch yourself that thin, and Parker fell in love with *Endora*—not with a children's book author, or a fantastic organizer, or even a preacher's wife."

Endora had always taken comfort in talking to her

sisters, whether it was Rae and Bo, who were only a year older than she and Luna, or the three who were above them in age. They had been the ones, along with her parents, who had helped her move on from the ordeal with her previous fiancé.

"Here's the new rules," Rae declared. "When you put someone in charge of a project, like me teaching the little kids' Sunday school class, you don't get to pop in to see how things are going. Trust whoever has that responsibility to do their job."

"Yes!" Bo agreed. "We are not like the elementary students you used to teach who had to have their work checked. We can handle the job."

Endora took another deep breath and let it out slowly. "Y'all are right. I just want everything to be perfect."

"Life ain't perfect, kiddo," Rae told her. "I understand why you are feeling like this, though. You feel like you failed with your first engagement…"

Endora nodded with every word.

"But you didn't," Bo finished the sentence. "Let go of that and move on to a relationship with Parker. You don't need that baggage hanging around your neck like an albatross."

Endora wrapped an arm around each sister. "Thank you both, and you are right. I just need to concentrate on being a wife and mother first and foremost."

Rae's eyes widened. "Are you?"

"Is that why you don't want to wait until…?" Bo gasped.

"No, and no, but I've tossed my birth control pills in

the trash. Parker and I want to start our family as soon as we are married." The dark cloud that had been hanging over Endora for weeks disappeared, and suddenly her heart and soul felt lighter at the very mention of having a family in the near future.

"What about between now and March?" Rae asked.

"Neither of us is a virgin, but we decided to wait until our wedding night." Endora said and felt the heat of a blush filling her cheeks. "That sounds so crazy in today's world, doesn't it?"

Rae shook her head. "I probably couldn't do that, but I think it's sweet. Just remember one thing through all this. It's your life and your wedding, so don't let anyone else's opinion worry you."

"No wonder you don't want to wait!" Bo said. "Holy smoke! You've been dating for months. Are you afraid that he's going to do what Kevin did?"

"No," Endora answered. "I trust Parker, but we want to…" She paused. "It's complicated. There's no way we could go to the parsonage and spend the night. We dang sure can't have sex on a church pew or in my bedroom here at the Paradise. The simple answer was just to wait until we're married."

"There's a barn out back," Rae suggested.

"And Aunt Bernie's trailer is only fifty yards from there," Endora reminded her. "Believe me, I've thought of everything."

Bo raised an eyebrow. "Hotel room."

Endora set her mouth in a firm line. "It's like I'm a teenager again. This county is so small that someone would see us for sure. I haven't talked to Parker yet, but I was thinking maybe we'd have a surprise wedding like Ophelia and Tertia had."

"When?" Rae asked.

"Right after the Christmas program. Our old preacher will be there, so we'll have someone to do the ceremony. Parker's family are all coming. Our whole crew will be there, and there's a potluck afterwards in the fellowship hall so we can call that our reception. I could 'borrow'"—she air quoted the last word—"Luna's dress and even her bouquet. They are both stored in her old bedroom."

Bo patted Endora on the knee. "We'll keep your secret and even help get the dress to the church."

"I'll order a cake from Wichita Falls and make sure it's in the fellowship hall. The children in my class will have their part in the program at the first, so I'll have time to take care of that," Rae said.

"And you won't tell anyone else?" Endora asked.

Rae held up her little finger. "Pinkie swear that it'll just be between us three. Us twins have to all stick together."

"Not even Luna?" Endora begged. "She'll want to drag out all her wedding floral arrangements and decorate the fellowship hall. Everything will get out of hand."

"Not even," Rae and Bo said in unison as they all three locked their little fingers together.

Endora stood up and headed for the door. "I'll talk to

Parker right after church and let y'all know if it's a go, and thank you from the bottom of my heart."

"You are so welcome," Rae said. "Besides, from the way Maverick was looking at Bo last night, we may have a spring wedding anyway."

"In your dreams," Bo said.

Endora could hear them bantering back and forth as she made her way downstairs. The sweet smell of cinnamon floated up the stairs. That meant French toast, or else cinnamon rolls if Tertia and Noah had brought them from the café across the road. She stopped in the foyer for a moment to send up a silent prayer that she was making the right decision about an early wedding.

Tertia waved from across the big country kitchen. That morning she had swept up her ultra-curly brown hair into a messy bun on top of her head. "It's about time someone showed up. I was afraid that you were all going to sleep until time to rush out of here to church."

Noah's brown eyes twinkled. "She thought just the aroma of fresh-baked cinnamon buns and coffee would have everyone storming the kitchen before now." He had been a star football player in high school, and then had coached and been the Saint Jo High School principal until last summer, when he and Tertia got married and opened a café.

"Not even Mama or Daddy have gotten up," Tertia said.

Mary Jane entered the kitchen and covered a yawn with her hand. "Did I hear my name? That was some storm last night. Kept me awake until almost dawn."

Noah kissed Tertia on the forehead. "See, there's a reason no one is up at the crack of dawn like we are. And yes, ma'am, Mama Carter, you heard your name. You got here just in time for breakfast to come out of the oven so you can have a steaming hot cinnamon roll. Have a seat, and I'll pour coffee for you and Endora."

That's the kind of marriage I want, Endora thought.

Quit fretting about every little thing, and you will have it, Aunt Bernie's voice popped into her head.

———————

Rae walked into the classroom on Sunday morning with the teacher's study guide for that day's lesson in her hands. A memory surfaced of two sets of twins—she and Bo, and Endora and Luna—coming in that same room years ago. If any one of the four had had a halo, it would have been dusty and crooked for sure. Surely, she assured herself, she could manage Daisy and Heather Watson.

Everything was in place when six more little kids—two little girls and four boys—arrived.

"Good morning," Rae said. "If everyone will take a seat, we'll begin this morning by introducing ourselves. My name is Rae and I'm Endora's sister. I am your new Sunday school teacher."

A freckle-faced little boy raised his hand. "I'm Gary, and where is Miz Endora?"

"She's busy with some other things," Rae said. "I'm glad to meet you, Gary."

"I'm Calvin," the next little boy said.

The tallest of all the boys spoke up, "I'm Richie, and this is my brother, Donnie. He's younger than me, so Mama says I have to watch out for him. If Heather or Daisy are mean to him, she says I have to take up for him."

"Brothers *should* stick together." Rae wondered where the twins were that morning but was secretly glad that they weren't there.

"I'm Annie, and this is my cousin Bella. We're in the first grade at school, but Heather and Daisy aren't in our class." With her curly red hair and round face, the child could have easily played the part of Annie in a Broadway play. Her cousin Bella was a blond with blue eyes and reminded Rae of Endora at that age.

"All right then, Gary, Calvin, Richie, Donnie, Annie, and Bella, let's get started on the lesson for today," Rae said.

"How did you remember all our names like that?" Annie asked.

"It's just something I'm able to do," Rae answered.

"We're here!" Heather and Daisy said in unison as they slung the door open and slammed it behind them. "Did you bring cookies?"

"No, did you?" Rae asked.

Heather crossed her arms over her chest. "The teacher is supposed to bring cookies."

"Why would you think that, Heather?" Rae asked.

"I'm Daisy," she protested. "And the teacher brings cookies or candy to give us when we are good."

"No, darlin', you are Heather," Rae told her. "And you should be good because it's the right thing to do, not because you want a reward."

Daisy narrowed her eyes and glared at Rae. "I want Miz Endora to be our teacher."

"We don't always get what we want," Rae said, and then lowered her voice to a whisper. "Sit down and we will talk about baby Jesus, and then my twin sister, Bo, will come in here and you will all practice the two songs you are going to sing for the Christmas program."

Heather plopped down in a chair. "Do what she says, Daisy. She might have a gun on her leg like cops on television, and she might shoot you. That would make Daddy sad."

"But Aunt Rosie wouldn't care," Daisy said. "She likes you better than me."

"I do not have a gun. I won't shoot you, but if you don't behave, I will send you out to sit with your aunt Rosie for the next month. You won't get to be in the Christmas program, and that will really make your daddy sad. Do you want your daddy to be sad?" Rae stared right into Heather's pretty blue eyes.

"You win," the child said with a long sigh.

"Besides, I don't like sitting with those old women," Daisy said. "They smell funny."

"All right then, who either read our lesson for today or listened when their parents read it to them?" Rae asked.

All eight raised their hands. Rae asked questions and the

kids really got into the discussion, sometimes to the point of arguing and talking over each other. The next fifteen minutes went so quickly that Rae was surprised when Bo knocked on the door and peeked inside.

"Are y'all ready to do some singing?" she asked.

Several of the children nodded, but the Watson twins glared at her.

"You can't be Miz Rae's twin," Heather said.

"You don't look like her," Daisy added.

Rae shrugged when Bo raised an eyebrow. "You can take that one, sister."

"We are twins, but we are not identical," Bo said. "You can talk to your parents about the difference in fraternal and maternal twins after church. For right now, we're going to sing, so march single file out to the sanctuary."

"Why?" Gary asked. "We been singin' in here."

Bo opened the door wide and stood to the side. "You need to see where you will be standing and get used to the piano music with the songs."

"This is supposed to be fun, not like school," Heather grumbled.

Rae winked at her sister but didn't say a word. She had made a little progress with the ornery twins, but she would pick her battles. Thank goodness for that freckle below Heather's ear that let her tell them apart. That was the first baby step forward.

After Sunday school, Bo took her place at the piano on the right side of the sanctuary. Singing at Whiskey Bent the night before and then playing for church services that morning reminded her of a country song, "One Wing in the Fire." Lightning didn't come down from the rafters and turn her into a pile of ash, so she figured that God wasn't too upset with her. The congregation sang a couple of hymns and then Parker took his place behind the lectern. Bo quietly slipped down the narrow outside aisle to find a place to sit since there were no empty places in the front pew, where she usually sat with Endora.

Parker read something about when God visited Mary and told her that she would have a son, but past that Bo didn't hear a single word. Right there in front of her, standing up to allow her to sit down on a pew was Maverick Gibson with a big smile on his face. The aisle was so narrow that she couldn't go around him. To make a fuss would make everyone in the church stare at her even more than they already were. The cell phones would come out, thumbs would be a blur as folks ignored Parker's sermon, and texts would fly around the sanctuary like an annoying fly.

She nodded at Maverick and slid onto the old oak pew. Maverick sat down beside her and whispered. "You sure look pretty today. That sweater matches your eyes."

"*Thank you*," she mouthed and kept her eyes straight forward. That did not mean she didn't notice that his thick hair was flowing down to his shoulders and that his beard had been trimmed. Or that his dark-green-and-gold-plaid shirt, starched and ironed no less, brought out the flecks in his eyes. His jeans were creased, and his boots were so shiny she could have used them to apply her makeup.

"You played those hymns beautifully," he said out the corner of his mouth.

"What are you doing here?" she asked.

"Bar is closed on Sunday. Thought maybe I could talk you into going to lunch with me," he answered.

"Thanks, but not today," she said.

"Maybe another time," Maverick said with a grin that almost made her change her mind.

Somehow she made it through the next thirty minutes, but if she had to die or pass a test on what the sermon was that morning, she would have had to crawl up in a casket and cross her arms over her chest. Her eyes kept sneaking peeks over at Maverick, who stared straight ahead and either heard every word of the sermon or pretended that he did.

After the benediction, she stood up and turned around to find her oldest sister, Ursula, grinning at her from the pew right behind her. "Who's your friend?"

Maverick stuck out his hand. "I'm Maverick Gibson. Are you one of the sisters?"

"I'm the oldest, Ursula." She shook hands with him. "This is my husband, Remy, and that little guy with him is our son, Clayton. Are you new to this area?"

"Yes," Maverick answered. "I'm the manager of the bar where Bo had the meet and greet last night. I've never been to Spanish Fort. Seems like a nice little town."

Remy waved with his free hand. "Best-kept secret in Texas. Got any plans for the afternoon?"

"Not a one since Bo turned me down for lunch," Maverick grinned.

Bo could already see where Remy was going and tried to give him a look that told him to stop in his tracks and not do it. Aunt Bernie would have a fit if she knew Maverick was at the Paradise.

"You should come home with us to the Paradise for lunch," Ursula said. "It's just family, and afterwards we'll enlist your muscles to help finish decorating for Christmas. I understand you and Bo did a bang-up job of fixing up the bar last night."

"It's going to look good right through the holidays," Maverick said, "and I would love to go to dinner." He turned to focus on Bo. "If it's all right with you. I wouldn't want to intrude."

"It's fine with me," she said with her best fake smile. "I'm sorry that I didn't ask you myself. I rode with Rae this morning, but maybe I could go with you and show you the way?"

"That would be great," Maverick said.

When he turned his back, Bo used her thumb and forefinger to pretend to shoot Ursula. All she got in return was a head wiggle.

Chapter 7

PARKER LACED HIS FINGERS with Endora's on the way across the church parking lot, removed his tie with his free hand, and tucked it into his coat pocket. "You are the absolute bright spot in this cloudy day."

"You are a hopeless romantic," Endora said, "and I love every minute of it."

"Just the truth the way I see it," he told her as he opened the truck door for her, dropped her hand, and cupped her chin with his fist. His mouth found hers in a long kiss that left her knees weak. "I love you so much," he whispered when the kiss ended. Then he slipped his hands around her waist and lifted her up into the passenger seat.

Every hormone in her body whined for her to ask him to drive to Nocona or to Wichita Falls and book them into a hotel room. She wanted to go somewhere and snuggle down with her head on his chest and listen to the steady beat of his heart. To wake up in the morning cuddled up next to his back with an arm around his broad chest.

"I love you, too, and March seems like an eternity away from now," she panted.

"It does, but it will pass, and you'll have time to plan your perfect wedding." He slammed the door shut and whistled all the way around the vehicle.

"Let's really get married right after the Christmas program like we've teased about doing," she blurted out when he slid under the wheel. "All our families and friends will be at the church. Our old pastor is coming back to visit during that time, so we have a preacher to perform the ceremony. The potluck can be our reception. We can surprise everyone, have a couple of days' honeymoon at the parsonage, and..."

Parker's hazel eyes widened, and the edges of his mouth turned up in a smile. "Are you serious? What would your mama say?"

"I am very serious, and Mama has two more daughters. She can plan big weddings for Bo and Rae," Endora answered.

"Then let's do it," Parker said. "We can tell your folks at dinner."

"Oh, no!" Endora shook her head. "Mama and Luna will freak out. They'll start worrying about centerpieces and shopping for the dress and all that. Let's surprise everyone— except Rae and Bo. They're going to help me get the dress to the church and sneak a cake into the reception hall."

"Best man and maid of honor?" Parker asked.

"The only real reason we need them is so they can sign the license as witnesses. We'll pick a couple of folks to do that after the wedding," Endora suggested. "Maybe Aunt Bernie, since she's been fussing to be a part of one of our weddings, and your dad or grandpa?"

Parker got out of the truck, walked around it, and opened the passenger door. "I want to seal this plan with a real kiss, and not with a console between us."

He drew her so close that neither air nor light could have gotten between them and kissed her with so much passion that her knees went weak. When the kiss ended, she had to lean against him to keep from melting into a pile of hot hormones right there in the church parking lot.

"Just three weeks," she whispered.

Parker took a step back and stared into her eyes. "Sounds better than three months. Have I told you today how beautiful you are, and what a lucky man I am?"

"Only a few times." Endora didn't blink but let her soul blend with his for several seconds. "But I never get tired of hearing it."

Parker put his hands on her waist and lifted her back up into the passenger's seat. "Let's always be this much in love."

"We will because we are soulmates," she said.

―――――――――

"Aunt Bernie and Gladys have boarded the ship. She called me a few minutes ago to send a picture of how enormous the ship is and the two of them having their first drink— something called a dirty banana," Rae announced as she and Bo entered the kitchen together, "and Bo brought a guest to dinner."

"Aunt Bernie sent me a text, and I believe our new guest is Maverick Gibson. Your daddy and I met him in the church parking lot. We didn't make it to Sunday school," Mary Jane said.

Bo focused on her twin sister without blinking. "Did you tell Aunt Bernie that Maverick is here?"

Rae shook her head. "The boat doesn't sail until four o'clock."

"What does that have to do with anything?" Bo asked.

"If she thought Maverick was here, she would get off and come straight home to talk some sense into you," Rae answered.

"What are y'all gossiping about?" Endora asked and then lowered her voice. "Parker agrees with the plan."

"Hall-le—" Rae shouted.

"Lujah!" Bo finished for her.

"What are y'all celebrating?" Ursula asked as the rest of the sisters and Mary Jane turned to stare at them.

"Three things," Rae answered. "Dinner is almost ready. Aunt Bernie is ecstatic to be on the boat, and…" She looked right at Bo.

"And Endora tells us that"—Bo smiled at the crowd— "she and Parker want to start a family really soon, but don't tell anyone in case it takes a while."

Endora shrugged. "Mama, you've been saying that you wish you had a houseful of grandbabies. Maybe Parker and I will get lucky and have twins."

"I can't think of any better news than having more grandbabies," Mary Jane beamed and then took in Luna, Ophelia, and Tertia with a frown.

Luna threw up both palms in a defensive gesture. "Those other two are older than me. They should get to start families first."

"But you got married before us," Tertia argued.

"Only by half an hour," Luna shot back.

"You owe me," Bo whispered for Endora's ears only.

"We both should disown Rae for starting the problem," Endora snapped. "I thought for sure you were going to let the cat out of the bag. I really don't want the hassle from everyone for the next three weeks."

Rae filled glasses with ice for sweet tea and said in a low voice. "Sorry about almost letting that slip. It won't happen again, I promise. I'm so excited for you, Endora, and…"

"What are y'all whispering about now?" Mary Jane asked as she took a huge pan of roast beef from the oven.

"I swear, Mama!" Rae shook her head. "There is nothing wrong with your hearing."

"Baby names," Bo said in a hurry.

"Don't count your chickens before they are hatched," Mary Jane warned. "And for all of your information, I did not like the empty nest when all of you left home. Joe Clay and I will love having more grandchildren whenever they get here."

"We are here," Tertia yelled from the back door, "and bringing a couple of peach cobblers we had left over from the café yesterday."

"And we have three more guests, so set some more plates," Noah said as he ushered Gunner and the twins into the kitchen through the back door. "These folks forgot that the café is closed on Sundays and showed up for lunch, so we invited them to join us."

Bo nudged Rae on the shoulder. "Comeuppance just walked in the door to punish you for the way you've teased me about Maverick," she whispered just for Rae's ear. "I'm going to tell Aunt Bernie when she gets back. I bet she doesn't go off and leave us again."

"Welcome to the Paradise, Gunner," Mary Jane said. "We just have a buffet meal on Sundays. Everyone sits wherever they can find a place—dining room, kitchen or even out on the back porch. There's a blaze in the firepit, so it should be fairly warm out there."

Nothing had ever seemed to faze Mary Jane, but then she had raised seven girls and managed to write several bestselling novels all at the same time. Looking back, Rae wondered how her mother managed to meet all her writing deadlines, put three meals on the table every day, keep up with laundry and whiny or giggly girls—leaning heavy on the whining some days. More importantly, she did it all with a smile on her face. Rae had never admired her mother more than she did right at that moment.

"Miz Rae!" Heather squealed and skipped across the kitchen. "I didn't know you were going to be here. Am I Daisy or Heather?"

Before Rae could answer, Daisy asked, "Is this your house? Is it a farm? Do you have little kids? Why don't you bring them to church?"

"You are Heather," Rae said and pointed at the right twin. "And this is where I live, Daisy. I grew up in this house. It's not a farm, but my sister lives on a ranch next door. I don't have any children."

"How do you know us apart?" Heather asked.

Rae squatted down and looked the little girl right in the eye. "Do you know what *classified* means?"

Heather shook her head.

"It means that it's a secret so big I can't tell you what it is." Rae stood back up.

"Why can't you tell us?" Daisy asked.

"*Classified* says I don't tell anyone," Rae said with a smile.

"Can we go outside and look at all the decorations, Daddy?" Heather asked.

The expression on Bo's face told Rae that she worried about what might happen if those two little girls were turned loose unsupervised.

"How about we eat first, and then you can go with Bo to take Pepper for a walk, if that's all right with your dad?" Rae answered.

"Who is Pepper? Is it a dog? I want a puppy for Christmas. Daddy says puppies aren't in Santa's sleigh because they'd be afraid to fly that high." Daisy stopped for a breath and then went on. "Do you think puppies are scared? I wouldn't ever take one up in a tree if I had one. Do we have to have a Sunday school lesson in your house?"

"Whoa!" Gunner held up both palms. "Enough questions for the whole day."

"But, Daddy..." Heather argued.

Gunner tucked his chin down slightly and looked down at both his girls with a look that Rae remembered all too well from her own childhood. When Mary Jane cut her eyes around or down on one of the sisters, the argument was over—no *ifs*, *ands*, or *buts*. Heather and Daisy snapped their mouths shut. She heard her mother chuckle in the background and caught a wink when she glanced that way.

"Pepper is a Chihuahua that belongs to our Aunt Bernie. Bo takes care of him while Aunt Bernie is away, but I bet she would let you go with her to take him for a walk after dinner," Rae said and shot a smile over at Bo.

She got a double dose of stink eye for her suggestion.

"Really?" Daisy's eyes widened. "Is Pepper a big or a little dog? Do you got any more animals?"

"He's a little bitty dog, but he thinks he's as big as a lion," Bo answered. "After we take him for a walk, Rae might let you pet our cat, Sassy."

"I don't know what kind of magic you sprinkled over my girls in the Sunday school room, but they sure do like you," Gunner whispered close to Rae's ear.

"I'm not only a twin, but I also have a set of identical twin sisters," Rae told him. "Guess it's a genetic thing that causes us to recognize that."

"I think it's more than that," Gunner said. "It's because they can't fool you. They respect that."

"I hope so. You do know that *classified* is a very good

thing, right?" Rae stepped away from him to avoid the sweet little tingles created by his warm breath on her neck.

"Yep, and I intend to use that word more often in the future," Gunner answered.

Bo sidled up next to Rae and said, "I will get even."

"Hey," Rae protested. "I didn't cause Gunner and his girls to be here, or for that matter, I didn't invite Maverick either. Blame two of our other sisters for that, not me. Evidently, they've been standing too close to Aunt Bernie, and some of her matchmaking mojo has rubbed off on them. Besides, you have already got me back by saying I'd let them pet Sassy. You know she hates kids of any caliber or size."

"You started it when you volunteered me to let the twins go with me to walk Pepper." Bo reminded her in a cold tone.

Rae hip bumped her. "Take Maverick with you too. If he can keep peace in a bar, he should be able to handle a couple of rowdy girls."

———

Bo thought she was sneaking away from everyone when she carried her plate of food to the screened-in porch. Maybe she would even get lucky, and Gunner would take the little girls home before it was time for Pepper's afternoon walk.

"Well, hello." Maverick waved up from the picnic table, which sat not far from the firepit. His smile caused a vision of him tangled up in bedsheets, with his hair flowing out over a pillow, and those long eyelashes resting on his high cheekbones. She hoped that he blamed the heat in her cheeks on the blaze in the pit.

Bo nodded and sat down across from him. "What brought you out here?"

"Remy said he and Ursula would join me in a few minutes," Maverick said. "This is some mighty fine food. It's not often I get home cooking like this, and I understand there's cobblers for dessert?"

"That's right. Tertia brought them over. She and her husband, Noah, own the café across the road from the Paradise. If you want good old southern food, then drop by there any day of the week except Sunday. They serve breakfast and lunch every day." Bo realized she was babbling and stopped talking abruptly.

"I will remember that, but..." He paused. "There's something about being around a big family that makes the food even better."

"Do you come from a big family?" Bo asked.

"Kind of," Maverick answered. "I only have one brother—the good kid in the family. He followed in Dad's footprints and is a banker. I'm the rebel child who wanted to see the world and try new things."

"Are you about finished seeing the world?" she asked.

He took a long drink of his tea. "I'll never know until I get the right feeling."

"And what would that be?"

"You already know the answer." Maverick took a drink of his sweet tea and then set his tea glass to the side of his plate.

"You had it when you realized you were tired of chasing a dream and came back to Texas."

"Does that mean you are still running after your dream?"

"Yep, but I will know it when I find it," he answered.

Ursula came through the door with Remy right behind her. "Sorry it took us so long. Clayton wanted me to hold him until he went to sleep."

"No one else but his mommy would do." Remy chuckled.

"No complaints," Maverick said. "Not when I can spend time with a big family and get a meal like this to boot. Plus, Bo and I have been getting to know each other. I do have a question. Is Bo your real name, or is it a nickname?"

"It's what's on my birth certificate," she answered. "Bo Arlene Simmons. All seven of us are named after the heroines in whatever book Mama was writing at the time. Bo was a singer, and Rae was a detective. They weren't twins in her story, but they were cousins who solved crimes together."

"Was there a happy-ever-after?" Maverick asked.

"Always," Ursula answered.

"You might change your mind about having a good home-cooked meal after you spend the afternoon helping us put up the rest of the Christmas decorations," Remy teased as he sat down beside Maverick.

Maverick's eyes widened. "How could there be more?"

"There's always room for one more thing when it comes to getting the Paradise ready for Christmas," Ursula answered and slid onto the bench beside Bo. "You'll have to stick around until dark. We always turn on the lights on Sunday night after Thanksgiving."

If Bo could have figured out how to kick her sister sideways without causing a scene, she would have done so. "You were about to tell me how you only have one brother, and yet you have been to big family dinners."

"My dad has eight brothers and one sister. My mother has four sisters and two brothers. Lots and lots of cousins, and both families get together for Thanksgiving and Easter. We have to rent a venue, but it's a wonderful, chaotic day," Maverick replied. "I haven't been out to the Panhandle for one of those reunions in five years, but today kind of reminds me of those times."

"Where in the Panhandle?" Remy asked. "Rae was just over the border in Oklahoma for a few years, and Tertia spent time in Vega, Texas."

"Dumas," Maverick answered. "From our house, you could almost throw a stick over into Colorado or New Mexico. How about y'all? Have you two always lived in Spanish Fort?"

"Most of the time for me," Remy answered. "Ursula was raised right here, left for a few years, and came back last year just before Christmas."

The door burst open and two little girls came rushing out of the kitchen and onto the porch so fast that they were a blur. They stopped right beside Bo and stared at her plate, which was still half-full of food.

"When can..." Heather started.

Daisy butted in. "We go with you…"

"To walk Pepper?" Heather finished.

Maverick picked up the pepper shaker from the middle of the table. "Here you go, ladies. You don't really need Bo to go with you to walk this. Just be careful and don't fall down or run with it. If you get too much of it up your nose, it will make you sneeze. You really should take salt too. She will be sad if she's left behind."

Heather covered a giggle with her hand. "You are silly. Pepper is the name of a dog."

Daisy crossed her arms over her chest. "Daddy says that a Chihuahua is a little dog. That's the kind we want for Christmas."

"Well, then"—Maverick slid a sly wink toward Bo—"you do know that you have to be extra good for Santa to bring you a puppy, don't you? He and his elves make toys all year, but they have to really work hard to find puppies and kittens."

Bo thought of the kittens she and her sisters had found in a box the previous year on their way home from a Christmas shopping trip. Endora had claimed them both, and somehow, those cats, along with Pepper and the Paradise cat, had inspired her to write children's books. Would a puppy help the twins get past losing their mother at such an early age? Bo couldn't imagine life without her mama, and she was staring thirty right in the face.

"Why don't you girls go sit on the swing while I finish eating?" Bo suggested with a nod toward the other end of the porch.

"Then we'll take the dog for a walk?" Daisy asked.

"That's right," Bo answered.

Heather's eyes twinkled. "Can I hold his leash first?"

"I'm the oldest!" Daisy declared. "So, I get to hold it first."

"Only by five minutes, so"—Heather did a perfect head wiggle—"it don't matter."

"I'll hold the leash," Bo said.

Daisy let out a lungful of air in a loud whoosh. "See what *you* caused."

Heather stormed over to the swing and plopped down. Daisy marched across the wooden porch floor and sat down as far from her sister as she could.

"Good luck." Maverick chuckled.

"Luck, nothing," Bo said. "I need a miracle."

———

Parker and Endora were among the few people sitting around the kitchen table. Several conversations were going on at the same time in both the kitchen and dining room. Endora didn't even try to keep up with them, but concentrated on the desire shooting through her body when Parker placed his hand on her knee.

"Are you sure about the Christmas program?" He leaned over and whispered in her ear, then kissed her in the soft spot on her neck, sending even more tingles down her spine.

If she hadn't been sure about the decision she had made to steal Luna's dress and get married before the original date, the touch of Parker's hand convinced her. She only wished that the wedding was that day instead of three weeks away. "I'm very, very sure," she whispered.

"What was that about the Christmas program?" Joe Clay asked. "I've been hearing that we might need to build a bigger church for all the people who are planning to be there."

Parker gave Endora's knee a gentle squeeze. "I've heard the same thing. We might have to put a screen up in the fellowship hall so the overflow can watch it."

Endora's chest tightened when a vision popped into her head of Joe Clay walking her down the aisle amongst all those people. The majority of them wouldn't have been invited to the wedding if she and Parker had kept the original date.

What all have I set in motion with the idea of getting married after the Christmas program? Endora asked herself.

"Sounds like I'd better be sure we have plenty of presents for Santa to give to the good little boys and girls"—Mary Jane smiled at Joe Clay—"and goody bags fixed up for the kids to take home."

"What about the bad ones?" Ursula asked.

"At Christmas all the children are good," Mary Jane said.

"We can always get Gunner and Maverick to help us with that," Joe Clay said with a wide smile.

Rae held up both palms. "Whoa now, Daddy! Before you talk them into saying yes, you better be honest and tell them what you made Shane and Remy do last year."

"Santa Claus"—Mary Jane nodded toward Joe

Clay—"always needs some extra help at the Christmas church party after the program is over. The helpers dress up like elves and hand out the presents."

"Are you helping with that this year, Parker?" Joe Clay asked.

Endora covered his hand with hers. "Not this time, Daddy. We'll need to mingle with the people, but we'll be there for pictures. We all know how much Mama loves her photographs every year."

"Yes, I do," Mary Jane said with a nod. "Y'all want me to drag out a few from years ago to look at this afternoon?"

"No!" several of the sisters said in unison.

"We've got to finish the decorations this afternoon," Endora reminded her mother, "while we've got all these strong men to help us."

"Another time, but we will get them out and look at them before the holiday ends." Mary Jane's tone didn't leave room for argument.

"I'd love to see them," Gunner said and grinned. "My mother gave me all the family photo albums a few years ago. The twins think it's a hoot to see me when I was a kid."

"We've got one that our mama made, too," Heather said.

Daisy held up her hand but didn't wait for anyone to notice. "We got a picture of our mama in our bedroom."

Endora's eyes glazed over at the idea of Heather and Daisy—ornery as they were—losing their mother at such a young age. Without Mary Jane, Endora might have never moved on after the terrible experience she had gone through with her fiancé and best friend. Worse, yet, thinking about having to live with her biological father, Martin, and his wife made her shiver.

"Are you chilly?" Parker asked.

"No, just a terrible thought went through my mind and caused me to shiver," Endora answered. "I'll tell you about it later."

Joe Clay finished off the last of his coffee. "It gets dark early, so I reckon we'd better get busy if we're going to put the final touches on the Paradise. We want it all done and ready to flip the switch on the lights by nightfall."

"And this year, I don't get to do that, do I, Daddy?" Endora asked.

"Nope," Joe Clay shook his head. "You are no longer the youngest member of the family."

"Ursula will hold Clayton's little hand, and help him do the honors this year," Mary Jane said and then swept a look down the table at Tertia, Ophelia, Luna, and Endora, "and maybe next year we'll have a new youngest member to do the honors."

"One can hope," Joe Clay added. "But that's in the future. Today is the present, and we've still got to string lights around the porch posts and put up the greenery on the railings out there."

Parker removed his hand from Endora's knee, pushed back his chair, and stood up. "Let's get to it, then. I want to be here when everything is lit up. Endora and I have to be at the church at six thirty for evening services."

Endora missed his touch when he headed toward the door. "Great dinner, Mama, and wonderful pie, Tertia."

"Family and friends always make everything taste better," Mary Jane said. "Rae, you and Endora are on cleanup duty today."

"We can do that," Endora agreed. "You will need to help Daddy supervise, and everyone else can follow your orders."

"Does that mean you can't?" Luna asked.

"You should know the answer to that question," Endora answered. "After all we have always been two peas in a pod."

"Just like my girls," Gunner said with half a sigh. "What one can't think of, the other can."

"I remember those days," Mary Jane said as she led the way to the foyer, where everyone put on their jackets and followed her outside.

Endora waited until she and Rae were alone and asked, "Did you see the way Maverick kept sneaking looks at Bo all evening?"

"Yep," Rae answered.

"Aunt Bernie is going to have a fit," Endora said and then lowered her voice when Maverick, Remy, and Ursula came inside from the porch. "She's already laid down the law, just like she did when Noah and Tertia were flirting."

"What are we talking about?" Ursula asked.

"Shhh…" Endora rolled her eyes toward Maverick and Remy.

"Okay, now they are outside," Ursula said a couple of minutes later. "Did y'all see the way Maverick was looking at Bo?"

"Yep, but we aren't telling Aunt Bernie, are we?" Endora answered.

Ursula put leftovers in containers for the refrigerator. "Maybe it's that reverse thing she pulled with Tertia and Noah."

"Could be, but…" Rae said.

"No one wants to test her." Ursula giggled.

"Amen." Endora said, remembering that Aunt Bernie had been so disappointed she couldn't be the maid of honor at any of the four previous weddings. Endora did not like to break promises, but she would have if she had promised her great-aunt a position at her wedding. Suffering the wrath of Aunt Bernie wouldn't even make her change her mind about moving up the date several months.

"I hear Clayton fussing in the living room," Ursula said. "Sorry, but I have to go."

Endora handed the empty green-bean bowl to Rae to rinse and put into the dishwasher. Then she shredded what was left of the roast, scraped it into a slow cooker, and added a bottle of barbecue sauce.

"You sure are quiet," Rae said. "Do you have wedding jitters now that you've made up your mind?"

"Nope," Endora answered. "I was actually hoping that Aunt Bernie wouldn't be disappointed. She wants to be a bridesmaid or a flower girl in one of our weddings. But"—she giggled—"I'm leaving that to you and Bo."

"In your dreams, Sister!" Rae snapped.

Chapter 8

PEPPER PULLED AGAINST HIS leash when he saw a squirrel run up one of the pecan trees that lined both sides of the lane. The trees had to be over a hundred years old. Bo wondered if maybe Miz Raven, the madam of the Paradise back when it was a brothel, had planted them. Or had they already been there and she had simply cleared out to make a path wide enough for a wagon or a horse to travel through for customers to get to her place of business?

"Silly boy," Heather said. "That squirrel is almost as big as you."

As if he understood what she had said, Pepper stopped in his tracks and growled at the girl.

Daisy stooped down and scratched the dog's ears. "You don't like her as good as me, do you? I don't think you are silly. You were protecting us from that mean old squirrel, weren't you?"

Pepper wagged his tail and took a few more steps.

"He does not like you better!" Heather argued. "He wasn't growling at me anyway. He was talking to us and saying that he wouldn't let anything hurt us. Dogs can't use words."

This must be what Mama had to deal with when she had to raise two sets of twins only a little more than a year apart in age. Bo thought about the times when she and Rae had argued over things that seemed important at the time—like who got to name the old mama cat and the kittens that Joe Clay brought into the house.

The girls argued about everything all the way to the end of the lane, but Bo tuned them out and thought about the excitement there had been in the Paradise when the kittens finally opened their eyes and she and her sisters got to touch them.

"Hey, Miz Bo!" Heather tugged at the tail of Bo's jacket and pointed toward the three guys walking toward them. "Tell Daddy that we have to help take Pepper back. We don't want to go home, yet, and he has to work tonight, and can we please stay longer?"

"We want to see the lights that your daddy talked about," Daisy said.

Heather crossed her arms over her chest. "We want to tell everyone at school tomorrow that we saw lights before they did."

"Why?" Bo asked.

"Everyone talks about going to see the lights, and..." Daisy stopped when Gunner, Maverick and Remy were close.

"And"—Heather frowned—"Aunt Rosie don't feel like driving us around."

Maverick bent down and rubbed Pepper's ears. "So, this is Pepper?"

"I told you he was a dog and not in a shaker thing," Heather declared.

"Yes, you did." Maverick grinned and straightened up.

"Daddy," both girls said at once, and began talking at the same time.

All the words that filled the air, Pepper's barking at a rabbit that ran across the lane, and even her phone buzzing in her hip pocket disappeared when Maverick locked gazes with her. They were in a bubble with only room for two people.

"What do you think, Bo?" Remy asked.

His deep voice jerked her back to reality, and for a split second, she was angry with him. "About what?" she asked.

"These girls are begging Gunner to let them stay for the lighting ceremony this evening, and Gunner has to go to work at five," Remy said.

Bo nodded in agreement. "Of course, they can stay."

I'll get even with you, Rae, for volunteering me to take Pepper for a walk, Bo thought.

"I'll use my break to drive up here and get them right after the lighting," Gunner said. "I appreciate this, Bo."

"No problem, but Rae will be glad to take them home," Bo said. "I would volunteer, but I have to go to the church. I need to work on the Christmas cookbooks a little this evening.

"Thank you again," Gunner said with a nod. "I can stay until four, so they'll only be here a couple of hours."

"Yay!" The girls said at the same time and did a fist bump with each other.

"We'll be the first ones to see any lights this year," Heather said.

"Our friends are going to be so jealous! I wish Daddy would let us have a cell phone so we could take pictures and show them," Daisy said with a dramatic sigh.

"No cell phones," Gunner said in a serious tone.

"Enjoy being little girls," Maverick told them. "When you grow up, you don't get to go back and be a little kid again."

Gunner patted Maverick on the shoulder. "Amen and thank you!"

Bo almost nodded in agreement. Growing up in an old brothel located in a near-ghost town with six sisters had been tough, but she wouldn't want a do-over for even one day of her childhood. If her absentee father hadn't divorced her mother, then they would have never gotten Joe Clay for a stepfather. He was the best thing—other than having Mary Jane for a mother—that had ever happened to the whole family.

Heather rolled her eyes. "Come on, Daisy. I bet I can beat you back to the house. Whoever gets there first can tell Miz Rae the good news."

They bent forward and Heather counted. "One. Two. Three. Go!"

Gunner shook his head and sighed. "How did your mama ever raise two sets of twins?"

Bo tugged on Pepper's leash and turned around. The girls were just a blur of red and green plaid as they ran, neck and neck, down the lane. "And we were only a little more than a year apart."

Gunner took a step forward. "No wonder she's got the patience of a saint."

Remy fell into step beside him. "If that's what it takes, I think I'll just be satisfied with a little impatience."

"Y'all go on ahead. Pepper's little legs can't keep up with you," Bo told them.

"I'll hang back with you, then," Maverick said. "This has been a wonderful afternoon, Bo. I can never repay y'all for today, but next Sunday, please let me take you to dinner after church."

"Okay, and thank you." Bo accepted his invitation, and then wished she hadn't agreed so readily, but she had experienced a feeling when they shared that moment a few minutes earlier—one that she had never known before.

Chapter 9

RAE NEVER DOUBTED FOR a minute that Bo would find a way to get even, but in her wildest dreams she didn't imagine that her sister would send her to Nocona with those rowdy girls after they'd had an afternoon at the Paradise.

"You are the devil's sister," she hissed at Bo when she finally found her and Maverick on the back porch—sitting on either end of the swing.

Bo shook a finger at her. "Be careful. You are my twin, so that would give you the same DNA. You shouldn't be surprised. I told you I would get even."

"But this is worse than what I did, so I get another shot at you," Rae said.

"I bet y'all were just like Gunner's twins when you were little girls," Maverick said.

Both women turned to focus on him, and then giggled.

"Yep," Bo said with a nod.

"And those two couldn't ever compete with all seven of us when we joined forces." Rae agreed, remembering when she and all six of her sisters had committee meetings to discuss how to get Joe Clay to marry their mother.

"Want to go into detail?" Maverick asked.

"That's a story for another day," Rae answered. "Mama sent me out here to get y'all to come in for supper, and then we'll turn on the lights. It's cloudy, so it's getting dark earlier than we expected, which is good because Endora and Parker want to see everything all lit up before they have to leave for church."

Maverick put a boot out to stop the swing and stood up. "I wasn't expecting to have supper too. This has been a great day."

"Mama loves having a big crowd for meals." Bo started to stand up, but her toe caught on a crack in the wooden floor, and she plunged forward.

"Whoa!" Maverick caught her and pulled her tightly against his chest.

"Thank you," she muttered, and when she took a step back, she set the swing in motion with the back of her leg, and it slung her forward into his arms again.

"I believe that swing wants us to dance," he teased. "If you'll come by Whiskey Bent, I promise not to step on your toes."

"'Whiskey Bent and Hell Bound,'" Rae said.

Maverick released his hold on Bo and took a step back. "That song is on the jukebox. I wouldn't be surprised if it's not where Dave got the name for the bar."

"Can't have one without the other," Rae said and felt just a little sorry for her sister. She could almost feel the invisible heat between Bo and Maverick. Bo had spread her wings and followed her dream when she moved to Nashville. Even though she gave it all she had, it hadn't worked out, and now she needed to put down roots. Aunt Bernie had been right when she said Maverick wasn't the man for Bo. Chemistry or not, Bo would simply have to pour cold water on the sparks.

Rae followed Bo and Maverick into the kitchen, where supper was laid out on the bar—barbecue sandwiches made with the leftover roast beef, baked beans, potato salad, and warm brownies topped with ice cream for dessert. Endora had taken the twins under her wing while Rae was hunting down Bo and Maverick and had the rowdy girls corralled sitting at the kitchen table with plates of food in front of them.

The room went quiet when Joe Clay bowed his head. After he said a short grace, Daisy smiled at him. "Aunt Rosie always says the blessing unless Daddy is home. I like your prayer better. Aunt Rosie talks too long."

Joe Clay chuckled. "I figured you girls might be hungry, so I kept it short."

Heather nodded seriously. "God don't care how long you pray. He just wants to hear your voice. That's what Miz Endora told us in Sunday school."

"Amen," Parker agreed.

Rae remembered a conversation she and her sisters had had when a preacher more or less invited himself to Sunday dinner. All seven of them united together in a campaign to get rid of him so that he wouldn't get in the way of Joe Clay being their new daddy—and it worked. The preacher couldn't wait to get out of the house when he finished eating that day.

Thank God Parker isn't like that man was, Rae thought as she took her plate to the table and sat down with Daisy and Heather.

"Have you girls had a good time this afternoon?" she asked. "You didn't get bored, did you?"

"Oh, no!" Daisy declared.

"We could live here," Heather said. "Can you take a picture of us out by that sleigh before we go home, and maybe send it to Daddy?"

"I sure can," Rae agreed.

Even if they were ornery and always into some kind of mischief, she felt sorry for them. Her father had been absent for most of her life—always studying to be a doctor, and later at the hospital or clinic—and seemed to only pop in sporadically. Her mother had been the rock that held the family together. These poor little girls would never have a mother in their lives again and, quite possibly, didn't even have a lot of memories of her.

"I wish he was here to see the lights when they come on," Daisy sighed. "That might make him happy."

"We can take pictures as we drive away so he can see how the whole place looks," Rae offered.

Bo nudged her on the shoulder and whispered, "They're growing on you, aren't they? Think Aunt Bernie would agree to a spring or summer wedding between you and Gunner?"

"Bite your tongue," Rae snapped.

"Mama has her heart set on one, and since…" Bo rolled

her eyes toward Parker and Endora, with their heads together at the dining room table.

"I'm passing that honor on to you," Rae said with a wicked grin.

"In your dreams," Bo said.

"Dreams?" Daisy said. "I am going to dream about this day."

"Me, too," Heather agreed.

When the sun finally dropped below the bare trees and the horizon, everyone gathered out in the middle of the yard. If the two little girls holding Rae's hands had been hers, she wouldn't have been nearly as interested in a posed picture of them as she would be in a candid shot of their eyes when they first saw all the decorations lit up. With that in mind and hoping that she was able to catch the expressions on their faces, she aimed her phone at them and waited.

"Okay, everyone." Joe Clay raised his voice. "The tradition has always been that the youngest in the family gets to do the honor of turning on the lights. Endora has held that place in the past, but this year the honor is passed down to baby Carlton. Since he's really too young to do the job on his own, Ursula is going to help him. Are we ready?"

The twins yelled, "Yes!"

Joe Clay cupped his hand over his ear. "I couldn't hear that. Are...we...ready?"

Everyone screamed. "We are ready!"

Rae let go of the girls' hands and got their faces in focus on her phone. She remembered the first time she and her sisters had to go home with their biological father after they moved to Spanish Fort. The weekend had bordered on miserable, but Joe Clay had delivered what he had promised Endora. He had stopped the reconstruction work and had the Paradise decorated when they returned on Sunday evening. Every year since then, he had built new cutouts, and Mary Jane had bought even more lights and pretty Christmas things to add to the collection.

Rae could still see the look of pure joy in Endora's and Luna's eyes when Martin, their father, had turned down the lane that first Christmas they all lived at the Paradise. She quickly flipped through the pictures she'd just taken, which captured the same look in Daisy and Heather's eyes that evening. Yes, they were ornery, and yes, they got into lots of trouble, but the sweetness of that moment made up for everything—almost.

Endora broke into her thoughts when she asked, "Cute, huh?"

"Reminds me of a couple of other little girls," Rae answered.

"Does it make you want a family of your own?" Endora pressed.

"Maybe, but you get to have a little one to turn on the lights next year," Rae said with a smile and then pointed toward the sleigh. "Do you girls still want a picture by the sleigh?"

A bitter cold wind made the music from the wind chimes that were shaped like candy canes and hung between the porch posts. Heather shivered, nodded, and dragged her sister across the yard to stand beside the sleigh that Joe Clay had built several years before.

"Can we sit in it?" Daisy asked.

Endora raised her voice and said, "Of course, and Rae can sit with you. I'll take the picture." She slipped the phone from Rae's hand and gave her a push. "Go on. This could be the start of your own family."

Rae shook head. "Oh, no! Not in a million years."

"Never say never," Endora giggled.

"One Sunday dinner doth not a relationship make," Rae quoted.

Endora's giggle turned into laughter. "That sounds like the day when the preacher came to dinner, and we told him that we were Baptist nuns. Go get up in the sleigh with those girls, so I can take a picture. You are their Sunday school teacher, so that makes y'all at least a church family."

"Temporarily," Rae said and climbed into the sleigh. She positioned herself between the twins and wrapped an arm around each of them. "As soon as the holidays are over, you can have your job back."

"We'll see about that," Endora said as she took several pictures.

"Miz Rae, will you make me some pictures you took today?" Daisy asked. "I want to fix an album so me and Heather can look at it every day."

Heather hopped down from the sleigh and looked up at Rae with a sweet smile. "You can have all the money in my piggy bank to pay for them."

"You can keep your money," Rae told them. "I'll get some pictures made for you, anyway."

"Hey, wait up!" Mary Jane yelled as she jogged across the yard. "I didn't get my goodbye hugs from you girls, and I have a plate of brownies for you to take home to Rosie."

Daisy met Mary Jane halfway and barreled into her. Then Heather added her fierce hugs. Rae slipped her phone from the hip pocket of her jeans and took several shots of the three of them. If she and her sisters had gotten married young—like Mary Jane had the first time—they would possibly have children who were that age.

Do you have regrets? the pesky voice inside her head asked.

"No, I do not have any regrets," she muttered. "There were six more sisters who could have taken care of that."

Chapter 10

AFTER THE LIGHT HAD been turned on, and Rae had driven away with the girls, Maverick laid a hand on Bo's shoulder. "I've already said this a couple of times, but this has been a great day. And"—he removed his hand and headed toward his truck—"I'm looking forward to next week. Do you have any food that you hate? I wouldn't want to take you to an Italian place only to find that you don't like it."

"Nope." Bo could still feel the warmth of his hand. "I lived on a shoestring so long in Nashville that I can even appreciate bologna sandwiches—as long as I have mustard."

Maverick opened the driver's door and slid in under the steering wheel. "I think I can do a little better than that. I make a mean ham-and-cheese sandwich." He turned his focus toward Bo. "This sight is absolutely breathtaking, and I'm not just talking about the decorations."

"Is that your best pickup line?" she teased.

"I'm not shooting you a line," Maverick protested. "I'm telling the truth. See you next weekend if not before."

Before she could answer, he closed the truck door. Before the vehicle disappeared completely, he stuck his hand out the window and waved. Bo threw up a hand and watched the taillights of his truck blend in with the thousands of lights strung from the house to the road. He had proven there was chemistry by that last comment, and his touch when he kept her from falling left no doubt that she felt it too.

"Can't do it!" She sighed as she turned around and headed for the house. "Aunt Bernie warned me, but it's more than that. I came home to put down roots, not go off chasing butterflies with a sexy bartender."

Flirting is fun and doesn't mean shopping for a white dress or wedding cake. The voice in her head sounded a lot like Rae's.

Bo was jerked right back into reality when Endora touched her on the back.

"Didn't mean to startle you," Endora apologized and held up her car keys. "Parker and I are leaving for church. Would you drive my…?"

"I'll be along in a little while in my own vehicle. You can ride home with me," Bo said.

"Oh, I almost forgot," Endora said. "The cookbook committee is meeting at ten o'clock tomorrow morning instead of tonight. I appreciate the ride home."

Bo sucked in a lungful of air and let it out in a loud whoosh.

"I heard that." Endora laughed and walked away. "Going to church twice in one day won't hurt you. You can ask God to take away that attraction you have for Maverick."

"What are you talking about?" Bo asked.

Endora stopped and turned around. "The sparks dancing around the house today almost burned me."

"You are confused. What you saw was sparks between Gunner and Rae, not me and Maverick," Bo declared, but she crossed her fingers behind her back.

"You can fool yourself if you want. See you in church. I'll save you a seat on the front pew. Don't be late," Endora told her.

The chatter of little girls in the back seat of Rae's truck brought back memories of when Joe Clay would load the family up in the van. Whether they were going to a softball game to watch Tertia play or just driving to Nocona for burgers and ice cream at the Dairy Queen, there were always several conversations going on in the back seats.

"If you turn right there, it will take you to our school," Daisy said and pointed to the right. "We had the same teacher for kindergarten, but we didn't the first two days of first grade," Daisy said. "They put us in two different rooms."

"I cried so hard that I threw up all my lunch," Heather said, "and it smelled so bad that a bunch of other kids puked too. The floor was a mess, and they had to call Daddy to come get me and…"

"So…" Daisy butted in for her turn. "Daddy told the school to put us in the same room. Aunt Rosie lives down that road." She pointed to the left. "She smells funny."

"Like old people, and her toenails are ugly," Daisy said.

Rae bit back a giggle. "What do old people smell like?"

"That stuff they rub on when their Uncle 'Ritis comes to visit them. He might like them better if they would use some perfume like your mama does."

"Turn right here before you get to the Dairy Queen and go down this road."

Rae made a left turn and drove a few blocks before Heather said, "That white one with a red mailbox is where we live."

Rae turned into the next driveway. "What makes her toenails ugly?"

Daisy sighed in an exasperated way that only a child her age could produce. "Chipped polish. She says that she can't wear anything but sandals because she's got 'ohpathanee in her feet."

Rae parked behind a small compact car, got out of her truck, and walked the girls up onto the porch. The cold north wind rattled the bare tree limbs and scooted dead leaves from one side of the yard to the other. Rae flipped the hood up on her coat, but the little girls didn't seem to mind the cold at all.

Daisy slung the door open and called out, "Aunt Rosie, we are home."

"And we brought brownies!" Heather ran into the living room right behind her sister.

Rosie groaned when she got up out of the recliner. "Thank you for keeping them this evening. Gunner said they were having a wonderful time."

The pungent aroma of Bengay, or some other such arthritis medication, filled the room as Rosie shuffled across the floor. "I swear, a ninety-year-old woman can't keep up with two rowdy girls, but I guess I can be thankful that they weren't triplets. You girls go get your baths, and then you can have a brownie."

"Can Miz Rae come see our room before we do that?" Heather begged.

Rosie eased down onto the sofa. "Yes, she can. I forget that it gets dark too early for their bedtime. I'll be glad when Gunner finds someone to take over for me. I told him after Christmas he's on his own, even if he has to take them to work with him. My arthritis gets worse every month and the neuropathy in my feet is terrible. I'm in no shape to keep these girls. If you know someone who wants a babysitting job, tell them there's one available right here."

"I'li put the word out," Rae said as she took in the small living area in one sweep. She could write her name in the dust, but everything else was in order. Children's books in a basket by Rosie's chair proved that she read to them before bedtime. Through an archway, the kitchen countertops were clean, and there were no dirty dishes in sight.

"Come on!" Daisy tugged at her hand.

"We're supposed to read tonight?" Heather led the way down the hall. "Will you listen to us? Aunt Rosie falls asleep sometimes when we read to her."

Daisy threw open the door. "Not until after we show her our room."

Twin beds were covered with matching pink-and-white-striped comforters. Stuffed animals covered a bookcase on one side of the room. Puzzles and toys filled a second one on the other side.

Heather pointed to one of the beds. "You can sit right here on my bed."

Rae opened her mouth to say that she really had to go, but Daisy's expression made her clamp it shut and sit down on the edge of the bed. "I can't stay long, but I could listen to you girls read."

"And you'll sign the paper that says we did?" Heather asked.

"Yes, I will." Rae made a mental note to ask her mother and Aunt Bernie if they knew someone who would babysit the girls. What they really needed was a mother, but in a pinch a babysitter younger than Rosie would do.

"If we hurry with our bath, will you brush our hair?" Daisy asked.

Heather cupped her hand over Rae's ear and whispered, "Aunt Rosie don't like it if we cry when she gets the tangles out."

Daisy nodded in agreement. "Daddy says we have to be nice and not yell when she does that because"—she glanced at the door—"she's so good to help us."

"If you hurry, I guess that would work," Rae agreed, and wondered if it would be interfering too much if she found a babysitter for the girls.

That is none of your business. Bo's voice popped into her head.

Rae ignored her sister's voice.

"Let's do this," she said. "Heather, you go take your bath now. I will listen to Daisy read while you do that. Then I will listen to you read and comb out your hair when you get done. Daisy will be finished, and I'll comb her hair, and we can all have a brownie before I go home."

"Yes!" Heather removed her jacket and hung it on a hook on the back of the door. Her footsteps made a *rat-a-tat* noise on the hardwood floor as she ran down the hallway and into the bathroom.

Daisy climbed into Rae's lap with a book. "Me and Heather could read before we started to school, so this is kind of like a baby book, but the teacher says we got to read three pages for tomorrow." She opened to where a bookmark was located.

Rae didn't have to help her sound out a single word and was amazed at how well the child read—even putting inflections and voices to the characters in the story that was about a mouse and a lion. When she finished the three pages, she wrapped her arms around Rae's neck and hugged her.

"Sometimes, I'm the lion and Heather is the mouse," she said.

"And other times?" Rae inhaled the scent of wind in the child's hair mixed with the barbecue sandwich she'd had for supper. She wondered if her mother had gotten whiffs of whatever her girls had eaten for supper when they were little, and that's how she knew if they had really brushed their teeth?

Daisy sighed. "We look alike, and our beds are alike,

and"—another sigh—"Daddy buys us matching clothes, but I wish we could be different. I want my own room, and I want a red comforter, and I don't want to dress just like Heather every day."

"Is there another bedroom in the house?" Rae asked.

Daisy nodded and pointed across the hall. "That's where our mama was before she died and went to heaven. We don't go in there because it makes Daddy sad."

"How old were you when your mama went away?" Rae asked.

Daisy shrugged. "Me and Heather don't remember her, but we have a picture." She slid off Rae's lap and picked up a photograph in a frame of a lovely dark-haired woman with deep brown eyes holding two toddlers.

"She was pretty like you," Daisy said. "Aunt Rosie says that we look like her except for our eyes. We got them from Daddy."

Rae had to fight a sudden overwhelming desire to run out of the house and never look back. These kids were not her responsibility when they left her Sunday school classroom. She didn't need to fix their problems, or even talk to Gunner about a sitter. That was way out of the purview of what a Sunday school teacher should do.

"My turn!" Heather appeared at the door wrapped up in a thick terry-cloth robe. "When you get my hair done, I'll put on my jammies. What color are we wearing tonight, Daisy?"

"Red!"

"I hate red," Heather declared.

"It's my night to choose," Daisy reminded her. "You picked purple last night."

"Then tomorrow night, we will wear pink," Heather threatened.

"I might puke!" Daisy grumbled as she left the room.

Rae appreciated that her mother had made it possible for all seven of the girls to have their own bedrooms more right then than she ever had before.

———

Bo wrapped a quilt around herself, sat down in one of the rocking chairs on the front porch, and set it in motion with her foot. This was Pepper's time for a bit of fresh air, according to Aunt Bernie. One of the gazillion sticky notes Aunt Bernie had plastered to her refrigerator for Bo said that it didn't matter if it was freezing cold with a hint of rain in the air, or if it was scorching hot, the dog was to have his half hour on the front porch every night.

"And I thought being free from her sass was going to be wonderful," Bo grumbled. Then she saw the headlights of a vehicle coming down the lane. "Please, Lord, don't let that be Maverick. I need some time to talk myself out of this chemistry I feel when he's around."

Rae parked beside half a dozen other vehicles and made her way to the porch. "What are you…? Oh, it's Pepper time. Aunt Bernie's entire schedule is governed by that dog." She sat down in the rocking chair beside her sister and drew her coat tighter over her chest.

"So much for not having Aunt Bernie around," Bo said. "I bet Pepper figures out a way to tattle on all of us when she gets home. You were gone for a long time. What happened?"

Rae gave her a quick rundown of her time with the girls. "I feel so sorry for them. Rosie isn't really able to watch them at all. She told me that she's ninety and that Gunner's got to find another sitter by Christmas. You know how you always told me that I could not fix everything even though I tried to? I need to hear it again."

"You can*not* fix everything," Bo said, putting emphasis and even air quotes on the *not*, "but I wish you could."

Rae pulled her chair closer to Bo's and tugged part of the quilt over her legs. "Did I hear a bit of wistfulness in your voice? Do you have a problem that you need help with?"

"Yep, and his name is Maverick," Bo answered.

"Have you had a single date since you left Nashville?"

Bo shook her head. "And not for over a year before I left. Times were tough out there these past couple of years. I wasn't getting any gigs, and I was working double shifts just to pay rent and eat off-brand ramen noodles. I didn't have time for romance."

"Then you come home and dive into helping Aunt Bernie with her advice blog and working on romantic events. What you need is a hot fling, not a relationship," Rae said.

"And you?" Bo asked.

"We're talking about you, not me. I am *not* going to let those little girls steal my heart."

"Looks like that ship already sailed tonight." Bo giggled.

Chapter 11

THE BONE-CHILLING FEEL OF moisture in the air, be it rain or snow, hit Bo when she stepped out of the house on Monday evening. Even all the warm lights around the wooden cut-outs of Santa and Mrs. Santa and the elves didn't give off a glow that evening. A puff of breath filled the air with every exhale as she jogged out to Tertia's SUV.

"Remember when we used to think it was cool to play like we were smoking in weather like this?" Tertia asked when Bo opened the passenger door and slid into the seat.

Bo chuckled at the memory. "Oh yeah, and we used twigs for cigarettes."

Tertia had gotten her name from an Irish trilogy that Mary Jane was writing at the time. Tertia was the last book in the series, and since she was also the third daughter in the Simmons family, her name had a double meaning. Her curly brown hair was pulled up in a messy bun on top of her head, and her aqua eyes looked tired that evening.

She put her truck in gear and drove slowly down the lane. "Why were we in such a hurry to grow up? Those were good days."

"Are you all right?" Bo asked.

"Just tired, but the remodeling on our house is done, and we've got our Christmas tree up and decorated. We probably won't have time to do much outside this year, but I do plan to wrap the porch posts with lights." Tertia covered a yawn with the back of her hand.

"Sister, you've been working six days a week at the café, and every evening and Sunday either doing food prep for the next day or helping get your house fixed up. You aren't leaving any time to catch your breath," Bo fussed at her. "Rae doesn't have a job yet. Put her to work doing something."

"She needs to have time to find herself like I did." Tertia's voice quivered, and she wiped away a tear.

Bo laid a hand on her sister's shoulder. "Out with it. What is really wrong?"

"Noah and I…we…I feel like we're drifting apart, and we've only been married a few months. At this rate, we won't even have a relationship in five years," Tertia said. "He used to look at me like Maverick looked at you yesterday, but now we are so weary from all we've been doing that we barely even say, 'Good morning,' to each other."

Bo remembered several questions from Aunt Bernie's blog about that same thing—what to do when the relationship isn't new and shiny anymore. "Without time together, and I don't mean in the work situation, you are going to have these problems. Maybe since Sunday is the only day that you have away from the café, you should do something fun."

"But we always have dinner at the Paradise, and…" Tertia made a turn into the church parking lot.

Bo didn't give her time to finish the sentence. "And we will all understand if you and Noah want to spend the day eating strawberries in bed. Mama will never get any more grandkids if all you married sisters are too tired to even get one started."

Tertia finally smiled. "If we had a whole afternoon, we would probably forego the strawberries and sleep."

"Then when you awake, you could cuddle and maybe make a grandbaby for Mama and Daddy to spoil," Bo said.

"We both want to start a family, but how could we ever give children the time and attention they need when we can't even give each other a few minutes a day? How did Mama and Daddy ever raise us seven girls and keep their marriage fresh? He still looks at her like she's made of pure gold."

"You remember what Mama told us about Sundays?" Bo asked.

"Every other day of the week belonged to her work and to us girls, but Sunday was Daddy's day. After church and dinner, they would go for long walks or just sit on the back porch and talk," Tertia said with a nod.

"They flirted with each other all the time, and still do, but those Sundays set the mood for the romance later that night, I'm sure." Bo smiled.

Tertia almost giggled. "Even though we don't like to think about that part of their relationship."

"I know." Bo nodded. "The stork brought all seven of us, I'm sure."

"Or Mama found us under a cabbage out in the garden." Tertia's mood seemed a bit lighter.

"You should have seen the sixty-and-older women at the meet and greet," Bo said. "They were just a little older than Mama and Daddy, and honey, they could give us some lessons on flirting."

"Okay, okay!" Tertia said as she parked in front of the church. "I'll flirt, but right now, we've got to go inside the church and put our stamp of approval on the cookbooks."

"Then you are finished with your church duties. My advice is that you do *not* let Endora talk you into another job here. After Christmas, I'm just the piano player for Sunday morning services, not the coordinator for the Christmas music," Bo said.

Both women opened the truck doors at the same time, and a gust of cold wind with a hint of misty rain swept away any of the warmth inside. Bo glanced at the temperature on the dashboard just before it went dark—thirty degrees.

"We're liable to be driving home on slippery roads," Tertia said. "Instead of a white Christmas, we could have an icy one."

Bo hopped out onto the ground, slammed the door, and jogged toward the church. "I hope Aunt Bernie is enjoying better weather than this."

"Me too." Tertia followed close behind her sister.

"Hey," Endora said, slinging open the door. "We're all in the fellowship hall waiting to open the boxes until y'all got here."

"Sorry we're late," Bo said. "The time got away from us. Before we go in and join the rest of the committee, how do you and Parker plan to keep the romance in your marriage?"

Endora whipped a strand of her long blond hair over her shoulder and closed the door. "Are you already thinking that far ahead with Maverick?"

"No, but I might need to know for Aunt Bernie's blog while she's gone," Bo answered.

"We've talked about that, and we will follow Mama's old rule." Endora motioned for them to follow her and headed to the fellowship hall. "Sunday afternoons belong to us unless there is an emergency of some kind, so for the first little while, don't even expect us for Sunday dinner at Mama's house. And another rule we have promised each other is that we will never go to bed angry with each other. We'll settle the argument and then…" She blushed.

"Have wild, passionate makeup sex even if you are tired?" Bo finished for her.

"Something like that." Endora opened the door and stood to the side to let them enter the room ahead of her.

Several women waved.

"We didn't peek. Since Tertia put so many of her recipes and so much work into the making of the cookbooks, we wanted her to see the finished product first," Frannie said. "Too bad Bernie isn't here. We'll miss her Thursday night at the final quilting bee before the holidays. We should do very well with the silent auction."

Bo removed her coat and hung it on the back of a chair.

"She's got some good ideas for a spring quilt to auction off for the missionary fund. I bet she won't be off cruising to warmer climates when you put that one up at Easter."

"Let's hope she doesn't get addicted to living on a ship," Frannie said.

Tertia set a box up on one of the tables and used a pair of scissors to cut the tape away from the top. She removed a wad of packing paper and smiled when she saw the book's cover, with its picture of a metal Christmas tree in the middle of a table and with Christmas cookies and pies surrounding it. Bo couldn't remember a time when a tree just like that one hadn't been on the holiday table at the Paradise.

"Now for the big surprise," Frannie said. "We had an anonymous donor who paid for the publication of the cookbook, and all the work and recipes were donated by us church women. So, the proceeds are all profit, which will go to Endora and Parker to use to redo the parsonage."

Endora eyes widened and she slapped a hand over her mouth. Tears streamed down her face and she shook her head. "But that's money for the missionary fund…"

"No, that was just what we told you so we could surprise you," Frannie said. "The quilt money will go to that fund. This is for you and Parker. We ordered five hundred copies, and three hundred of them are already sold. The others will go fast, and our donor has said that if we need to have a second printing, it will also be paid for," Frannie said. "No arguing about this. We have had so much fun doing it."

Vera crossed the room and hugged Endora. "Keeping it a

secret wasn't easy when I was in Wyoming, and even harder when we came back to Spanish Fort for part of the year. You don't know how many times I nearly told Ursula and Remy. I didn't even tell Alan."

If Bo had been married, she probably wouldn't be able to keep a secret from her husband, or her son and daughter-in-law, like Vera had for all the weeks and months that went into putting the cookbook together. She gave Vera a hug, and whispered, "If I ever have a secret I need to tell someone, I'm coming to talk to you."

"Anytime, darlin', anytime," Vera said with a smile.

Bo turned to face Endora and whispered, "Just say thank you."

Endora wiped the tears away with the back of her hand. "Thank you isn't enough. The money from it will be put to good use, and I will remember the love and labor that you all put into making this every time I use one of the recipes."

A round of applause filled the fellowship hall, and then the women all gathered around to take a book from the first box and go through it. After a few minutes, Vera laid the copy she had been looking at aside and said, "We can't have our last cookbook committee meeting without refreshments, so I brought my pumpkin bundt cake—recipe is in the book of course—and everything is set up back in the kitchen."

"And my pecan tassies are there," Frannie said. "Gladys is off on the cruise with Bernie, but she asked me to make Grammie's gingerbread—and both of those recipes are in the book too."

Bo almost said that Bernie would have sent a bottle of tequila if she'd been home, but she just smiled. "Did someone make coffee to go with all these lovely desserts?"

"Yes, ma'am," Frannie answered and headed toward the kitchen. "I preordered a copy of this book, Tertia. Don't let me get out the door without paying for it."

"Me too," half a dozen other committee members said.

Bo's phone buzzed in her hip pocket. She slid it out, saw Bernie's name on the screen, and carried the phone to the back of the fellowship hall so she could hear better. "Hey, are you enjoying the cruise? Have you made any matches since you've been out to sea? I figure you've at least put a couple of folks together for their happy-ever-after."

"I am not and I have not!" Bernie's voice sounded horrible.

"What's wrong?" Bo worry meter jacked up a hundred percent.

"Me and Gladys are both taking turns throwing up in the bathroom. We're either not cut out for ship travel or we've picked up a stomach bug. We saw the ship doctor, and he gave us medicine, but it's not doing a blessed thing," Bernie answered.

"Maybe it's just a twenty-four-hour stomach bug, and you'll feel all better by tomorrow." Bo remembered an article she had read about women's symptoms of a heart attack, and one of them was severe nausea. Bernie was past eighty and Gladys was most like about that same age. What on earth would they do if one of them had a cardiac arrest on the ship?

I'll just have to fly to wherever they dock and take care of them until they are able to fly home, Bo thought.

"We make our first stop on land tomorrow morning. I hope we feel better by then," Bernie said. "We haven't been able to eat anything but crackers and sweet tea since we set sail."

"I'm so sorry," Bo said. "This was supposed to be a wonderful experience, not a nightmare."

"And we missed the unveiling of the cookbooks and the surprise for Endora for this," Bernie groaned. "Talk to you tomorrow if we're able to make it off this death trap. Bye now."

"Hope you are well soon. I'll be looking for your call." Bo heard a gagging noise, and the phone went dark.

"Poor Aunt Bernie," Bo muttered, and then felt guilty that she had wished her elderly aunt would be gone for even longer than the cruise.

She stood up and the phone rang again. Expecting it to be Aunt Bernie telling her that her fast trot to the bathroom was just a false alarm, she answered it without even checking the caller ID.

"Feeling better?" she asked.

"I would be if it were next Sunday instead of just Monday." Maverick's deep voice threw an extra beat into her heart.

"I'm sorry," Bo said. "I thought you were my aunt... How did you get this number?"

"I have my ways, and you have six sisters." He chuckled.

"I'm getting the bar ready to open, and my mind keeps going to all the fun we had yesterday. That was the best first date ever."

"That was not a date," she protested. "It was simply a Sunday dinner."

"Potato, po-tah-toh," he said. "I'm calling it a date."

"Nope, a date is when a good-night kiss is involved," she told him, and wondered if she'd actually said that out loud.

"We'll remedy that on the second date," he shot back. "I just wanted you to know I'm thinking about you. Have a good evening, Miz Bo Simmons."

"You, too, Mr. Maverick Gibson," she said.

He chuckled again and the screen went dark. She stared at it for several minutes before she shoved it back in her pocket.

Rae snapped the leash on Pepper's collar and walked behind him as the dog pranced from Bernie's trailer to the nearest bush and hiked his leg on it. Five feet farther down the well-beaten trail to the house, he had to water a weed. Another few yards and he hiked up a hind leg but had nothing to offer the base of a hackberry tree.

"I should have gone to church rather than taking on Pepper duty," she grumbled.

The north wind swept her black hair across her face, but she couldn't do anything with it as long as she had a leash in one hand. Finally, after a few more dry attempts at Mary Jane's dormant rosebushes, she and Pepper reached the front porch. She attached the end of his leash to a porch post and sat down in a nearby rocking chair. Endora's cats, Poppy and Misty, came up the steps and curled around Pepper when he lay down on the porch.

"That's not very nice," Rae said. "You could keep my legs or even my lap warm instead of feeling sorry for Pepper."

Tertia's vehicle pulled up in front of the house. Bo got out and jogged up to the porch.

"I'm glad you are here." Rae stood up. "Pepper has had about ten minutes of his evening outing. You can take over now. Did you bring my cookbook?"

"I'll get two quilts if you will stay and talk to me," Bo said. "And I didn't bring mine or yours. We can pick them up next Sunday after church."

"I'll get the quilts and make a couple of mugs of hot chocolate." Rae went inside and was heating water in the microwave when her phone rang. She didn't recognize the number, so she answered it cautiously. "Hello?"

"Miz Rae?" Heather asked.

"Yes, is something wrong, Heather?"

"How did you know it was me and not Daisy?" she asked.

"I told you the first time you came into the Sunday school class that I could tell y'all apart," Rae answered. "How did you get my phone number?"

"I called the church and Miz Bo answered, and she said your number was the same as the church except the last four were five, two, one, six," she answered. "Daddy says that we have to go to a new school next year."

Rae tried to console her by saying, "Maybe you'll like it better than the one you are going to now."

"Daisy is happy because she gets her own room, but I don't want to be in a room all by myself in the dark." Her words came between sobs.

"Where's my phone?" Gunner's deep Texas voice overpowered Heather's weeping. "Heather, who are you talking to?"

"Miz Rae," she answered.

"Give me the phone and go on to bed, sweetheart. You will love the new place, I promise, and we aren't moving until school is out at the end of this semester," Gunner assured her. "Rae, are you still there? Got time to talk for a few minutes? Do you mind if I switch it over to FaceTime?"

"Yes, I'm still here, and I don't mind FaceTime. What's on your mind?"

His face looked rugged, as if he was carrying the weight of the world on his shoulders. "I'm between a rock and a hard place."

"Talk to me," she said. "Maybe I can help."

He closed his eyes and shook his head. "I went to college with Remy. I didn't know him well, but we were acquainted. I run into him every now and then at church when I can go with the girls."

Rae used to tell her old partner that he started every conversation with "on the sixth day God made dirt," so she was used to what seemed like a discombobulated beginning.

"Why do you drive all the way up here when there are churches in Nocona?" she asked.

"My wife was raised on a little farm between here and there, and that's where she went. Aunt Rosie is actually her great-aunt, not mine," Gunner answered and then paused. "I shouldn't be bringing my worries to your doorstep."

"When I brought the girls home last night, Rosie told me that you have until Christmas to find a babysitter," Rae admitted. "Is that what you are fretting about?"

Gunner raked his fingers through his dark hair. "That's just part of my problem."

Rae couldn't imagine what Remy had to do with the whole story, but she was patient. He had at least gotten past the day that dirt was created. "Go on."

"I rent this house. The owner died and his kids have a buyer for it." Gunner said. "It's time for me to…"

"Move on, right? But it's tough living in a place where your wife's memory is around every corner," Rae finished the sentence for him.

"Yes, it is." He nodded. "And here lately I feel like she is telling me that she can't rest in peace until I have moved on, not just where houses are concerned, but in life."

Rae carried two quilts out to the porch and laid them on an empty rocking chair while she talked. "I understand where you are coming from. I got that message—maybe not from a spouse or even a boyfriend—but it was a strong feeling that it was time for me to move back to Spanish Fort."

Bo raised an eyebrow. "Gunner?"

"Do you need to go?" he asked.

"No, I'm here and listening to whatever you want to talk

about. Heather was upset when she called," Rae said. "Have they lived in that same house all their lives?"

"Yes, they have," Gunner answered. "They've shared the same room too. I told them they could have their own rooms in the new place. Daisy seemed happy with the idea, but Heather got tears in her eyes. I hugged them both and assured them that the school is a lot smaller than the one they are attending now and told them they would love it."

"They're young," Rae said. "We moved to the Paradise when I was about their age, and it didn't take any of us long to adjust. Kids are resilient."

"Heather asked me if they could still go to the same church." His tone got more exasperated with each word, and sighed again. "I think the girls really, really like you, Rae. Maybe that will make the move easier, just knowing that you'll still be their Sunday school teacher."

Rae went upstairs to her room. When she kicked off her shoes and sat cross-legged in the middle of her bed, Gunner was explaining that as the Nocona police chief, he had to stay in Montague County. Knowing that she would still get to see the girls on Sunday put a smile on her face. But she still wondered what Remy had to do with the story.

"So, anyway, to make a long story short"—he finally smiled—"or a short story long like I just did, Remy and I were talking yesterday afternoon while I helped with decorations. He has an empty house adjacent to his property that he bought up when the previous people living there decided to leave town, and he's willing to rent it to me. I called him this afternoon, and the girls and I will be moving into it in a week or two. Now, all I need is a babysitter for a few hours after school, all day on Saturday, and a few hours Sunday evening. Do you know anyone who might be interested in that kind of job?"

"I'll do it," Rae volunteered. "They can ride the bus here to the Paradise, and you can get them here at the end of your workday."

"Are you serious?" Gunner's face showed pure shock.

Rae didn't understand what he was saying until she realized she had said the words out loud without even thinking about it. "I guess I am, if you will trust me with your daughters."

"Thank you, thank you!" Gunner said. "I'll tell the girls. They kind of fell in love with you at the house yesterday. All they've talked about is how you let them read to you and even brushed their hair. Heather probably won't even mind the move if she gets to see you every day. I'll call you tomorrow with more details."

"Daddy, will you come tuck us in?"

Rae could see the child in the background, and her heart went out to her. "You've got girls to kiss good night. We can talk more later."

"Thank you again, and good night."

"Good night, Gunner, and give the girls a kiss from me."

Bo knocked on the door and peeked inside.

Rae tossed her phone onto a pillow, threw her hand over her forehead, and groaned. "What have I done?"

Chapter 12

SOMETIMES WHEN BO GOT homesick in her efficiency apartment in Nashville, she would go into the tiny kitchen that was on one end of the room and pretend she was back at the Paradise making breakfast or lunch with her mother. She would even talk to Mary Jane as if she were in the room with her during their virtual time together, and they would solve all kinds of problems.

She checked the kitchen calendar while she was making sausage gravy and biscuits that morning and was surprised to see that it was already Wednesday. It seemed like they had just had Sunday dinner with all the family the day before. Even with her busy schedule of working as much as she could in Nashville, and the occasional gig, time didn't pass as quickly as it did when she was in Spanish Fort.

But, then, you aren't having nearly as much fun out there without family as you do here. Aunt Bernie's voice was so vivid that Bo stopped stirring the gravy and checked to be sure her aunt hadn't flown home on a magic carpet, or maybe a witch's broom.

"Good mornin'," Mary Jane said as she entered the room.

"Mornin'." Bo set a cast-iron skillet full of gravy on a

warming burner and gave her mother a hug. "What's on your agenda today?"

"I finished the last chapter in the book I've been working on, so I'm taking from now to Christmas off to enjoy the family and the holidays. I thought I might go with you girls to the church quilting bee this morning," she answered.

"That would be wonderful."

The timer on the stove dinged, so Bo removed a pan of biscuits from the oven. "How many eggs do you think I should scramble?"

"Ten should be plenty," Mary Jane answered.

"Hello, the house!" Bernie yelled as she entered the kitchen by the door leading out to the screened-in porch. "I could smell breakfast cooking halfway across the yard. God…bless the home…" She giggled. "You thought I was going to say a cuss word, didn't you? Well, you were right! I have not been a good girl. I cussed seasickness so much that I almost blistered the paint right off my truck on the way home from Galveston."

"Make that an even dozen," Mary Jane whispered.

Bo thought that she was imagining things for a split second. Aunt Bernie was supposed to be on a ship headed to somewhere in Mexico—or was it Belize?—that day. Bo closed her eyes for a moment, but when she opened them, Bernie was still there, and Pepper had chased Sassy out from under the table and into the foyer.

"He's missed me," Bernie said. "I will never go anywhere again if he can't go with me. He said that if I stayed out another four days, he would die."

"Aunt Bernie!" Bo crossed the room and gave her a hug. "How did you…?"

Bernie held up a palm. "I'll tell my story when the rest of the family gets here. Right now, I'm going to get a cup of coffee and wallow in the good feeling that I am back home."

Bo took a couple of steps back and thought of the old adage about dynamite coming in small packages. "Did you threaten to bomb the ship if they didn't turn around and bring you home?"

"Of course not," Bernie snapped. "Get me a cup of coffee and make it right. That stuff y'all drink and what they had on the ship was just murdered water. No wonder me and Gladys got sick."

"Yes, ma'am." Bo poured a mug full of black coffee and added a heaping teaspoon of instant coffee to it.

She set it in front of Bernie, who immediately took a sip. "Perfect! I've trained you well. Are you ready to get back to work?"

"I've been working every single day except Sunday since you've been gone," Bo snapped. "I've got all the questions from your followers typed up and ready to put on your blog when you decide which ones go when."

"Don't get sassy with me, girl. I can always fire you and hire Rae to take your place."

"Don't threaten me," Bo shot back at her. "I can always work at the bar with Maverick. He offered me a job and even said I could sing whenever I wanted."

Bernie's finger shot up close to Bo's nose. "I forbid you

to go near Whiskey Bent ever again. That piece of eye candy that works in there is bad news."

"Maybe I just need a little dose of bad boy in my life," Bo said.

"If you two want to argue, then you'll have to sit on the sofa and hold hands," Mary Jane threatened.

"Yes, ma'am," Bo nodded. "One more thing and then I'll hush. Rae wouldn't work for you in a million years. She hates computer work. She whined like a little girl when she had to learn how to run the program at the police department, and she wouldn't even help me decorate the bar."

A wide grin spread over Bernie's face. "I'm so glad to be home again, and, honey, I knew I was leaving my business in good hands." She took a sip of her coffee. "Now, tell me all about the meet-and-greet event. Did anyone hook up after it was over?"

"As in exchange phone numbers or as in the real sense?" Bo asked.

"Either one," Bernie answered.

"Rae saw a couple out in the parking lot making out like teenagers, and a woman named Dixie was pretty determined not to go home alone," Bo told her. "I told a couple of women that we might do an event for married couples. Kind of like a fall-in-love-all-over-again event."

"Yes!" Bernie clapped her hands. "I've been trying to think of something during Valentine's. That would be wonderful. We could have a nice dinner catered, and… But whoa! You are changing the subject away from Maverick." Her eyes narrowed and she shook her finger at Bo. "You didn't fall in love with that sexy Maverick while I was gone did you? I heard that he and Gunner Watson came to Sunday dinner. I knew if I wasn't here something like this would happen. But I'm home now, and I can nip in the bud anything that might have gotten started. Rae has always loved little kids, but those two little hellions that Gunner has…" She clucked her tongue like an old hen gathering in her chick before a storm. "Well, suffice it to say, Rae doesn't want to take that job on. Well? What about you?"

"What about me?" Bo asked.

"Did you get all tingly when you were around Maverick?"

"I did, but you didn't leave your teddy behind, so I couldn't seduce him," Bo answered.

"Aunt Bernie!" Endora squealed when she and Rae came into the room.

"What are you doing home today?" Rae rubbed her eyes. "Did I sleep for four days?"

"Hey, look what Pepper dragged in." Joe Clay teased and then kissed his wife on the cheek before heading toward the coffeepot.

Bo busied herself fixing eggs and putting everything on the bar for a buffet breakfast. Even though she would be getting calls at least once an hour from her aunt, she could be thankful that Aunt Bernie refused to climb stairs to Bo's little office in Tertia's old room. If Bernie's knees were good, she would spend the whole day in the room with Bo.

I know, Bo thought, *but even with that, I'm kind of glad she's home. Never thought I would say it, but Mama is right about liking the way she spices up the Paradise.*

———

Rae caught Bo's eye and winked at her. They might not be identical twins like Luna and Endora, but she could still read her sister's mind most of the time. "You just thought you were going to have a few days to run from her matchmaking."

"Don't tease me about such a serious matter," Bo said out the corner of her mouth. "You're on the hot seat just as much as I am."

"Okay, the gang is all here," Bernie said. "So, I'll tell my story while y'all help yourselves to the food. It's not a long tale, but we can talk while we eat, and then I can go to the quilting bee this morning with y'all. Lord, but I'm glad to be back. I thought I'd died and gone to heaven when I made the turn down the lane and saw the Paradise all lit up for Christmas. Gladys said to tell you that she's not going to the quilting bee. She's still a little under the weather."

Rae took the coffeepot and pitchers of milk and orange juice to the table, then went to the bar and filled her plate. "Is that the whole story?"

"Good God, no!" Bernie declared. "We were so excited to get on the ship. We didn't even unpack before we went to the lido deck, got us a dirty banana drink, and joined in the fun of waving at the people who were on the pier. We kind of felt sorry for them because they couldn't go with us. We had supper, watched a movie under the stars, and had another drink or two, then went to our cabin. By midnight we were taking turns in the bathroom, and I wondered if we hadn't gotten a taste of what hell felt like. The nausea didn't let up until yesterday morning when we made land. We got off that miserable ship, went ashore, and actually felt better," she stopped and took a sip of coffee. "Bo, honey, will you make me a plate?"

"Glad to," Bo said with a smile and pushed back from the table.

"So, where was I?" Bernie frowned. "Oh, yeah, we got off the ship, felt better, got back on and were sick again, so we told our steward that we would be getting off permanently. He knew someone who knew someone and got us a cab to the nearest airport. We had to wait for the next flight, which took us to Miami, and then wait for another one to get us to Galveston, but when we got there, we'd had enough of flying and cruising. We got home about two o'clock this morning. I thought I would sleep until noon at the least, but at seven o'clock my eyes popped wide open, and here I am."

Bo set a plate in front of Bernie and eased back down into her chair. "You think maybe it was just a stomach bug?"

"I don't know what it was, but me and Gladys ain't goin' on no more cruises. I might go to a beach in Florida in the spring, but only if we make it a road trip, and Pepper can go with me," she answered. "I get a little queasy every time I even think about a dirty banana or a ship."

Rae finished off her last bite of food and was on the way

to the sink with her dirty plate when the house phone rang. She picked the remote receiver off the base and said, "Hello."

"Hello, may I please speak to Rae Simmons?"

"This is Rae." Something about the voice sounded vaguely familiar.

"This is Holly Daniels," the lady said. "I don't know if you remember me or not. I was Holly Sullivan, and I graduated with your older sister, Ursula."

A picture of a tall girl with red hair popped into Rae's head. "Yes, I remember you. You ran cross-country in high school and brought home a lot of trophies for the school."

"That was a long time ago," Holly said with a chuckle. "I'm the principal at Prairie Valley School now. Ursula told me that you are back in this area, and that you are certified in early childhood development. I need a long-term substitute for a kindergarten teacher. Probably for all of next semester. Would you be interested? The teacher is pregnant and having problems, and there's a possibility she won't return next year, so this could develop into a full-time teaching job."

"When would I start?"

"I've got someone lined up to take over for her until the Christmas break. So right after that?" Holly asked.

Rae took a deep breath, thought about the offer for a minute, and let her breath out slowly. She could easily watch the twins. They would have the same hours, so that would make it easy, and the job would give her an opportunity to see if she would even like to get into the teaching field.

"Yes," Rae said, "I would like to take you up on that offer."

"Can you come by the school this afternoon about three thirty to fill out some paperwork?" Holly asked.

"I can do that," Rae said. "See you then."

"You have no idea what a load of worry you just took off me," Holly said. "I'll see you soon and thank you so much!"

"What did you just do?" Bo asked when Rae put the receiver back on the base.

"I'm going to see if I like being a kindergarten teacher," Rae answered and explained what had just happened.

"I thought you were going to take a few months to regroup," Bo said. "And now you've taken on two jobs in less than twenty-four hours."

Bernie's fork clattered when she dropped it on the table. "What is this about two?"

"Gunner is moving into the rental house on the back side of Jake and Ophelia's land," Rae answered and went on to tell them that she would be taking care of the twins. "It will all work out. I can pick them up for school and after school, I'll have them for a couple of hours. Mama, I can always keep them at his place if..."

Mary Jane waved the idea away with the back of her hand. "Nonsense. My schedule was set when you girls were all in school. I started writing when you all left for school and finished with whatever chapter or scene I was working on about the time you got home. That way I could spend more time with you. I still call it a day by three o'clock most of the time, and I will love having kids in the house."

Bernie picked up her fork and sighed. "Bo, won't those wild girls be too noisy for you to get any work done?"

"No, ma'am," Bo answered. "They are rowdy and remind me of Luna and Endora when they were younger, but Rae can keep them in line. After all, her last job was keeping the peace in a whole city. Surely, she can manage a couple of ornery girls."

"Thank you, Sister, for that vote of confidence. Does that mean I can call on you if I need you?"

Bo shook her head. "It most certainly does not."

Mary Jane laughed out loud. "I hope they give all of you a run for your money. It will be wonderful comeuppance for all the times when I almost pulled my hair out."

"Endora, how are you coming on the children's books?" Bernie asked.

Rae didn't need a third degree in rocket science to know that her aunt was trying to get some negative responses out of someone. "Aunt Bernie, the girls don't have horns, and they don't carry around a pitchfork. They might even walk Pepper for you in the afternoons. They fell in love with him last Sunday."

"You keep those two away from Pepper!" Bernie accentuated every word by poking her fork toward Rae. "They might corrupt my poor baby."

Joe Clay chuckled as he got up to refill his plate with a second helping of biscuits and gravy. "Congratulations!"

"What's funny, and why are you congratulating us?" Endora asked.

Joe Clay brought his plate back to the table. "We've got girls getting out of the teaching field to do something else, and here is Rae going into it. I hope you are as happy as a teacher as they are in their new fields."

"Thank you, Daddy," Rae said. "But if I don't like the job, it's only for one semester. This is kind of like a little test to see if teaching is what I want to do."

"When do you start the nanny business with those kids?" Bernie asked.

"As soon as school is out for the Christmas break. That will involve having them underfoot all day. I'll take them with me to the church to decorate. Maybe they'll even be a help."

"That will work out just fine," Mary Jane said. "I'm not starting a new book until after the new year. We'll be busy with the Paradise Christmas party and the church program. My thoughts on ornery kids is to keep them occupied and feeling like they are helping."

Bernie's sigh came out more like a snort. "Just keep them out of my trailer and away from Pepper."

"They can play with my cats and Sassy," Endora offered. "And we could turn one of the spare rooms into a playroom for them."

"Thank you all," Rae said. "If it gets to be too much around here, y'all be honest with me, and I'll take them somewhere."

"You aren't talking about my place, are you?" Bernie gasped.

"Of course, she is," Bo teased. "You can read to them or, better yet, let them read to you. Rae says they are very smart."

"I'll cut you out of my will if you do something that stupid," Bernie threatened.

"You'll do that anyway," Bo said, "when you find out I'm going to go wandering about the world with Maverick. Can I have your teddy when we leave?"

Bernie rolled her eyes toward the ceiling. "Sweet Jesus! Send that man on down the road before my niece gets into trouble."

"Was that a prayer or a demand?" Rae asked.

"Both, and you better not get involved with Gunner either," Bernie growled.

Hmm…why not? Rae thought.

Chapter 13

RAE DELIBERATELY WAITED UNTIL the other four were in Endora's car before she came down the stairs. When she went outside, Bo rolled down the window and yelled, "We've got a full car. You'll have to take your truck, but we're all planning to catch a ride back with you."

"Why?" Rae asked.

"Endora needs to take care of a few things at the church," Bo answered.

"I got half my wish," Rae mumbled as she braced herself against the cold wind and jogged out to her vehicle. Her phone rang before she could start the engine, and Gunner's name popped up on the screen.

"Hello," she answered. "I'm glad you called. There's been a slight change of plans with the girls."

"Please don't tell me that you can't keep them," Gunner groaned. "They're on cloud nine, and now they don't even mind going to a new school."

"No, I've got the schedule all worked out," Rae answered. "I'll be substitute teaching the pre-K and kindergarten classes at Prairie Valley School next semester. They can come to my classroom after school, and I'll take them home."

"Are you sure that's not...?" Gunner started.

Rae butted in and said, "It's not too much for me. Did I tell you that I have a double degree? One is in criminology and the other is in early childhood. I didn't know which way I wanted to go back then. I tried the police work for a while, but now I want to dip my toes in the teaching field."

"Thank you, thank you, thank you," Gunner said. "The reason I called is to ask you if you would be willing to meet me at the house this afternoon. I rented it sight unseen because of the location and availability. I'd like to get an idea of what I need to move before I start packing. Aunt Rosie is already bringing boxes and packing things like stuffed animals from the girls' room. It's like she's saying that she will miss us, but it's time to get the hell out of Dodge...or in this case Nocona. I don't think she would have cared if we were moving into a tree house as long as she doesn't have to babysit anymore."

"I've got to be at the school at three thirty, but I can meet you right after lunch. Say one o'clock?"

"Great," Gunner said. "I'll see you there. I'm not even sure where it is, so could we meet at the winery and go together from there? I'll be the one in the car with 'Police' written on the side."

"Then that's what I'll look for, and why did Rosie...?" She paused, not knowing whether the question she was about to ask was too personal.

"Why did she keep the girls in the first place?" He finished for her. "She and Stacey were very close, and she wanted to come help with the girls when Stacey took sick. One thing led to another, and when the girls' mother died, Rosie insisted on helping even though her health wasn't good. I've got a call coming in, so I should go. See you soon. Bye and thank you again."

Rae tossed the phone over onto the passenger seat and headed to the church. She had never been in the rental house, so she couldn't tell Gunner how it was laid out. Jake's cousin, Conor, and his girlfriend came to Spanish Fort six months ago to help in the winery. By the middle of the summer, she was pregnant and homesick, so they sold the house to Jake and moved back around her parents.

Everything happens for a reason. Rae's old partner's words popped into her head.

———

"Bo, you did a wonderful job making the quilt top," Mary Jane said when she took one of the chairs circling the quilt frame and threaded a needle.

"Thank you, Mama," Bo said. "My sewing machine was the one thing I was determined not to leave in Nashville, and I'm glad I brought it along." She heard a vehicle door slam, and then someone coming down the hallway. Rae pushed open the door and sat down in the last chair.

"What took you so long?" Endora asked. "I was about to call you to be sure you didn't have a flat tire or that you hadn't caught a stomach bug from Aunt Bernie."

Bernie handed a threaded needle to her friend and

Ursula's mother-in-law, Vera. "I did not bring home a bug. Gladys and I had a dose of seasickness, which was a sign that we should never get on another boat. I figured as skinny as you are that the wind blew you all the way over the river and into Oklahoma."

"I'm not skinny," Rae protested. "I had a phone call, but according to the weatherman I heard on the radio, this wind is going to blow in a storm later this evening. Good thing our Paradise Christmas party isn't until the end of next week."

"The almanac says we're in for a hard winter," Frannie said. A tall woman with a pixie haircut and big pink-framed glasses, she was one of Bernie's best friends.

"Maybe it'll freeze out the mosquitoes and ticks," Vera said. "Next year, our precious grandson, Clayton, will be walking, and I hate to think of those miserable insects biting him."

"Ain't that the truth," Bernie added. "Do you think it will be cold enough to murder all the fire ants? I hate them even worse than ticks."

"At least all of those things have died out for this year and won't bother us during the holidays. I'm excited about the Paradise party. It's the one time during the holidays that I get to dress up," Frannie said.

"Me too," Bernie agreed. "I always look forward to it."

"Good save by changing the subject to the weather," Bo whispered to Rae, and then lowered her voice even more. "You were talking to Gunner, weren't you? Sit down here beside me and start hemming the edges. Aunt Bernie has offered to keep needles threaded for all of us so we can keep working."

"We want to have the quilt done today so we can display it on Sunday out in the foyer for the silent auction," Endora said without even looking up from her place on the other side of the quilt frame. "It's sure worked out to be a piece of art with all the pretty holiday fabric that Bo found."

Frannie raised her hand. "I believe that we should vote Bo in as the head of the quilting committee. She's the one who does such a lovely job of making the quilt tops, and there ain't a one of us can match her stitches."

"I second the motion," Bernie said as she changed out Frannie's empty needle for a fully threaded one.

Bo stopped hemming for a minute to shake her finger at her aunt. "You just want me to be committed to something so I don't leave."

"Yep, but you are good at this, and Endora needs help," Bernie declared. "And besides, I will hog-tie you and chain you to the walls in the barn if you start up anything with Maverick Gibson."

"If you don't want him, you can throw him across the fence to me," Frannie said.

"How do you know Maverick?" Bo asked.

"His boss, Dave, is my cousin, and he introduced us. I'm old enough to be his grandma, but oh, honey…" Frannie used her hand like a fan to cool her face.

"Good Lord, Frannie!" Vera scolded.

"Wait until you see him," Frannie snapped. "He'd make a

nun's underbritches fall down around her knees, and honey, there's not a holy woman sitting amongst us, even if we are in a church house."

"Hold on," Endora said. "My mama has a halo that shines in the dark."

"That's sweet," Mary Jane said, "and I'm really glad I've got you fooled, but, darlin' daughter, if I have a halo, it is crooked and probably has some scorch around the edges. Now let's turn this conversation to next year's cookbook committee and electing a president for the quilting business."

"That's not nearly as much fun," Rae said, "but since Aunt Bernie is opposed, I suppose we should think of something other than crawlin' between the sheets with Maverick or else Bo might get jealous."

Bo reached over and slapped her sister on the arm. "You just don't want us to get started on you and Gunner."

"We'll save that for the next meeting," Endora said. "Rae should head up next year's cookbook committee, and Bo should take over the quilting. That will free me up for the other duties that a preacher's wife has."

Rae shook her head. "Starting next week, I will be babysitting, and then after the holidays, I have agreed to do some long-term substitute teaching. Choose someone else for the cookbook business."

"I'll do it!" Bo threw up her hand and volunteered. "I've already got the templates made in my computer, so the next one won't be as tough or time-consuming as the Christmas one. Maybe we could just do something like *Grannies from Spanish Fort Cookbook*."

Several conversations began about who could contribute their ancestors' old recipes. Bo didn't even try to listen to them, but leaned over and whispered to Rae, "You owe me one. Who were you talking to on the phone?"

"Thank you, and it was Gunner. He wants me to go see the rental house with him before he moves into it. I'm meeting him at the winery at one, and then I'm talking to Holly at the school at three thirty," Rae answered.

"Two hours is enough time to get into trouble." Bo grinned. "Maybe you should take Ursula with you."

"Hush!" Rae snapped. "You sound like Aunt Bernie. Gunner and I barely even know each other."

"That's about to change whether Aunt Bernie likes it or not," Bo told her.

She had barely gotten the words out of her mouth when a vision of Maverick came to her mind. *Now where did that come from?* she wondered.

The last stitch was put into the hem by Endora, and then she took a picture of the quilt in the frame and one with each of the ladies holding up a section before it was hung in the foyer for the auction. "I want all of you to know how much I appreciate all the work that's gone into this project. The missionary family our little church supports over in Thailand is going to be so tickled to get the money the quilt brings in. I hope that we can construct two next year: one in the summer and one at Christmas. Another special thanks to Bo for sewing up the top. To get all those corners even would have tested every ounce of Jesus that I have in me."

"Amen!" Mary Jane said. "Bo is the only one in the whole family who enjoys sewing."

The ladies showed their appreciation with a round of applause.

Bo did a perfect curtsy. "Thank you. After that much attention, I'll have to really outdo myself to make the summer quilt even better and prettier than this one. Now can we adjourn to the fellowship hall? Tertia can't be here, so she whipped up some finger foods for us for lunch."

———

Lightning zipped through the sky when Rae skipped the lunch and slipped out the front door. The thunder that followed was so loud that it rattled the windows of the church and sent her running across the parking lot. Cold wind was supposed to bring snowflakes or sleet, not a rainstorm. But then Texas weather had always been, and would most likely always be, as unpredictable as a pregnant woman's food cravings.

Her phone rang as she slid behind the steering wheel, and by the time she picked it up from the passenger's seat, huge raindrops had begun to hit the windshield.

"Hello, Mama," she said on the third ring.

"Where are you?" Mary Jane asked. "We're waiting on you and Bo to say grace so we can start eating."

"I told Bo I had to skip lunch," she answered. "I'm

meeting Gunner at one o'clock to go see Jake's rental house, and then I have a meeting at the school after that."

"I see," Mary Jane said.

"Aunt Bernie is close, isn't she?" Rae whispered.

"Yes," Mary Jane answered. "I see Bo coming now. But I understand. Tell Holly hello for me. See you at home later this afternoon."

The windshield wipers had to work double time, and she had to drive slower than she would have, but she still made it to the winery with a few minutes to spare. The vehicles that were parked outside said that people were waiting for the rain to slack up before they made a mad dash for their vehicles.

Her phone rang again, and this time it was Ophelia wanting to FaceTime. She touched the screen and her sister's face appeared. "I'll bring an umbrella if you want to come inside."

Rae shook her head. "No, thanks. I'm meeting Gunner here in a few minutes. He asked me to go look at the house with him."

Ophelia raised an eyebrow. "Oh, really?"

"It's not like that," Rae frowned. "He needs to make some decisions about the girls' rooms, and he wants my opinion since they seem to like me."

Ophelia grinned. "If you say so. He's already got the keys and paid the rent. Is Rosie moving in with him?"

"No," Rae answered. "I'm going to keep the girls for him after school and when he has to work on weekends. I'm surprised that Mama hasn't called you already."

"About what?" Ophelia tilted her head to the side.

Rae told her about working at the school, and how she was arranging her schedule to keep the twins.

"You are one brave woman," Ophelia said. "I hear those little girls are a handful."

"I already know that from having them in Sunday school class, but like I said, they seem to like me, and here's Gunner pulling up right beside me," Rae said.

"Be careful." Ophelia giggled. "He has handcuffs."

"So do I. See you later," Rae said with a giggle and ended the call.

She only had to take a couple of steps from her vehicle to his, and for a split second, a little nostalgia washed over her. "I kind of miss my police car," she admitted.

"There's a place for you on my staff if you want it," Gunner said.

"Thanks, but no thanks. I really am excited about giving this teaching position a try," she said as she fastened her seat belt. "The path will be a little bumpy, especially since few people have even traveled back here since Conor left."

By the time they reached the house, the rain had stopped as suddenly as it began, and the sun popped out in a pale winter-blue sky. A lovely rainbow appeared right over the pretty little ranch house. The bare trees glistened with water droplets, and at the sound of a truck's engine, a flock of cardinals took flight. A couple of cottontail rabbits hopped out from under the porch and stared at the truck for a full minute before they disappeared out into the thicket on the other side of the road.

"The girls are going to love this," Gunner whispered. "It will so be worth the extra miles I have to drive to work."

Rae was totally speechless at the sight before her. With the light shining down on the pale-yellow house, it truly looked like it was the pot of gold at the end of the rainbow. Was it a sign or just a coincidence?

"It's so peaceful," Rae finally whispered. "It kind of reminds me of a Thomas Kinkade painting."

"You are right," Gunner said. "Aunt Rosie gave me a calendar last year with his works on it. Birds, bunnies, and a rainbow. Think it's a sign that I'm making the right choice?"

"It just might be," Rae said with a nod as she opened the door on her side of the truck, got out, and started toward the porch.

"Thank goodness for the grass, even if it's dead," Gunner said. "After that rain we could be walking in mud. As it is, we probably should take our shoes and boots off at the door."

"I was just thinking the same thing," Rae said.

Gunner's eyes darted around as if he was trying to take in everything at once and plan for the future at the same time. "The girls could have a swing set—and maybe an above-ground pool next summer."

"Do they have bikes?" Rae remembered how riding her first bike up the lane to the road to get the mail had been a really big deal.

"Not yet," Gunner answered. "But they should be safe out here."

"I would think so," Rae agreed, "but they might like a four-wheeler better."

Gunner pulled a key from his pocket, unlocked the door, and swung it open. "Oh, no! I love my girls, but I also know them, and anything bigger than a bike would be asking for double trouble, probably in the form of emergency room visits for broken arms or ankles." He stopped just inside the room and removed his boots. "The living room is bigger than the one in the house I'm living in, and thank goodness, it's got vinyl flooring. I've always felt like keeping the carpet clean in the house is like having a second job."

Rae followed his lead and put her boots beside his. How many times had she seen Mary Jane's shoes and Joe Clay's placed side by side in the foyer? Sometimes with all seven girls' footwear sitting beside them. She was always reminded of those decals on the back windows of vehicles that had figures of a daddy, a mama, and however many kids were in the family all lined up in a row.

Just a mama and daddy today, the voice in her head whispered.

Don't go there. I'm just a part-time nanny, she thought as she followed Gunner down the hallway.

She stood by the door when Gunner went inside the first bedroom on the right. "Bunk beds will fit very well in both bedrooms, and with the built-ins, we won't have to move the dresser that's in their room now."

"They might each have room for their bookcases at the end of the beds," Rae suggested.

"Do you believe in omens, Rae?"

"I do," she answered. "Why do you ask?"

"When I drove up here, I felt a sense of peace I haven't known in years. I got the same feeling when I walked into this house," he said and left that room to open the next door down the hallway.

"Well, look at that," he pointed at the washer and dryer. "I won't have to move any appliances."

"Looks like your move gets easier by the minute." Rae remembered all the things she had given away when she left Boise City. "If you've got things you don't want, you might donate them to a women's shelter. That's what I did when I left Boise City."

"That's a great idea," Gunner said and peeked into the next room. "Identical to the one next door, but I betcha that the girls argue over which one gets which room." He moved on again to open another door. "This just gets better and better. Look, Rae! They each get their own sink."

"Another sign that you are doing the right thing," Rae told him.

The last door opened into the master bedroom. "And would you look at the size of this room, and it's got its own full bathroom. I feel like I just found the pot of gold at the end of that rainbow out there."

Seeing a grown man, a police chief at that, so excited over a house put a smile on Rae's face. "You have found the pot of gold. Now you just have to make the move."

"What is the biggest omen is that you will be watching

over the girls for me." He turned around, took a couple of steps forward, and wrapped Rae up in a hug. "This wouldn't be possible if you weren't willing to help me."

Rae's heart threw in an extra beat when her cheek was against Gunner's chest. Her pulse jacked up a few notches, and her knees went weak. Her mind told her to take a step back, but her heart gave her a different message. She listened to the latter and leaned into the hug even more. Her mind said that she could not get involved with a man who was just now moving on after his wife's death. She did not want to be the rebound woman, and he would most likely never have a whole heart to give to anyone again. Plus, he needed to spend all his spare time with his girls. They would be grown someday, and he couldn't reclaim the time he lost.

She leaned back and looked up at him in time to see his eyes flutter shut. She barely had time to moisten her lips before he kissed her. Suddenly, the rest of the world disappeared, and they were the only two people in the whole state of Texas. For the short moment that his lips were on hers, she was transported into the middle of an unfamiliar place—like a tornado had picked her up from her little world and tossed her into a whirlwind. She had been kissed before—many times. She had been in a couple of relationships, but nothing had ever made her forget everything and everyone in her life the way Gunner Watson's kiss did.

When the kiss ended, he ran the back of his hand down over her cheekbone. "I've wanted to do that ever since I met you for the first time in Saint Jo."

"Really?" Rae tried to keep her voice steady, but catching her breath was tough.

"Yes, really," Gunner said. "Are you going to slap me for...?"

"No, I am not." Rae rolled up on her toes, cupped his cheeks in her hands, and brushed a soft kiss across his lips. Even that much sent a rush through her body. "But before we do that again, we need to talk about where it could lead."

Chapter 14

IN SPITE OF THE cold weather, when she reached the school that afternoon, Rae's insides were still warm from the kisses she had shared with Gunner. She had hoped to have time to discuss their future—if there was one for them—but he had gotten called out for a domestic disturbance and had to leave.

Since she wasn't ready to go home or even stop in at the winery and visit Ophelia, she drove to the school parking lot and sat in her car for an hour. She weighed the pros and cons of a relationship with Gunner and asked herself if she could merely be feeling sorry for him and his daughters. She didn't have a single answer when the end-of-the-day bell rang and kids began to swarm out of the building. Teenagers who had vehicles tossed books and backpacks into their cars or trucks and drove away from the parking lot. Some of the younger children were picked up by their parents. Others climbed onto the yellow school bus that waited to take them home.

Rae remembered hating the fact that the Paradise was close to the last stop for the bus she and her sisters had taken home each afternoon. She couldn't wait to get off at the end of the lane and walk to the house, most of the time lingering behind the other six to suck in the fresh air and get away from the sweaty smell of a busload of kids.

"And yet, sitting here for more than an hour in the quiet hasn't gotten me a bit closer to an answer for my dilemma about Gunner," she said out loud, and then another question popped into her mind. "Do I really want to teach little kids, or even keep those girls?"

Are you having regrets? the voice in her head asked.

"No, I am not! Just as surely as that rainbow over Gunner's new home was an omen for him, all these things falling into place in my life are signs that I'm going in the right direction," she answered.

The parking lot cleared out and left only a few cars behind. The buses had driven away, and no more parents waited for their children. Yet, Rae still couldn't answer the question that kept playing on repeat in her head. Finally, with only five minutes left until her appointment time, she opened the truck door and slid out of the driver's seat.

She opened the front door, and the familiar smell of the school wafted down the hall to meet her. She took a few steps toward the principal's office—a place that Bo actually knew much better than she did—and Holly came out of a classroom right ahead of her.

"I was just finishing up with the sub who's working for the kindergarten teacher. She just told me that she won't be back tomorrow. Think you could go to work earlier than we talked about?" Holly asked.

"Are you serious?" Rae asked.

"Very much so," Holly answered. "Walk with me up to my office. Pre-K and kindergarten together have a total of ten kids. Five in each grade. Christmas break starts at the end of the day on Friday, December twentieth. We resume classes on January sixth for the second semester. You would only have to work two weeks and two days until the holiday starts. That would give you a chance..."

"I'm in," Rae said before Holly could finish.

Holly opened the door into her office and stopped dead in her tracks. "Are you serious?"

"I don't have anything else to do for the rest of this week, and I think you were about to say that these next two weeks and two days would give me a chance to see what teaching is all about." Rae went on into the office and sat down. "Where and what do I need to sign?"

Holly sat down at her desk. "If things work out for you to teach full-time next year, we'll need copies of your transcript and credentials. Did you take the Texas tests?"

"I did, and I've kept my teaching certificate current. I'll email it over to you when I get home," Rae said.

"Why did you do that when you...?" Holly frowned and paused.

"When I worked on the police force?" Rae finished for her and shrugged. "I have no idea because once I started, I really thought I'd always be a policewoman for the rest of my life, but I'm glad I did. If your teacher decides to return next year, maybe there will be another position opening up that I can fill. Or I might take the test to teach forensic criminology at the high school level. I have a lot of options, but this job will give me a feel for teaching."

"Sub work does not come with benefits, but if things work out for you to teach next year, we'll get all that going then," Holly said.

"I understand that," Rae told her. "I'm covering my own insurance for now."

"We sure miss your two sisters here at the school. They were excellent teachers," Holly said.

"Do I have to live up to their standards?" Rae joked.

"Of course not," Holly was quick to answer with a nervous giggle. "I'm sure that, with your background, you will do a fine job of corralling and teaching the kids."

"Thank you," Rae said, "and I was teasing."

"I knew that," Holly declared.

"Anything else?" Rae asked.

"I hear that Gunner Watson is moving to this area and bringing his twin girls to enroll them in Prairie Valley School in the next few days," Holly blurted out.

"Yep, and I'll be helping take care of them. I'll take them home each evening and keep them until Gunner gets there," Rae said. "I'm sure he'll fill out the permissions paperwork when he comes in to talk to you."

"Are y'all dating?" Holly asked.

"No, but I've been teaching the girls' Sunday school class," Rae answered.

Holly picked up a pencil and fiddled with it. "Do you realize how ornery they are?"

"I understand they can be, but they seem to like me, and I'll be here to help with any problems," Rae assured her.

Holly tucked a strand of her chin-length red hair behind her ear and then pushed her glasses up further on her nose. "Gunner's wife, Stacey, and I are...were...cousins. Aunt Rosie is a sister to our grandmother who passed away a few years ago. Stacey was the love of Gunner's life, and he was devastated when she got cancer. That's probably why he lets those girls get away with their antics."

Holy smoke, Rae thought, *everyone seems to be related in this whole county—if not by blood, then shirttail kin.*

Was Holly giving her a subtle warning that she didn't know what she was getting into by taking on the babysitting job?

"Aunt Rosie brings them to the family reunion, and we are all on pins and needles until they leave, and that is putting it mildly," Holly said with a long sigh. "I hate to say it, but I'm not looking forward to having them in my school. I had no idea he was moving up here until this morning when Aunt Rosie called to warn me."

"Maybe a move to a smaller school is just what they need." Rae had to fight to keep the chill from her tone. If she taught at the elementary level, this woman would be her supervisor, so she had to be nice, but her first instinct was to tell Holly where she could go and what kind of sunblock she might need. With Rae's education, she could always homeschool the twins.

Holly barely nodded. "Gunner has dated a few women in

the past couple of years. Aunt Rosie says he won't ever have a chance at another relationship until the twins are grown. They sabotage every woman he gets close to. Just giving you a heads-up and fair warning in case he does happen to ask you out."

"Thank you," Rae said with a graciousness that she sure didn't feel. "So, back to the job. May I see my classroom?"

"Sure thing. The janitors haven't cleaned it yet so it's a little messy," Holly stood up and led the way back down the hall.

All the way home that afternoon, Rae kept telling herself that Holly had a right to her opinion. She couldn't fault the woman for thinking the way she did since she had spent time around Daisy and Heather at family reunions. Rae was sure that Aunt Rosie kept her up on the gossip about Gunner's girlfriends and about how much she didn't want to keep the twins anymore.

"I handled them in Sunday school," Rae told herself, and then Endora's words about how badly the girls behaved at church came back to her as she turned into the lane leading back to the Paradise. Bo had come close to calling them hellions, but Rae saw something else in them—pain and a need to be loved.

"Cut them some slack," Rae said as she parked in front of the Paradise. Seeing all the Christmas decorations lit up softened her mood a little bit. No doubt about it, she was in bad need of a shot of holiday spirit. She had had the right attitude when the committee told Endora about the cookbook funds, and that morning when they had finished the Christmas quilt to auction off for the missionaries. Then there was the peace that Gunner talked about and she had felt at his new house, and the breathlessness of his kisses.

"Then Holly sucked it all right out of me," Rae said.

You are not their mother and never will be, so slow your roll. Aunt Bernie's voice was so real that Rae looked over her shoulder to see if the old gal was in the back seat.

"Hey!" Bo slung the truck door open and slid into the passenger seat.

"You startled me," Rae said.

"You look like you could chew bark off the pecan trees and spit out toothpicks," Bo said. "You better start talking or you're going to explode."

Rae's could hear her own voice getting colder with each sentence when she told Bo about what Holly had said, and she finished with a sigh. "And I agreed to start working for her tomorrow. She's going to be my boss."

"Endora and Luna loved her, so give her a chance," Bo said. "You are just being defensive because you've fallen in love with those girls. Honey, they *can* be little terrors. Believe me, I know from working with them at the church these past six months. But you must have gotten your bluff in on them, or else they need someone like you to guide them."

"I know, but…"

Bo patted her on the shoulder. "But you are playing mama bear, right?"

"Gunner kissed me," Rae blurted out, "and I liked it, and now I don't know what to do about my own feelings. Maybe that's why I'm so..."

"Worried about whether you might just be a rebound since he's finally moving on?" Bo asked.

"That entered my mind," Rae admitted with a long sigh.

"Think, Sister," Bo said. "You just told me that Holly said he had dated a few women, but the girls sabotaged them all. He's already moved on in his heart if he went out with others. Getting out of the house he shared with his wife is simply the physical part of what has already happened. If you like him, then..."

"Open the door and invite him in, right?" Rae asked.

"Yep, just like Mama said about opportunity. It's tough to chase it when it's a mile down the road."

"But what if...?" Rae started.

"If we built our lives on what-ifs, we would live in isolation."

"Are you preachin' to me or to yourself?" Rae asked.

"Mostly you, but I need to hear the sermon too. I could really like Maverick, but my mind tells me that if I'm here in this area to settle down, I had better steer clear of him." Bo opened the door and got out of the truck. "It's cold out here. Let's take this conversation inside where it's warm."

Just thinking of Gunner's kisses chases away all the cold and warms me up, Rae thought as she followed her sister into the house.

Chapter 15

DISAPPOINTMENT WASHED OVER RAE as she and the rest of the family gathered round the trailer that evening to go on the annual family Christmas caroling trip. Gunner had promised Rae that he and the girls would do their best to join them, but the sun had almost set, and they still weren't here. She had worked on the police force long enough to know that the chief was basically on call most of the time, especially in emergencies. She had completely given up on seeing them when Bo nodded toward headlights coming down the lane.

"Turn that frown upside down," she teased. "Looks like your boyfriend made it, and just in time. Mama is bringing out the hats and candles. Once she hands them out, we'll load up and be on our way."

"Gunner is not my boyfriend," Rae argued.

"What do you call him, then?" Bo asked. "You've talked to him more than you have me in the past few days."

Bernie wedged her way between them. "I heard what y'all said. Gunner is a good man, but he is really, really not *the* man for you, Rae. You are mixing up your feelings for his motherless girls with feelings of love for him. That's never a smart thing to do. Besides that, he's a policeman. Every time he walked out the door to go to work, you would worry that he would get shot or hurt before he came home in the evening. That's not even mentioning all the emergency calls that he would have to go out on in the middle of the night."

Bernie's red velvet pantsuit showed in flashes under a floor-length dark-green cape with a white fur lining and a hood. She wore red satin gloves and rings on every finger, including her thumbs. Her earrings—jingle bells, of course—gave off a tinkling sound with every movement of her head. The matching necklace added to the noise. Then to top it all off, she had piled her dyed red hair up on top of her head and was wearing a glittering tiara around the messy bun.

"How do you intend to get a Santa hat on over that tiara?" Rae asked.

Bernie lifted her chin a notch. "If I can make two people fall in love, or keep a couple from falling in love, a tiara is no match for my magic."

"We're here! Don't go without us!" Heather yelled as she jumped out of the truck as soon as it was parked and ran across the yard. She wrapped her arms around Rae's waist and hugged her.

Daisy ran up beside her and grabbed Aunt Bernie in a bear hug. Then she took a step back, looked up at Bernie, and her eyes got big. "You aren't Miz Bo. You are a princess." She slapped her hand over her mouth and whispered. "Heather, this is the famous princess that we saw on television."

Heather took a step back and gasped. "No, that's not the princess, Daisy. That's the queen."

Both of them did a perfect curtsy.

"Can we sit beside you?" Daisy asked.

"Can we take a picture with you to show all our friends?" Heather asked. "Do you live here?"

"Yes, I do, and I'm Queen Bernie," she said.

"Wow!" Heather exclaimed. "We are moving to the town where Queen Bernie lives."

"Yes, you are," Bernie told them. "Who are you two little girls?"

"I'm..." Her eyes twinkled. "Which one am I, Miz Rae?"

Rae could hardly keep the laughter at bay as she looked from one girl to the other. Queen Bernie indeed! After that meeting, she wondered how long it would take her aunt to warm up to the little imps. She finally caught a glimpse of the freckle below Heather's ear.

"Let's see." She tapped her chin. "Daisy is wearing a red stocking hat, and Heather's is pink. I can't believe you aren't dressed alike."

"Daddy let us choose our own clothes tonight," Heather declared proudly. "But if we'd a-knowed we were meeting the queen, we would have dressed up. Guess what? I've got a loose tooth. See?" She opened her mouth wide and touched a tooth. "I'm going to pull one before Daisy does."

Daisy tipped up her chin and narrowed her eyes. "Then she won't be able to grin for school pictures, and everyone will be able to tell us apart because I always smile."

"I'll smile anyway," Heather declared.

"Guess what else?" Daisy changed the subject. "We are moving and going to a school where you are going to be the teacher."

"They are just alike," Bernie whispered. "How do you ever tell them apart?"

"Rae is one of the only ones who can," Bo answered and looped her arm into Bernie's. "Your lady-in-waiting is here to help you up to your hay-bale throne."

Daisy and Heather stood to the side, their little faces still a picture of pure awe.

"Can we sit beside the queen?" Heather asked.

"You can ask her," Rae answered.

If that didn't win Bernie over to thinking they were angels instead of hooligans, there would never be any hope.

"All aboard!" Joe Clay called out. "This wagon train leaves in five minutes for Spanish Fort and beyond."

"That's our cue to find a hay bale to sit on and get ready to sing," Rae told the twins.

Mary Jane brought out two tote bags. "Everyone needs to line up right here and get your hat and candle." The flame looked real when she flipped a switch on the bottom of each candle.

"Do we get one?" Daisy asked Rae.

"Of course, you do," Rae told them. "And a Santa hat too."

Bernie was first in line to get her hat and candle. She removed her tiara, affixed it to the Santa hat and then put it on her head. "There now, I'm ready to sing."

Heather was next, and when she'd crammed the red and white hat down over her stocking hat, she took a deep breath and looked up at Bernie. "Can we sit beside you?"

"If you promise to be good little girls," Bernie answered. "And if Rae wants, she can bring you to my house sometime when she's keeping you after school. It's not very big, but we have to keep where I live a secret. If everyone knew the queen lived here, they would swarm this area."

Heather made the sign of the cross over her heart. "I promise."

"It will be our secret," Daisy whispered.

"We might even have a dress-up party and take pictures," Bernie told them and then shot a look toward Rae that said she had better not say a word.

Bo reached down to get four hats and as many candles. "Hey, Rae, remember the first time we did this?"

"Yep," Rae said. "The nursing home staff had hot chocolate and cookies ready for us in the lobby."

"Do we get some, too?" Daisy asked as she waited for Bernie to take her place on a bale of hay. Then she sat down as close as she could on Bernie's right side. Heather hurried over and claimed a spot to her left.

"Everyone does," Bernie answered. "We go inside the lobby, and they have refreshments for us."

"Do they know you are the queen?" Heather asked.

Rae was so busy enjoying the show with Bernie and the twins that she didn't hear Gunner coming until he was right beside her. Who would have ever thought that two little girls' reaction to a costume that an octogenarian pulled together would have turned Bernie's attitude about the twins completely around? Certainly not Rae, nor her own twin from that smile on Bo's face.

"I feel like just saying the words are never enough," Gunner whispered. "But thank you once again for inviting me and the girls to the Christmas caroling tonight. Since they found out you are a teacher at their new school, they are actually looking forward to the move. How did your first two days go?"

"So far, so good," Rae said. "I'm really enjoying the job. How are the girls handling the idea of having their own rooms?"

"Daisy is over the moon about it, and Heather..." He paused. "She's getting into the spirit better than I hoped."

Rae was concerned about Heather, but she really wanted to wrap her arms around Gunner and drag him off to the barn for a make-out session, even after all her aunt's warnings.

"Daisy actually kind of took care of that issue," Gunner answered with a chuckle. "She asked if she could have bunk beds. Heather jumped on the idea and asked for the same thing so that she and her sister could have sleepovers on stormy nights. Neither of them likes thunder nor lightning."

"That is great!" Rae took her hat and candle from her mother and started to step up on the trailer. But her foot slipped, and she fell backward, right into Gunner's arms.

"We've got to stop meeting like this," Gunner teased as he picked her up and set her firmly on the bed of the trailer, then took the hat and candle from Mary Jane. "Folks are going to believe that you are either clumsy or flirting with me."

"I've never been known for being graceful, so they'll probably think that's the issue." Rae's words came out between breaths. "That was scary for a split second. This time I'm the one thanking you."

"My pleasure, but I was sure hoping you were flirting with me." Gunner grinned.

"Everyone is ready now. Ursula and baby Clayton are in the back seat. It's too cold for him to ride back here." Mary Jane winked at her and headed toward the truck where Joe Clay held the door open for her.

Rae couldn't remember the last time she had blushed, and she hoped that everyone who was already seated thought the cold wind was the cause of her red cheeks. She eased down on a bale of hay, and Gunner sat down right beside her.

"If Rae is finished showing us that she hasn't outgrown her clumsiness, we will get warmed up by singing 'Jingle Bells,'" Bo said and then glanced over at Bernie. "Is the queen ready to go?"

Bernie did a perfect royal wave. "I'm on my throne and since my official lady-in-waiting is busy leading singing tonight, these two lovely little girls will be filling in for her."

Daisy and Heather beamed and snuggled in closer to Aunt Bernie. If only something as simple as a little adoration could make her aunt like Gunner, all would be well.

Endora nudged Rae on the arm. "Are you okay? That

was a close call. If Gunner hadn't caught you, you would have hit your head on the trailer hitch."

"I'm fine," Rae answered.

"Can you believe Aunt Bernie?" Endora lowered her voice. "She's been cussin' mad about you keeping Gunner's kids, and now they are allowed to sit beside her, and she called them her ladies-in-waiting."

"Amazin' how being called a queen will change a person, isn't it?" Rae chuckled.

"Downright fascinating," Endora said.

Rae focused her attention on Bo and said, "You are welcome."

"For what?"

"For me taking the clumsy gene before we were ever born and giving you the musical ability," Rae answered.

Bo laughed out loud. "Well, then thank you. Daddy has started the truck engine, so here we go…" She hit a button on the karaoke machine and led the whole group in the first song.

Rae sang along until Gunner touched her on the shoulder. "The girls are having so much fun. Did your aunt dress up just for them?"

"No, Aunt Bernie is a little eccentric. She owned a bar up in southern Oklahoma for decades, and she loved to dress up on every holiday. Sometimes if there wasn't a special day, she invented one. They even had their own version of Mardi Gras. Is this the first time Daisy and Heather have been out Christmas caroling?" she asked.

"Honey, this is the first time I've done something like

this," he answered and sang another chorus of "Jingle Bells" before he said, "Seems like your family makes up most of Spanish Fort and are in this trailer or else in the bed of the truck. Who are we going to sing to?"

"The folks who live along the road to Nocona," she said. "Then we go out Main Street to the nursing home and make a loop through town on our way home. It's too cold for the folks who are able to come out on the lawn to listen to us, so we'll take our caroling into the lobby tonight. Afterwards we come back to the Paradise for sandwiches and chips. The family does this every year, but this is the first time Bo and I've gotten to be a part of it in a long time."

"I had no idea the ride would be this long," Gunner said. "I should have bundled the girls up a little more."

"The queen might wrap them up in her fur cape if they get too cold." Rae pointed to blankets and quilts stacked up beside Bo. "But if she doesn't, that's what those are for."

"I might not need one if I can snuggle up close to you," he said.

The heat from Bernie's stink-eye glare reached across the truck bed, but Rae merely shot a sweet smile at her and turned toward Gunner. "Is that a pickup line?"

Evidently, Aunt Bernie was fine with two little adoring girls to fawn over her, but the issue of a relationship with Gunner was still off the table.

"Maybe," he answered. "I'm a little rusty. How am I doing?"

Rae scooted over a little closer to his side. "Not too bad

for someone who says he's out of practice, but we better start singing or Aunt Bernie is going to burn this trailer down with her mean looks."

"What'd I do to warrant that?" Gunner asked.

"It's not you. It's me. She thinks I've fallen in love with your girls, and that I'm transferring that over to you. Besides you are a policeman, and your job is dangerous. I guess she thought all I did was rescue baby kittens when I worked for the police force," Rae said and started singing "Frosty the Snowman" with the rest of the group.

"I'll have to work on her opinion, and Aunt Rosie told me the same thing. She says that since you are good to my girls that it's influencing my way of thinking about you," he said and joined in the singing.

"Are they right or wrong?" Rae asked.

"Guess we'll have to give it some time," Gunner answered.

Endora grabbed a fluffy red-and-black-plaid throw and wrapped it around her and Parker's shoulders. "Gunner is flirting with Rae."

"I noticed," Parker said. "They're almost as well suited to each other as we are."

"Aunt Bernie does not agree," Endora told him. "Look at the fire shooting out of her eyes."

"She was wrong about Tertia and Noah," Parker reminded her. "But it seems like she's changed her mind about the twins. They are definitely behaving better these days, but that credit goes to Rae. I didn't even find wads of gum stuck to the church pews where they sat with Rosie last Sunday."

"Bernie said that she was using reverse psychology on Tertia and Noah, but this time, she's just downright against Rae and Gunner having a relationship," Endora said.

He leaned over and kissed her on the cheek. "Then from what I'm seeing, she better get ready to agree to disagree on the matter. Tonight, the sparks around us have as much to do with what's between them as the ones that belong to us."

"Two weeks from Sunday," Endora whispered.

"You won't change your mind, will you?" Parker asked. "I've made a short-timer's calendar, and every day I mark off a day."

"Not a chance." She laid her head on his shoulder and sang "It's Beginning to Look a Lot Like Christmas" with the rest of the folks.

Several songs later, Joe Clay turned east on Highway 82, which was where a lot of the businesses were located. He drove below the speed limit, and when a vehicle passed them, most of the time they either honked or rolled down their windows and waved. The folks at a barbecue restaurant came out and yelled, "Merry Christmas." The news must have spread because from there, more and more people came out on the street, some taking photographs, and others merely waving the flashlight on their phones like they were at a concert.

"Will our picture be in the newspaper?" Daisy asked.

"It could be," Endora answered.

"Daddy!" Heather stood up and walked the short distance to her father and sat down on his knee. "Our picture might get in the paper with the queen of Paradise."

"What makes you think that?" Gunner asked.

"People are taking pictures of us," Heather answered.

"We're going to be famous," Daisy added.

Endora couldn't believe that this was the same set of twins who gave her such a hard time when she taught their Sunday school class. Had she known that it would just take Rae's magical touch to turn their horns into halos, she would have begged her sister to come home and take over the class sooner.

"What's the chances we'll have twins?" Parker asked.

"It could happen," Endora answered. "Aunt Bernie was a twin to my grandmother. Mama had two sets, so who knows?"

"I would love to have two sets," Parker said.

"Be careful," Rae said. "You might get what you wish for. Mama said that at one time our dad brought home two tricycles for my and Bo's birthday presents. After an afternoon with two kids riding and two crying—that would be Endora and Luna—she told him not to buy anything if he couldn't get four."

Parker chuckled. "I'll keep that in mind if we are blessed with twins twice."

"Hey, now!" Bernie said. "I know Mary Jane wants lots of grandbabies, but we should get to spoil them one at a time. And besides, you aren't even married yet. You need a couple or three years to enjoy being together before you even think about having children."

"We're almost to the nursing home now," Bo said into the microphone. "Raise your voices and sing. Let's put on a concert all the way into town."

"My lady-in-waiting is telling us to stop talking and sing," Bernie said.

Endora snuggled in closer to Parker. She sang the carols as they finished the drive down Nocona's Main Street, but her thoughts were on moving into the parsonage and beginning her life with Parker.

A jealous streak shot through Bo when Joe Clay parked the truck and trailer in front of the nursing home. Everyone, including Aunt Bernie with her two new little buddies, had someone that evening. All Bo had was a microphone. When she first went to Nashville, that's all she wanted, but sitting there on a bale of hay with her family all around her, she changed her mind.

Bo led the group in singing "Silent Night" as they all climbed out of the trailer and truck and filed into the lobby as they sang. Joe Clay and Mary Jane led the group, with Ursula, Remy, and the baby right behind them. Bo brought up the rear, still leading the singing with another carol.

Music brings joy, she thought as she looked around at the old folks—some in wheelchairs and some with walkers. The brightness in their eyes and the way they swayed in time with the melody testified that the carolers had brought happiness into the nursing home that evening. Several of them sang right along with the family who had now gathered in a semicircle around the front of the lobby.

Joy and jealousy can't live in the same heart any more than love and hate.

She was multitasking, as Oprah called it—singing and thinking at the same time. She had given up on her dream of being a big star, but in all her gigs she had never seen a crowd so enamored. All in all, the little voice in her head said that she hadn't given up as much as she was getting.

They sang several songs, and then a nurse with LESLIE on her name tag stepped up to the front of the room. "Hasn't this been wonderful? Let's give this family a big hand."

Bo knew she had made the right decision to move back to north Texas when the applause and whistles rattled the glass windows. She might never be a Nashville star, but being so loved right there in a small nursing home was even better.

"And now," Leslie said, "we have hot chocolate and cookies laid out on the table at the back of the room for everyone. Maybe we can talk our guests into staying a little longer to visit with all y'all. I see two little girls and a baby among the group…"

"And Queen Bernie," Daisy said loudly and then did another cute little curtsy.

"She got all dressed up just for y'all," Heather said.

"And we got dressed up for y'all," one little lady dressed in a hot-pink velvet robe said from the back of the room.

"I would love for the beautiful woman with the baby to sit beside me and just let me see that precious child."

Ursula made her way through the crowd, sat down beside the woman, and removed the blanket from baby Clayton.

"My name is Amelia," the woman introduced herself. "And that is the most beautiful child I've seen in years. He's going to have brown eyes."

"Just like his father," Ursula said.

"Which one is his daddy?" another lady asked as several other folks gathered around to look down on baby Clayton.

Ursula pointed to Remy. "The handsome one right over there talking to Leslie."

When he saw her, he smiled and blew her a kiss.

"You better start layin' in a supply of big sticks," Amelia said.

"Why's that?" Ursula asked.

"To beat off the girls that will come sniffin' around," one of the other women answered. "With a boy this pretty, they'll start early."

Bo touched Endora on the arm. "Baby Clayton is making quite the splash. And look at how Bernie is introducing the girls to that group of women on the other side. We should bring the Sunday school class to visit them at least once a year. Maybe they could even color pictures to give to the folks."

Endora nodded in agreement. "That's a wonderful idea. Do you think that the wise men looked at baby Jesus like that?"

"I imagine they did," Bo whispered.

"Ursula, Remy, and Clayton are going to make a wonderful Mary, Joseph, and baby Jesus in the Christmas program," Endora said. "I always imagined Mary being tall like Ursula. How are you coming along with their costumes?"

"All done with every one of them. They are pressed and hanging in the church choir room," Bo answered.

Parker crossed the room and draped his arm around Endora's shoulders. "I heard what you just said. Thank you, Bo, for all the sewing you've done. This is going to be an amazing program."

"And the after-party will be just as awesome." Bo grinned and then realized her mother was standing behind her. "I hear Santa Claus is going to be at the potluck. Are you going to sit on his knee, Endora?"

"Yes, I am, but I'm not telling you what I'm going to ask him for," Endora said. "How about you, Mama?"

"Honey, I can sit on Santa's knee anytime I want," Mary Jane teased.

"Did someone say Santa?" Bernie asked. "I sat on his knee one time, and oh, honey, that turned out to be one fantastic night."

"Aunt Bernie!" Bo nodded toward the children.

"Well, it was, and I got exactly what I asked for," she protested and then smiled at the twins. "If you are good, you might get what you want."

Daisy and Heather were vowing to be good when Bo headed for the refreshment table. Halfway across the floor, she turned back to look at the residents interacting with the little girls and the rest of the family. Yes, sir, she had made the right decision and was ready to settle down in or near Spanish Fort. She didn't want to miss times like this ever again.

Her phone buzzed in her hip pocket. She pulled it out, saw Maverick's name, and answered on the second ring. "Well, hello! Are things so slow at the bar that you are bored?"

"No, but I need your help, Bo." His voice sounded a little desperate.

"I'm out caroling with my family. There's no way…"

"Not tonight. Things are slow here, and I can handle it by myself. I need you tomorrow morning. Dave wants to have a float in the parade tomorrow. He's out of town for the weekend so he's given me the job. He says there's a flatbed in the storage shed out back. I took a look and it's pretty pitiful. Some ratty old garland is hanging around the edges and it's got a flat tire. I'm not sure what to do. Got any ideas?"

"The floats will probably line up at noon since the parade starts at one. I'll be there at seven in the morning with some leftover decorations from the Paradise. What's your theme?"

"The theme of the whole parade this year is Christmas carols, but other than that, I'm at a loss about what to do for a trailer. Should we just do something simple with my truck?"

"We've got a flatbed at the Paradise, and I can borrow Daddy's truck. We can decorate it. We'll have to make a run to the dollar store and get some candy to throw out for the little kids, and…" Her mind ran in circles, latching onto one idea and then another. "We have a Santa suit and a cute little Santa's helper costume that I can bring."

"You are a lifesaver, but what do we do other than pitch out pieces of candy?"

"Let's roll the piano out onto the flatbed," she suggested. "We can play and sing. We can put a sign on the side of the truck that says, 'Merry Whiskey Bent Christmas.' We should be able to decorate the trailer and make the sign by noon—easy peasy."

"That doesn't sound easy to me, but if you can help me do all that in five hours, you are beyond a lifesaver! I could kiss you," Maverick said.

"I don't kiss on the first date," Bo teased. "See you tomorrow morning bright and early."

Chapter 16

THE RIDE FROM NOCONA to Spanish Fort seemed to go far too fast for Rae. She would have liked more time with Gunner, even if they were in the midst of more than a dozen other people. But like the old saying that all good things must eventually come to an end, the caroling was over for another year. Tomorrow she might catch a glimpse or two of him at the Nocona Christmas Festival, but he would be on duty. She had volunteered to watch the girls for the day, but from the way her aunt was acting, she would probably have to share them with her.

Bernie stepped down off the trailer with two little girls right behind her "All that singing has built up my appetite. I'm glad that Mary Jane and Tertia put together some sandwiches and chips for us. Are you ladies hungry?"

Heather slipped her hand into Bernie's. "I hope she's got bologna. That's my favorite."

Daisy grabbed Bernie's other hand. "That stuff is yukky. I like peanut butter and jelly better."

"I believe she's got an assortment so each person can make their own," Bernie said and glanced over her shoulder at Rae and Gunner. "What are you smiling about, Rae?"

"You don't have to ask, do you?" Rae answered.

"Sometimes first impressions are wrong." Bernie narrowed her eyes and frowned. "I've got these two children. You can go help your mother."

Bo tapped Rae on the shoulder. "The rest of us sisters can help Mama get things put out if you want to linger back for a few minutes."

"Thank you." Rae eased down on one of the porch rockers and motioned for Gunner to sit on the one close by. "When is the move taking place?"

"Sunday, after church," he answered. "The furniture-store folks are delivering the bunk beds and setting them up tomorrow while we are at the Christmas Festival in Nocona. Remy, Shane, Noah, and Jake all offered to help me move the rest of the stuff. That way we can get it all in one trip. I know I've said it before, but this is one great family you've got."

"Even Aunt Bernie?" she asked with half a giggle.

"Oh, yes, ma'am. This evening has been better than a trip to Disney World for Daisy and Heather." Gunner reached across the distance and laid his hand on Rae's. "And getting to spend time with you... Well, I'm not sure there are words." He gently squeezed her hand.

"I agree, but..."

He brought her hand to his lips and kissed her knuckles. "No *buts* tonight. Just *ands*. *But* means there is something that isn't right. *And* means there's more to come."

"Okay, then..." Rae shivered, but it had nothing to do

with the chill in the night air. His touch and even a little kiss on the hand jacked up her pulse several notches. "And we probably should go inside, or else Aunt Bernie will shed her queen costume and put on war paint."

Bo opened the door and motioned for them. "Daddy is about to say grace. You'll have to steal a few minutes later."

Gunner held out his hand to help Rae up. When she was on her feet, he pulled her to his chest. "I don't want to go home without kissing you. I've wanted to hold you in my arms all evening."

"You did when I fell," she whispered just before his lips found hers in a passionate kiss.

She tiptoed and wrapped her arms around his neck. The feeling was exactly like before in the house, so that time wasn't just a one-and-done experience. There was true chemistry between her and Gunner, and no matter what Aunt Bernie said, she wanted—no, she needed—to see where it might lead.

***

Bo was up at the crack of dawn and spent an hour in the barn loading boxes of extra decorations into the bed of Joe Clay's truck. She was glad that the weatherman had called for a cold but sunny day with no chance of rain or snow in the forecast. There was nothing sadder than soggy floats and a muddy park for the festival.

She carried the last box out of the barn and smiled when she noticed the big Christmas wreath wired to the truck's front grill. That old song about a stepdad being the dad he didn't have to be came to her mind. That was Joe Clay in a nutshell.

The sun was a sliver of orange on the eastern horizon when she made the turn out of the lane and headed south. She hadn't driven a truck with a trailer hooked onto the back very often and had to remind herself to go slower than the speed limit allowed.

"Santa and his helper outfit, stuff for the trailer and to decorate the piano." She counted off what she had loaded as she watched the sun finish making its morning show. "I probably brought too much, but I can always bring what we don't use back to the barn. We'll have to make a run to the store for candy, and I should stop at the Dairy Queen and pick up some bacon, egg, and cheese biscuits for breakfast."

Your mama trained you well. Aunt Bernie's voice was back in her head.

"Yes, she did," Bo said out loud, "and she also trained me to listen to my heart and not to my aunt."

When she got into town, she made a stop by the Dairy Queen and picked up half a dozen breakfast biscuits and two large cups of coffee. She passed the Family Dollar store a few blocks later and noticed that the inside lights were on and the OPEN sign was in the window. She eased into the parking lot and hurried inside. She picked up two big bags of individually wrapped candy canes and several smaller ones with a variety of candy to throw out for the children. As she was leaving, she remembered the posterboard for the signs

208   Carolyn Brown

and went back inside to buy two of those. When she reached the bar, Maverick was leaning on a porch post with the piano on a dolly right beside him.

"You are here!" he called out as she got out of the truck. "Shall we just sit all this on the porch?" he asked and picked up the first box from the bed of the truck.

"Leave that there for a little bit. I brought breakfast and bought candy for us to throw. Not having to go back into town will save some time. Let's take ten minutes to eat before we get busy." She handed the brown sack with the food in it to him. "I'll bring the coffee. We've got almost five hours to get the piano loaded and the trailer decorated. We should be in good shape."

Maverick sat down on the back end of the trailer, took a breakfast sandwich from the sack, and handed it to her. "Thanks for all this, Bo. I was in a panic about how to get the job done."

"I would have been, too, but I know about what all we've got stored in the barn at the Paradise." Bo removed the paper from the outside and bit into the biscuit, chewed and swallowed, and then took a sip of coffee. "Every year Mama waits until the stores put all their decorations on sale at ninety percent off and makes quite a haul. I told you some of this already when we put up all the holiday stuff for the bar. Anyway, there's always extra in the barn. We'll get the trailer all gussied up and have the prettiest float in the parade. If there's one thing the seven sisters of Paradise are good at, it's making everything gaudy and glittery for the holidays."

"You've done all this on less than twenty-four-hour notice, and even remembered to bring breakfast?" Maverick sounded amazed.

"My mama raised me right." She quoted what Bernie always said.

"She sure did," Maverick agreed.

"I've got a question, though," Bo said. "Old pianos, especially uprights, can get out of tune if you sneeze on them. Jerking that one around today is going to cause problems. Do you know someone around these parts that can tune one?"

"Me," Maverick said. "I can tune it before we need to use it at the bar."

"For real?" Bo could hear amazement in her own voice.

"Yep, for real. I was trained by the best." He pulled a second biscuit from the sack. "Were you about to offer to do the job?"

Bo finished the last bite and took a sip of her coffee. "No. I can tune a guitar and a fiddle, but not a piano."

"What else can you play?" Maverick asked between bites.

"A little bit of five-string banjo, but I'm not very good with it, and the mandolin fairly well. My strong points are the fiddle and piano," she answered. "How about you?"

He stood up, went to the back of the truck, and unloaded all the boxes onto the porch. "Piano, banjo, and dobro with some degree of talent. Never could master the fiddle."

"Why didn't *you* go to Nashville?" she asked as she began to unpack the one that said GARLAND on the side.

"I wanted to see more than one place, work at more than

one job, and see more people," he answered. "Are we going to wrap battery-powered twinkle lights around the garland like we did in the bar?"

Bo nodded and opened the box of lights. "And maybe then we'll add some Christmas greenery around the piano along with more lights. There's ribbon and glitter for the signs. Did you come up with better wording for them?"

"I did not, but during slow times at the bar last night I came up with a couple of songs we could do. 'Rockin' around the Christmas Tree' and 'Christmas in Dixie.' We could change the word *Dixie* to *Texas*. Maybe Santa can play, and the helper can…"

"Oh!" she gasped before he could finish. "If we're going to play and sing about rockin' around the tree, we need one on the float, and I didn't think to bring one."

"There's a poor, pitiful-looking one in the storage room," Maverick said. "I was planning on putting it on the stage for the holidays before you arrived with better stuff."

Bo brought out long lengths of red garland and wrapped the battery-powered twinkle lights around them. "Let's drag that tree out here and rope it down on the trailer. I'll string some garland and lights around it and scatter a few bulbs here and there."

Maverick rolled the dolly off the porch and onto the trailer. He positioned it at the back and then used straps to keep it steady. "I'll depend on you to make it pretty while I go get the sorry excuse of a tree."

"Good idea." Bo remembered something her mother

said years ago. She couldn't quote it word for word, but the general idea was that if you really wanted to know someone, you could learn a lot about them by working with them a few days.

She had learned through the years that no truer words had ever been spoken. She had worked with jerks and at other times with some very nice people. Working with Maverick seemed to be on a different level. He even made a job like bartending or decorating an old flatbed trailer a lot of fun—and nobody could argue the fact that he was almighty easy on the eyes. Plus, when he looked at her with his piercing dark-green eyes, something ignited deep down in her body.

"Got it!" He raised the small tree above his head. "I told you it was ugly."

"Shh…" Bo shushed him. "You'll hurt its poor little feelings. We'll turn it from a bag lady into Cinderella with the right decorations."

Maverick laughed. "Sweetheart, if you can make this thing look good, you should go into interior design."

"Never interested me, not even as a little girl. When we all got our own rooms at the Paradise, my sisters were all about what color to paint the walls. I just wanted lots of electrical plugs."

"For your music stuff?" he asked.

"Yep," she answered and kept working. She stole glances at him and imagined all those bulging muscles and ripped abs without a shirt and jacket covering them up.

"Do you go to the gym? You've hoisted the piano and all the boxes like none of them were anything but a feather pillow."

"Nope," he answered as he set the tree in the middle of the trailer and roped it down. "My strength didn't come from a gym, but from some hard ranchin' work up in Montana in one of my jobs before I came down here. Hey, I've got a few hours after the parade is over. Can I buy you a hot dog or something from one of the vendors when it's all done with?"

"Sure, as long as we can come back here and change out of our costumes before we go to the festival." She didn't trust herself to look right at him again—not until she got control of the pictures flashing through her mind. "If we don't, you'll get swarmed by kids."

"That sounds like a plan," he said. "The floats are supposed to be left in the park for everyone to look at, but we can unhook the truck without a problem."

"Mama and Daddy are driving down here in my SUV. They'll take the truck and trailer home after the winners are announced, and I'll have a vehicle to drive home whenever I get ready to go," she said.

"What do we win?" Maverick asked.

"Our picture in the newspaper," Bo answered. "According to Gunner's girls, that's all it takes to be famous."

Maverick chuckled again. "See there. You go all the way to Nashville to get famous, and if we win, you'll get the title right here in Nocona, Texas."

"And you will be my band," she joked. "What shall we call ourselves?"

"Whiskey Bent Band," he suggested. "That's where we first met and had our first concert. Then today will be our first tour."

"I like it!" Bo agreed. "For our next concert, I'll bring my fiddle, and you should bring your banjo."

Maverick stopped tacking garland and lights around the edge of the trailer. He straightened his back and rolled the kinks out of his neck. "In all seriousness, what would you like to do with the rest of your life?"

"I have a job working for my aunt, but it's not what I want to do forever," she answered. "I'm not sure what I would do if I had the opportunity to choose, but I would still love to do something with music. Not much chance of that in Montague County, Texas, though. I can play for the church for free, or help with the Christmas program, or even ride on a float and sing, but..." She shrugged. "How about you?"

"I've given it a lot of thought, but I still don't know for sure," Maverick answered and abruptly changed the subject. "All done. Even that poor tree looks awesome, but the floor of the trailer looks bare."

Bo was a little disappointed in his answer. Aunt Bernie was probably right, but a little fling wouldn't be such a bad thing. If she fell in love with him along the way, she could very well just fall out of love with him when he moved on to the next job. She and Rae had had chicken pox when they were little girls, and even with all the whining and figuring that they would be ugly for the rest of their lives, they had survived. If Bo could live through that ordeal and then seeing her Nashville dream shattered, she could live through anything, including a broken heart.

"I can fix that," she finally said, and tore into a box marked SNOW. "We will have a white Christmas on our float. Help me cover the bed of the trailer with this quilt batting and then I'll sprinkle glitter on it to give it some pizzazz. Mama has used it on the tables at the Paradise party, and she bought too much."

They finished that job with only thirty minutes to spare. Bo grabbed the costumes from the back seat of the truck, kicked the empty boxes into the bar, and made a beeline for the bathroom.

"Use the bar to change," Maverick said as he headed back to his apartment. "You'll have more room. Just leave what you are wearing now on one of the tables."

She was outside snapping pictures of the trailer when Maverick came out in the Santa outfit with a big belly and a fake beard. He stopped on the porch and said, "Sweet Jesus, woman! You look like something that men only dream about."

"Well, darlin'," she drawled, "there ain't many women in the world who wouldn't want to sit on your lap."

Maverick wiggled his eyebrows. "How about my helper today? Would she sit on my lap and tell me what she wants for Christmas?"

"I don't date my boss," she teased.

"Then let it be known that I will never hire you," Maverick flirted.

━━━━━━━

They reached the Dairy Queen, where all the floats, the high school band, the local fire engine, and even a dozen or more horses from a riding club were milling around. A woman who carried herself like she was in charge of when the world ended marched around with a clipboard in her hands. She approached Bo and Maverick with a frown and ran a long, perfectly manicured purple fingernail down a list on a single sheet of paper.

"Here comes trouble," Bo whispered.

"Why do you say that?" Maverick asked.

"Just wait and see," Bo said and then smiled. "Good morning, Miz Helen."

"I see you are the Whiskey Bent Bar float. I can't believe Mary Jane is letting one of her girls ride on a bar float or…" She glared at the skimpy Santa helper costume Bo wore with a look that said she'd rather be chasing a skunk through fresh cow patties than have to see something so disgraceful. "Or wearing something that looks like that."

"Yes, Helen, that is the bar's float," Mary Jane yelled as she crossed the parking lot. "And dar…lin'…" She dragged out the last word. "Seems like I remember you wearing skirts a lot skimpier than that when we were in high school, and what you had under them didn't quite cover your butt. Now, let's talk about the float that Joe Clay and I will drive for them."

"Lower your voice," Helen hissed.

Not many people were brave enough to cross Helen, but Mary Jane crossed her arms over her chest and tilted her head to the side. "Don't put it at the end of the line in front of the fire truck bringing Santa to town or the music won't be heard."

Helen's grimace came far short of being a smile. "They were entered at the last minute, so I have to do what I have to do."

In a few long strides Joe Clay was right beside Mary Jane. "Hello, Helen. It's been a long minute since I've seen you. I bet it's been a while since you've seen our daughter, Bo. She is riding on the float and will be singing Christmas songs. And Santa is being played today by Maverick, the manager and bartender at Whiskey Bent. Remember when it was the Sugar Shack? We all had fake IDs and spent a lot of time there, didn't we?"

"I'm not here to talk about the past," Helen snapped. "The bar owner didn't enter the parade until yesterday, so they *cannot* have preferential treatment. By rights, they should be the last float before the fire truck."

"Yes, ma'am, but won't that confuse all the little kids?" Maverick asked. "They will see me as Santa Claus on the float, and then they'll see another Santa on the fire truck right behind me. Do you have grandchildren?"

"Yes, she does," Mary Jane answered.

"We'll be glad to fall in line wherever you think it best,"

Bo said with a shrug, "and you can explain to your sweet little kiddos about how two Santas are at the festival."

"But if we are near the front, then you can tell your grandkids a very different story," Maverick added.

"One that says Santa brought in the parade and then rushed back to ride the fire truck, so that he could usher in the parade and then end it," Joe Clay suggested.

"But it's your call." Bo tried to conjure up her most innocent expression. "Just tell us where to be, and we will do your bidding."

A little boy ran across the parking lot, wrapped his arms around Maverick, and looked up at Helen. "He's here, Granny. He's really here."

"Yes, he is and he's waiting to get on the fire engine." Helen's expression said that she was fabricating a story to tell the child. "You go let your mama help put your costume on for our church float."

"Yes, ma'am," he said and ran toward a float with a sign on the side that read JESUS IS THE REASON FOR THE SEASON.

Helen tapped her foot on the gravel parking lot and set her mouth in a firm line. Then she made some adjustments to the list and said, "The police chief will lead the parade like always. Then you will be right behind him. I'd planned to put my church float right behind him to remind people of the real reason for Christmas." She sucked in a lungful of cold air and a whoosh that left a puff in the cold air.

"Why, Helen!" Joe Clay chuckled. "I had no idea that you had started smoking again. Seems like I remember you having quite a habit when we were in high school." He lowered his voice to a whisper. "And it wasn't always *just* cigarettes."

Biting back laughter wasn't easy for Bo, but she managed. Everyone in all of north Texas knew that Helen was the head honcho of the Chamber of Commerce in Nocona. But Bo had no idea that she had gone to school with her mama and daddy. The woman looked twenty years older than either of her parents.

"Shhh…" Helen growled out the shushing noise. "That was a long time ago." She went back to marking out numbers and readjusting. "I can't put my float behind yours. That just wouldn't be right, so I'll put the Dairy Queen after you, then mine, and the high school band after that. Tell Dave that he better call me before the last minute if he wants to enter the parade next year."

"Yes, ma'am." Maverick nodded and tipped the ball of his Santa hat toward her. "I will do that."

Bo heard the door of a vehicle slam and saw Gunner coming across the parking lot. "Do you have the lineup all ready? It's a little past showtime."

"It's done," Helen said, "and I'll be staying right here and telling each float or group when to go next."

Mary Jane looped her arm into Bo's, led her away, and said, "That was fun."

"Oh, really? Maybe you better tell me more about the Sugar Shack and what went on there," Bo said.

"That is classified," Mary Jane declared and headed over to where Joe Clay held the truck door open for her.

"We'll unhook the trailer at the park and bring y'all back here to get Bo's vehicle," Joe Clay said as he came around the trailer. "Knock 'em dead, baby girl."

"Thanks, Daddy," Bo said with grin. "Drive slow. We don't want the piano to fall off and splinter into a thousand pieces."

Joe Clay gave her a thumbs-up and slid under the steering wheel. Gunner pulled out onto the street and turned the lights on, but he must have seen the piano because he didn't use the sirens. Bo caught sight of Helen's expression and giggled. Before, the police chief always led the parade, and always with the sirens blasting. Bo was sure that was why Helen had agreed to give the Whiskey Bent float the place she did, and now she was angry that her ugly plan didn't work.

"What's so funny?" Maverick asked as he sat down on the piano bench and began to play.

"I'll explain later," Bo answered.

She held the microphone in her left hand and got her footing on the moving trailer. She checked for her family in the crowds that had come out to enjoy the day. She found them, all in a bunch, in front of the flower shop. Aunt Bernie was sitting on a park bench with a little dark-haired girl on either side of her. They made quite the picture with Bernie wearing red-and-green-plaid bell-bottom pants that came from her hippie days and a denim duster that looked like something from an old western movie. Daisy's bright-red jacket and Heather's green one matched the colors in Bernie's pants.

"Miz Bo is Santa's helper!" Daisy squealed and pointed.

"And there's Santa Claus," Heather yelled over the applause. "I didn't know he played the piano."

There are a lot of things about Maverick that none of you know, Bo thought as she finished up that song, and Maverick played the opening notes of "I Saw Mommy Kissing Santa Claus."

Without missing a beat, Bo waved and then threw handfuls of candy in their direction. Apparently, Bernie had been teaching them the queen's wave because they each executed one perfectly.

Five songs later they reached the park, and Bo's moment of stardom was over, but it didn't matter. Her family had all been there to see her performance, which was something that had never happened in Nashville.

Joe Clay got out of the truck to help Maverick unhitch the trailer. "Y'all were really good. Bo, you must be freezing. Go on and get in the warm truck with your mother."

"I'm not even going to argue with you," Bo said.

Maverick hopped off the trailer and picked up Bo by the waist, swung her around a couple of times, and then set her on the ground. "That was so much fun. Think they would want us to play and sing some more for the festival? The piano is already here, and there's plenty of room for the two of us on the bench."

"Yes!" Mary Jane stuck her head out the window and raised her voice.

"I guess the real queen has spoken," Bo said and jogged

around the trailer. She hadn't even realized how cold she was until she started to shiver.

Mary Jane tossed a fluffy throw over the front seat. "You need this more than I do. I had thought I might sit on the sidelines with the family, but changed my mind when it turned off so cold. But at least the sun is out, and it's not raining. Y'all were so good. I'm proud of you both."

Bo wrapped the throw around her body. "Thank you, Mama."

"You are very welcome. I had no idea that Maverick could play the piano like that. Y'all should entertain at the Paradise Christmas party," Mary Jane said.

"I'll ask him if he can get off work that night, but there are conditions. You have to tell me a Sugar Shack story," Bo teased.

"Never going to happen," Mary Jane told her. "I also had no idea that you were going to wear that outfit today. Your legs have to be freezing."

"They are now, but I was so happy when I was performing that I didn't notice. When do they announce the winners?"

"As soon as they tally up the scores, so don't tarry too long when y'all are getting changed," Mary Jane answered.

Maverick barely made it into the back seat when the next float pulled up. "That was a close call," he said.

"Saved by a split second." Joe Clay chuckled. "Another minute and those little kids riding on that float would have swarmed you."

Maverick pulled off his fake beard and wire-rimmed glasses. "There can only be one 'real' Santa."

Bo stole a long sideways glance at Maverick. Santa was gone, replaced by a sexy bartender. She blamed her thoughts on the adrenaline high from performing, even if it was just on the back of a Christmas float.

Chapter 17

RAE TAPPED ON BO's bedroom door, and then opened it and peeked inside. "Are you awake?"

"I am now, and I may not forgive you for waking me up." Bo yawned, threw back the covers, and sat up. "I was reliving yesterday in my dreams."

Rae went on into the room and sat down on the edge of the bed. "Did Santa kiss his helper beside the Christmas tree when y'all took it off the trailer?"

"Did you get all tingly just looking at Gunner in his police uniform?" Bo shot back.

"Every single time." Rae had always been attracted to men in uniform—be it soldiers, firemen, or police—but there was more to what she felt for Gunner than what he was wearing. He looked just as handsome in his creased jeans and plaid shirt on Sunday as he did in his full policeman attire.

Bo rubbed the sleepiness out of her eyes. "Are you going to buck up against Aunt Bernie?"

Rae handed her phone to Bo. "Probably, how about you?"

"I haven't decided if I want a broken heart or not," Bo answered. "He could be the one, and it wouldn't take much to make me fall in love with him."

"Do I hear a *but* in there?" Rae asked.

"Maverick has admitted that he's not ready to settle in one place, and the writing on the wall says, 'Broken Heart' in big neon letters," Bo replied. "Now why am I holding your phone?"

"Sorry I ruined your dream, but if you check out the pictures on social media, you might forgive me. You and Maverick are the stars of the whole weekend. There are pictures and even videos everywhere. The newspaper editor posted that since y'all won first place for the best float, and you sang for a whole hour at the festival, you will be featured on the front page in tomorrow's edition."

"Holy smoke!" Bo flipped through dozens of pictures and posts.

"You might not be famous in Nashville, but, Sister, you made a name for yourself in Montague County. I bet folks will be calling you to sing at the county fair, weddings, and other events before long," Rae told her. "Daisy and Heather are going to be over the moon if they publish the picture of you throwing candy and kisses toward them in the paper."

"This is fantastic." Bo handed the phone back to Rae. "Did you see the post where it says that our float set the mood for the whole parade?"

"I sure did. Eat your pompousness, Helen!" Rae raised her hand for a high five.

Bo's slap made a cracking noise. "The mighty Helen has fallen off her pedestal."

Rae tucked her phone into the pocket of her flannel pajama

bottoms. "But now your fifteen minutes of fame and glory are over. I'm on breakfast duty, and then it's church. After services and dinner, I'm going to help Gunner and the girls move."

"Maverick is taking me to lunch," Bo said. "I was so involved with the parade yesterday that I haven't even had time to pick out an outfit. Help me, please."

Rae crossed the room and threw the closet doors open. "Where are you going?"

"I have no idea," Bo answered.

"Then we'll pick something in the middle. Nothing too fancy. Something easy to remove if you get lucky." Rae pulled out a dark-green sweater and a plaid skirt. "These look good together."

Bo must not have been fully awake, but suddenly she gasped. "What did you just say about getting lucky?"

"We have to be prepared," Rae answered without cracking a smile.

Bo's palms shot up in a defensive gesture. "This is our first date. I haven't even kissed him yet. All we've done is a little harmless flirting."

"This is your third date, darlin'." Rae slapped Bo's hands and then held up a finger. "Number one was when you had the event at Whiskey Bent." Another finger went up. "Number two was when he came to church and Sunday dinner." The third finger shot up. "Number three was actually when you rode on the float with him." She studied her hand and raised her pinkie. "I was wrong. This is the fourth date. I'm disappointed in you, Bo Simmons. You should have at least gotten a kiss or instigated one by now. He's got to be disappointed."

Bo laid the skirt and sweater on the bed. "His disappointment should make Aunt Bernie very happy. I would love waffles for breakfast." She turned around, put her hands on her sister's back, and pushed her toward the door.

Rae set her heels and held on to the doorjamb. "Hey, that's not nice. I brought you the reviews about your concert, and even picked out your outfit to seduce Maverick with, and you treat me like this."

Bo pushed even harder. "Have you and Gunner had sex?"

Rae laughed out loud and stepped out into the hallway. "No, but we have managed a few hot and steamy kisses, which is more than you've done. Stop pushing me. I'm going, but you are not getting waffles because you are mean. Give you a little fame and look what happens."

"I'm going to tell Mama on you," Bo told her.

"If you do, I'll tattle that you have deprived poor old Maverick of a kiss." Rae laughed all the way down the stairs.

―――――――――

That morning Maverick was five minutes early to pick Bo up for church services. He did everything a gentleman should do on a first date—knocked on the door instead of honking the horn, greeted Mary Jane and shook hands with Joe Clay, helped Bo with her coat, and kept his hand on the small of her back when he escorted her out to his truck.

"You are gorgeous," he said as he held the door open for

her. "I'll have trouble keeping my mind on Parker's sermon this morning."

"You clean up pretty good yourself, Mr. Gibson."

He tipped his cowboy hat with his free hand. "Thank you, ma'am, but that's just plain old Maverick to you. When I hear that name, I think my daddy is in the room."

"Okay, then, plain old Maverick, where are we going for Sunday dinner?" she asked.

He started the engine and drove down the lane. "To the bar."

"We're having beer for dinner?" she teased.

"Yes, but that's not our whole meal," he answered. "There is chili in the slow cooker. I made sourdough bread yesterday to go with it. If you are a vegetarian, I can stir-fry some vegetables."

"I'm not a vegetarian," she replied. "I love chili, but I didn't picture you as a guy who cooks."

"Remember that I've moved around a lot," Maverick told her. "I've wrangled cattle, bartended, and learned a little bit about cooking in a five-star restaurant in Las Vegas."

"How can you afford to do all that?" she asked.

"That's a story for a seventh date."

She raised her eyebrows. "Oh, so we're going to have that many, are we?"

"If you are willing, we just might. That's only one more after today, and seven is my lucky number," he replied.

Bo turned toward him and cocked her head to one side. "My sister said that this is our fourth date."

"You need to teach her to count better. We had date one when we decorated the bar, date two when you stuck around and helped me after the event, three when I went to church with you, four when we had Sunday dinner together, five when we decorated the trailer, and six when we had the first Whiskey Bent Band concert at the park. And I was mistaken. This *is* our seventh date," he told her.

He pointed to an old building on the left. "What's going on with that place? It looks like it's been there forever."

"Depends on your definition of *forever*," she answered. "It was here when we moved to Spanish Fort, and most likely it's old enough to be put on the historical register. Tertia and Noah wanted to put a café in the place, but it wouldn't pass inspection. Maybe someday, someone will figure out how to put it to use."

"It would make a good museum." Maverick made a turn into the church parking lot.

Bo would go to church and play the piano, but she didn't expect to get much out of the sermon that morning. She would sit beside Maverick and think about spending the afternoon with him in his apartment, but even if she did make out with him, she had no intention of kissing and telling—not even Rae. She had no doubt that Aunt Bernie would shoot evil glances at her, but she didn't care.

———

From the time Bo sat down beside Maverick until the bene-diction was given, she felt like time stood still and she had been sitting on the old oak pew for eternity plus three days. When everyone began to stand up, Tertia touched her on the shoulder and whispered, "Tell Mama that Noah and I won't be there for dinner. We have agreed that Sunday afternoons belong to us for some alone time for the next few weeks."

"Good for you, but you better let Ursula tell Mama. I'm going to dinner with Maverick," Bo told her.

Bernie grabbed her arm. "I heard that, and sorry, but you can't be runnin' off with anyone today. The two of us will be working on the advice column after we eat dinner at the Paradise. With all that's been going on, we are behind on getting questions asked."

"We can do that tomorrow," Bo said.

"You work for me, and I call the shots." Bernie's tone went cold. "You will come to Sunday dinner with the family, or maybe tomorrow you won't have a job."

Bo wrapped her arms around her aunt and hugged her. "You know you love me better than all the other sisters, and you would never fire me."

"Don't go testing the Jesus in me right here after that great sermon Parker delivered," Bernie growled.

"What did he preach on?" Bo stepped back.

"You tell me," Bernie's eyes narrowed into nothing but slits.

Bo glanced over her shoulder and caught Maverick's eye. He winked and then turned his attention back to the group of guys who had cornered him. *Thank goodness for brothers-in-law,* she thought.

"Well?" Aunt Bernie snapped.

"I wasn't listening to the sermon," Bo admitted. "I was thinking about borrowing your red lace teddy. I might need it wear it for dessert after Maverick and I have dinner together."

"You're aiming for a heartache," Bernie said.

"You've said that before," Bo told her. "I love you, Aunt Bernie, but this is my life. Maybe I'm like Maverick and haven't found my place in the world. I may need to move every six months or so, and like that old song says, I may need to chase some elusive butterflies before I settle down."

"All right." Bernie sighed. "But don't say I didn't warn you and know that I will say that I told you so when you have a broken heart."

"I wouldn't expect anything else, but if I do have a broken heart, will you bring the ice cream and two spoons?" Bo teased.

"I will not, and I won't share it with you either. You and Rae are going to ruin my winning streak with matchmaking," Bernie said and sighed again. "Strangers on my advice column listen to me better than y'all do."

"Queen Bernie!" Daisy and Heather yelled and ran down the aisle to curtsy.

"Some folks appreciate me," Bernie snapped and turned to smile at the little girls.

Maverick laced his fingers with Bo's and asked, "What was that all about?"

"Queen Bernie is having trouble with her lady-in-waiting," she answered. "I'll fill you in on more of her story on the way to Nocona."

Chapter 18

MAVERICK PARKED HIS TRUCK in front of the bar and turned to face Bo. "But she's such a sweet old lady. She's amazing with those little girls."

Bo told him how Bernie had been adamant about Rae not keeping the twins and, more importantly, not even dating Gunner. "She insists that she used her matchmaking skills to put my four sisters in touch with their husbands. When Endora and Parker get married, she'll raise her number to five."

Maverick opened the truck door and a rush of cold wind along with a few snowflakes rushed inside the cab. "Is that truth or just her reality?"

"Ursula and Remy knew each other in high school, and the sparks flew when they came home. Aunt Bernie had little to do with it, even if she does claim credit. Shane and Luna were already dating—albeit on the sly—when Bernie moved to Spanish Fort. She might have had something to do with Jake and Ophelia, but she says she used reverse psychology on Tertia and Noah," Bo answered and then shivered.

"I'm sorry," Maverick apologized. "I was engrossed in what you were saying." He slid out of his seat, closed the door, and then jogged around the truck to help Bo out. "It doesn't look like Gunner and Rae are paying much attention to her protests, or is she just doing some reverse psychology on you and Rae like she did Tertia and Noah?"

He unlocked the back door to the bar and stood to the side. The place felt different with no lights on, and no people around— as if it was empty and waiting, maybe hibernating for a day before the OPEN sign was turned on.

"I'm sorry," Bo said. "I was woolgathering. You asked me about me and Rae being subjects for reverse psychology. I don't think so this time. Aunt Bernie doesn't want my sister to be involved with a policeman."

"A few dates don't mean a committed relationship or marriage. It could just mean two adults having some fun," Maverick said. "What about you and me?"

"Like I told you before"—Bo followed him through the storage room—"she's ready for me to settle down like my sisters. You are not that kind of man, so this isn't reverse psychology. It's not that she doesn't like you. She just wants me to have someone who is ready to put down roots somewhere close to Spanish Fort."

"That's going into a relationship with marriage in mind. Where's the fun in that? And besides the *m*-word scares most men so badly they go into fight-or-flight mode." Maverick opened the door to his apartment and let her enter first. "Before that dreaded word, there should be first kisses, first time to make love, maybe moving in together—all those things that lead up to marriage."

Bo could almost hear Aunt Bernie gloating about being right, but like she had said, it was her life. She was going into whatever this was with her eyes wide open and no intention of trying to change Maverick.

She held up her hand. "This conversation is way too serious for a first real date, so I'm changing the subject. What were you and the brothers-in-law talking about after church services?"

Maverick helped remove her coat and draped it over the back of an overstuffed chair right inside the door and then tossed his denim jacket over the top of hers. "We were talking about helping move Gunner out of his house here in Nocona. They plan on being there about two thirty to start loading up his stuff in a couple of cattle trailers. I volunteered us to help on this end."

"Oh really?" Bo frowned. "Without asking me?"

Maverick shrugged. "You can stay here until I get back. I figure it will only take an hour, and Rae will be there with the little girls. Your family has done so much for me that pitching in is the least I could do."

"Well, Rae and I are better at organizing things than all you guys put together," she said with a smile.

Maverick crossed the room, filled two bowls with chili, and set them on the table. "You proved that when we decorated the bar for your meet-and-greet event."

"That was Aunt Bernie's notes, but honey, we'll have things loaded and be back here in less than an hour."

Bo took in the small living space in one quick glance. Living area with a brown-and-gold-plaid sofa that matched the chair—both of which had to be thirty or forty years old. A tiny table for two with a couple of mismatched wooden chairs, and a kitchen area that was really just a long cabinet big enough for a sink, an apartment-sized stove and a dorm-sized refrigerator. A king-sized bed took up most of the far end of the room. Except for the layout, it could easily have been her furnished apartment over a garage in Nashville.

"This place isn't much, but for the next few weeks, it's home," Maverick said. "It's like a five-star hotel after living in a bunkhouse with a dozen other men."

"I bet it is. That chili smells so good." What he had said about being around for the next few weeks kept playing in an endless circle in her head.

He sliced a round loaf of crusty sourdough bread and set it in the middle of the table, and then brought two bottles of beer from the refrigerator. "Dinner is served, madam." He pulled out a chair and seated her.

"Thank you," she said. "If I'd known we were eating here, I would have brought dessert."

He sat down in the other chair. "We have rocky road ice cream."

"My favorite." She took her first bite and hurriedly grabbed for the beer.

"That bad?" he asked.

"That good, but it's hot," she answered.

"Hot as in fire, or as in spicy?" He cooled his first spoonful by blowing on it.

"Both, but you got a good sting on it with the spices."

Maverick chuckled. "My grandmother used to say that. I haven't heard it since she passed away several years ago."

"Were you close to her?" Bo asked.

Maverick nodded. "Very. She lived with us after she retired. I was only four years old when she moved in. My brother, Denton, was sixteen and already preparing to step up into my dad's world."

"And you weren't expected to do the same as your brother?" Bo thought about all the different ways she and her sisters had gone after graduating from high school.

"Yes, but I was only a little kid then and Nana shaped my life more than she did Denton's. She read books to me about cowboys and chefs, and we watched old western movies with bars that had swinging doors. When I was older, she told me I didn't have to be a corporate banker, that I could be anything I wanted. She encouraged me to get out and experience life, and when she died, she made that possible. I was just graduating from high school when she passed away and left me a trust fund big enough to choke an elephant."

"Did you know that she was a rich woman all those years?" Bo asked.

"I knew that my father inherited the business from his dad," Maverick answered. "I didn't know that Nana's folks left her a fortune made from getting into the ground floor of the oil business. My brother only speaks to me when he has to be civil. He thought he should have inherited half the money she left to me. And that answers your question about how I can afford to do whatever I want."

"Where did you live and grow up?" Bo asked.

"You first. Have you always lived in Spanish Fort?"

"Nope," Bo answered. "We were in Dallas. Daddy was studying to be a doctor when he and Mama got married. Ursula says that we all had a different father. Mama was working when she was born, so her dad spent time with her while he studied. Ophelia's only got a little of his time because he was doing clinicals. Tertia got even less because he was on call so much as an ER doctor. By the time Rae and I came along, we hardly knew him, and the last set of twins were born in the dark days preceding divorce. But when we came to the Paradise, everything changed. Joe Clay became the daddy none of us ever really had."

"I was born—as an *oops* child—in Houston," Maverick said. "My mother only intended to give my father a son, and she got that job done on the first try. I was a surprise baby, but Nana took me under her wing and became a good role model. That's probably enough for a seventh date. I thought maybe we would come back here after we help with the moving business and watch a movie. I'm a culinary expert on microwave popcorn."

"What movie?"

"Since you aren't still mad at me over volunteering you to help with the move, you get to choose," he answered.

"How about *Quigley Down Under*?" She remembered an old western movie with Tom Selleck that Joe Clay had watched over and over again when she and her sisters were young.

"That's one of my favorites. Nana and I watched it often," he answered with a smile.

"Then a movie and your famous popcorn it is," she said.

―――――――

Daisy and Heather were bouncing with excitement when they crawled into the back seat of Rae's truck that afternoon when it was fully loaded. Rae wasn't sure that all the stuff she and Bo had helped pack into the two cattle trailers was going to fit in the new home. If it didn't, Gunner might have to rent a storage unit.

Bo tapped on the window seconds before Rae was about to pull out and bring up the rear of the caravan heading back to Spanish Fort.

"Did you forget something?" Rae asked as she lowered the window.

"Nope, not a thing," Bo said. "Just wanted to tell you that you can't count. Maverick says this is our seventh date."

"Oh, honey, do we need to see a doctor?" Rae teased.

"What for?"

"You must have something severely wrong if you can't close a deal in seven dates," Rae answered and quickly raised the window so that Bo wouldn't slap her on the shoulder.

"Is Miz Bo sick?" Daisy asked.

"Is she going to be at our Christmas program?" Heather's voice quivered.

"She's fine," Rae answered, and reminded herself to be

careful what she said in front of the girls. "Do you have any last words for the house you're leaving behind?"

Daisy shook her head. "I'm glad we are leaving."

Heather turned around and waved. "Bye, house."

Rae took her place in the long line of trucks going through town. Just yesterday the parade looked very different with all its fanfare, music, and even Santa Claus. "What about going to the new school on Monday? You thought you'd have a couple more weeks at the Nocona school, but with your aunt Rosie getting sick with the flu, you wouldn't have an after-school sitter."

Heather let out a long sigh. "You'll be there, won't you?"

"Yes, I will," Rae assured her. "Your dad has already gotten you enrolled, and he will take you, and you will come to my room after school."

"Will you be waiting for us at the door when we get there?" Daisy asked.

"I can do that," Rae agreed.

"Okay," Daisy said and then like most kids changed the subject completely. "Daddy said there's bunny rabbits that hop around outside our new house. Did you see them?"

Rae made the turn on the farm road heading north. "I did see them. You'll be living in the country, and you'll see lots of animals and birds." Those first weeks that the family had lived at the Paradise had been an adjustment from living on a street with several other houses. To have so much room to run and play hide-and-seek, to be able to sit on the porch and have time alone seemed like heaven.

"Are we there yet?" Heather asked after a few minutes.

Rae had asked her mother the same thing when she loaded up seven little girls and went grocery shopping in Nocona once a week, and she also remembered Mary Jane's answer and used it as she turned on the radio that played country Christmas songs from Thanksgiving until after the holidays.

"We'll be there in three more songs," Rae told them.

Daisy began a head wiggle to Blake Shelton's song "Up on the Housetop."

The song ended and the DJ announced that someone had called in a request for another song by Blake. "I wouldn't want to disappoint anyone at Christmastime, so here it is."

"I know this one," Heather squealed, and sang along to "Let It Snow! Let It Snow! Let It Snow!"

"Do you think it will snow at our new house?" Daisy asked.

"Bo told me there were a few flakes this afternoon," Rae answered. "We never know until Christmas gets here. Last year, we had a really big snowman over at the Paradise."

"This is the third song," Heather said when the fiddle started the music for "Two Step 'round the Christmas Tree."

"Daddy likes this song," Daisy said. "He taught me and Heather the two-step. Do you think you and Daddy will dance at the Paradise party? Queen Bernie said we could come to the party and sit by her."

"We'll have to wait and see." Rae made the turn down the gravel road that led back to the winery. At least she wouldn't be fighting a gray dust cloud once she started down the rutted path from there to the house.

"Is that a store?" Heather pointed at the Brennan Winery building.

"No, that's where Ophelia and Jake make wine," Rae answered.

"Yuck!" Daisy said. "I like beer better than that stuff."

Rae was so shocked that she almost choked. "When did you drink wine or beer?"

"Daddy likes a beer and sometimes he leaves a little in the bottle," Heather answered. "So, we tasted it."

"One of his girlfriends liked wine, and when she left, we tasted it," Daisy said. "Heather liked the wine best, but I liked the beer."

The orneriness has not been tamed yet, Rae thought.

"There it is," Daisy squealed when she could see the house. "It really is way, way in the country. I love it."

She and her sister had unbuckled their seat belts, hopped out of the truck, and beat Gunner to the porch. Rae stepped out to hear them both urging him to hurry up and get the door unlocked so they could get inside. She hung back, thinking that this should be his moment with his kids. He needed to be the first one to see the excitement on their faces when they discovered their bunk beds and the bathroom with two sinks. But he held on to the knob and motioned for her to join them.

"*Are you sure?*" she mouthed.

He nodded and she walked across the yard and put her hand in his outstretched one. "You'll want to see their faces too. Would you take pictures, please? Those you shot when the lights came on at the Paradise were amazing."

Daisy ran to Gunner and wrapped her arms around his waist. "Daddy, are we really going to live here?"

"Yes, we are." Gunner's voice sounded a little deeper than usual.

"Can we keep some of our books over there on the shelves by the fireplace?" Heather hurried across the room and made it a three-way hug.

"Of course, you can," Gunner answered and motioned for Rae to join them.

Rae slipped her phone into the pocket of her long denim skirt and wrapped all three of them in her arms.

"Thank you, once again," Gunner whispered.

"Someone open the door for us. We are bringing the sofa inside!" Remy yelled from the porch.

"You girls need to stand over there in the kitchen. The first piece of furniture is coming in. You don't want to miss this moment," Gunner said.

Rae broke free and held the front door open wide.

"Where do you want it?" Remy asked.

"Facing the fireplace," Gunner answered.

Daisy clapped her hands and ran into the kitchen. "This is like Christmas."

Heather followed her sister and peeked out over the island separating the kitchen and living areas. "Are we going to put up a tree? Did you tell the real Santa that we moved? What if he can't find us out here in the country?"

"We'll put up our tree this week. Santa told me that he already knows just where this place is." Gunner helped get the sofa positioned.

"Can we see our rooms now?" Daisy asked.

Remy laid a hand on Gunner's shoulder. "Go with them to see their rooms. That's a memory you'll want to keep."

"But…" Gunner started to argue.

"We can bring in boxes by ourselves for five minutes," Remy assured him.

"Thanks, man," Gunner said and turned to the girls. "Of course you can, and then you can start unpacking your toys and books."

Rae ran ahead to the end of the hallway and took pictures of them tearing down the hallway with their daddy right behind them. No doubt, the pictures would be a little blurry, but pure joy was written on all their faces. Rae videoed the squeals and expressions when they went into the first room and saw the set of bunk beds, and then they dashed off to find an identical setup in the next bedroom.

"Which one is mine?" Heather asked Gunner.

"They are identical, so y'all decide," Gunner answered, "but you have to do it quickly, because I'll bring in your boxes in just a couple of minutes. Once you decide, then you can't change your mind or argue about it."

"I don't care which one I get," Daisy said. "Miz Rae, will you help us unpack?"

Rae put her phone away and nodded. "Yes, I will. Let's

work together and put together one at a time. Who gets the first one?"

Daisy raised her hand.

Heather pointed at her.

"That was easy. Why did you make that decision?" Rae asked.

"I want the one closest to the living room, so I can hear Santa when he comes to leave our presents. I want a bike, and he'll make lots of noise bringing that into our new house," Daisy answered.

"I want the other one because it's between Daisy and Daddy. If I get scared, they will protect me," Heather declared.

"Fair enough," Rae said. "Let's do Daisy's room first, and then move on to Heather's."

Gunner came in with three boxes in his arms. "These are all marked "Daisy". Where do they go?"

"First bedroom," Rae answered.

He set them down on the floor and raised a dark eyebrow toward Rae. "No arguing?"

"Nope."

"You must keep a supply of miracles in your pockets," he said above the girls' chatter.

"Not miracles, but maybe a little of Queen Bernie's miracle dust. She likes to share it during the holidays—especially when it comes to the twins." She grinned.

"What does the smell of popcorn remind you of?" Bo asked Maverick that afternoon when they were back in his apartment.

"You go first." He removed the bag from the microwave and carefully opened the end. Steam rolled out and the smell permeated the whole apartment. "What kind of memories does it bring to your mind?"

She carried two bottles of sweet tea across the room, eased down on the sofa, and kicked off her boots. "Movies in Nashville, when I had the time or finances to go to one, but in the past, it was movies at home on Saturday nights or Sunday afternoons. I loved those times even better than going to see something at the theater."

Maverick sat down beside her and fed her a piece of the popcorn. "I didn't go to a theater until I was a teenager."

"Why?" she asked when she had swallowed and taken a sip of the tea.

"We had a theater in our house, and Dad had enough contacts that he could get copies of current movies for me and Nana to watch. Truth is, we liked our old westerns better than the new ones anyway, so I didn't ask for many. Nana would make popcorn and sweet tea for herself. Chocolate milk for me," Maverick said.

"Good grief! Just how big was your house?" Bo gasped and took stock of the small apartment once again.

He picked up the remote and started the movie. "Not as big as an English castle, but considerably larger than places I've lived in the last few years."

"That narrows it down," Bo said.

"Big enough that we had an indoor heated pool, a tennis court, and stables. My mother loves her horses. I had coaches for swimming, tennis, and riding," he said. "I don't usually tell anyone all that. Some of what I learned has helped me along my journeys."

"Why? Because gold diggers would come out of the woodwork?"

"Pretty much, but mostly because when I do decide to settle down, I want the woman to love me, not my trust fund," he answered.

Bo wanted to ask why he was telling her, but the still, small voice in her head reminded her that by saying what he did, he would be moving on. He wasn't ready to put down roots in Montague County, so telling her about his background didn't matter. At best, whatever relationship they had before he packed up his truck and left for another adventure would only be a short-lived fling.

"That sounds like a smart move," Bo said. "Hey, the Paradise Christmas party is next Friday night. Do you think Dave might work until midnight so you could come to it? It starts at six and everyone usually clears out by eleven or so."

Maverick scooted over closer to her and slipped an arm around her shoulders. "I'll be there."

The tingly feeling of his touch chased down her backbone. "But you didn't even ask Dave, yet."

"He's told me repeatedly that I can have a day off—other than Sunday—and I've never taken one, so I'm sure he won't object. Besides, I can always turn in my two-week notice if he does. I've got a job offer, working in Wyoming at a little bar in Jackson Hole. They need a part-time bartender and piano player. You want to go up there with me? You could dress up in an Old West barmaid outfit and sing."

Bo looked up at him and seriously considered his offer for a moment. "Thanks for inviting me, but I'll stay here. Aunt Bernie would chain me to the barn floor if I even mentioned such a thing. Besides, I'm ready to put down roots, whether it involves a relationship or not. I don't know what I want to do with the rest of my life, other than I would love for it to include music, but roaming all over the world doesn't fit into it."

She realized at the last second that he was about to kiss her, and barely had time to moisten her lips before his mouth closed on hers. She leaned in closer to him and forgot all about the movie. She was playing with fire, but she didn't care about getting burned. She just wanted more kisses, and what they would lead to in the end.

———

Thunder rumbling off in the distance awoke Bo long before daylight the next morning. She slowly opened her eyes and propped up on an elbow to stare at Maverick sleeping next to her. She had no regrets about the amazing night they had had, but now it was time to walk away. Too many more and she really would have to listen to Aunt Bernie telling her repeatedly that she had told her so.

His dark lashes fanned out over his high cheekbones, and a strand of his long hair was across his beard. She gently pushed it back and brushed a soft kiss on his forehead. He wiggled but didn't wake up.

She eased out of bed, got dressed, and was putting on her coat when he finally roused and sat up in bed. "It's not even daylight, Bo. Come back to bed, and I'll make breakfast for us in a little while."

"I need to get home," she said and blew him a kiss.

"That's a long way to walk." He grinned.

Bo frowned, and then remembered that she didn't have a vehicle in Nocona.

Maverick tossed back the covers and slung his long legs over the side of the bed. "Give me a minute to get some clothes on, and I'll take you home. I wouldn't want Aunt Bernie to shoot me for making you hitchhike."

Bo couldn't take her eyes off him when he slipped on a pair of jeans, jerked a shirt down over his head, and stomped his feet into his cowboy boots. He could have easily posed as a male model for a nude painting class with all those bulging muscles and ripped abs. But if he ever did take on that job, the art teacher would do well to hand out drooling bibs to each student.

"Should we talk about last night?" Maverick asked a few minutes later as he escorted Bo out to his truck.

"It was great, and it was a one-time thing," she replied as she settled into the passenger seat and fastened her seat belt.

"Must not have been that great if that's the way you feel," he said when he slid in behind the wheel.

"I love chocolate," she said, "but if I eat too much, it makes me sick. Too much of last night will only end in me wanting what I can't have and give me a heartache. It's best to end it now and have the beautiful memory to hang on to for the rest of my life."

"If only…" he said and then stopped.

"Care to finish that sentence?" she asked.

"If only the timing was right, I could fall in love with you," Maverick finished.

"Right back at you, Maverick," she said with a long sigh, and a few tears fell on her heart even if they didn't stream down her cheeks.

Chapter 19

ENDORA AWOKE TO THE sound of thunder and couldn't go back to sleep, so she padded quietly over to Luna's old bedroom and laid her sister's wedding dress on the bed. Luna had said when she came out of the dressing room that she had found her dream dress. Endora had been more than a little jealous because it was the exact style she had looked at back when she was engaged to her ex-fiancé. Another clap of thunder startled her. Was nature itself telling her that it would be bad luck to start a marriage in a dress that she had wanted when she was in love with a different man?

"This is what had brought on the antsy feeling, isn't it?" She heard the front door open and then close, and hurriedly hung the dress back in the closet. She slipped out into the hallway and gasped when she saw Bo tiptoeing up the stairs.

"Are you just now coming home?" she asked.

"I am," Bo answered. "What are you doing up this early?"

"Thunder woke me," Endora answered. "My mind wouldn't shut down, so I got up and sneaked a peek at Luna's wedding dress. I can't wear it, and I can't carry her bouquet. I'm getting married in less than two weeks. What am I going to do?"

"They sell dresses every day." Bo looped her arm into Endora's. "Let's put on a pot of coffee and talk."

"Let's have milk and cookies instead. The smell of coffee will wake up everyone in the house. We can take it to the back porch. There's a storm coming, and I just hope and pray that what's in the sky isn't an omen of an even bigger tempest in the family."

"I agree," Bo said with a nod.

While Bo filled two tall glasses with milk, Endora grabbed a package of chocolate chip cookies from the pantry, and they eased out the back door onto the screened-in porch. Bo set a glass of milk on each of the small tables at the end of the swing.

Endora tossed a soft throw over at her sister, wrapped a second one around her shoulders, and sat down on the end of the swing. "We can watch the sun come up if this bluster goes around us. Am I crazy? There's a perfectly good dress I can wear, and I love it, but..."

"Spit it out," Bo said.

"It's the same style I looked at when I was engaged to Kevin," Endora said. "I might be starting off my marriage on a bad sign. I've felt like there was a storm coming for days now, and wearing that dress just might be..."

Bo pulled her phone from her skirt pocket. "Let's go shopping. We can order a dress, have it sent here in my name, and no one will put the pieces together. How about white velvet since you're getting married during the holidays?"

Even though it was pouring down rain and lightning was

putting on a show, Endora felt like a weight had been lifted from her shoulders and, more importantly, from her heart. "Yes! I love that idea, and we could make my bouquet from the extra poinsettias in the barn. I saw some gold ones out there that Mama picked up last year."

Bo handed the phone to Endora. "This site promises to deliver in two days. If you pick out something that needs altering, I'll take care of it."

"Just like that!" Endora snapped her fingers.

"Thank goodness for the internet," Bo said.

"And for a sister who is a seamstress." Endora pointed at a long sheath-style dress with a princess neckline and long sleeves. "I really like this one, but the ball gown is beautiful too. What do you think?"

"It's your decision, but as tiny as you are, all that velvet in the full skirt will be really heavy," Bo answered.

"Then the first one is what I want, and just like that, my problem is solved. I'm so glad that I caught you sneaking in after spending the night with Maverick," Endora said.

Bo ordered the dress, laid the phone on the table, and took a drink of her milk. "Problem solved. Dress ordered. Bouquet can be made sometime this week. Do you have shoes? And, Endora, last night was a one-time thing."

"Thank you, yes, I have shoes, and I thought he might be the one," Endora said. "You were so cute together on the float and when you entertained at the festival."

"I need to put down roots. He has to keep his wings to fly."

"Did you tell him that?" Endora asked.

"Maybe not in those words, but I let him know that last night wouldn't happen again," Bo answered.

"Does it hurt?" Endora asked.

"Like hell," Bo admitted.

Endora opened the package of cookies and handed one to her sister. "Anytime you want to talk, I'm here for you."

Bo took the cookie with one hand and wiped away a single tear with her free hand. "Will you remind me in my weaker moments that I can't have both roots and wings?"

Endora laid a hand on her shoulder and gave it a gentle squeeze. "I promise I will."

———————

Rae reminded herself at the close of the day on Tuesday that the kids were getting antsy because the holidays were right around the corner, but it didn't help the tension in her neck and shoulders. Coloring sheets hung on the walls and windows of her classroom—Santa Claus, ornaments, Christmas trees—all done mostly in the abstract way that kids from four to six could produce. Their parents would collect the pictures on Friday of the next week after the little Christmas program in the auditorium, and hopefully take them home to proudly hang on their refrigerators. Then she would have two weeks at home, and a new semester would begin.

She loved her job, but when that day was done, she was more than glad to walk her students out to the front of the school. Some got on buses. Some had parents waiting to whisk them away in vehicles. When they were all gone, she just wanted to prop up her feet and have a good cold beer, but that wasn't possible when two little girls were waiting in her classroom.

When she opened the front doors, she could hear yelling coming from her room all the way down the hallway. She did a fast walk and hoped she would get there before the twins started throwing punches. She was out of breath when she arrived to find Daisy and Heather squared off with their noses just inches apart, hands clenched in fists and expressions that dared the other one to make the first move.

"Whoa!" Rae said from the doorway. "Take a step back and then take a long breath."

The girls whipped around to focus their anger toward her.

Rae pointed to a desk in the front row. "Daisy, you take a seat right there, and Heather, you sit on the one on the other end of the row. We'll take a moment to cool down, and then we'll talk about whatever it is that has you both riled up."

Heather let out a whoosh of air so hard that she snorted. "Daisy says that Millie can't be my friend because she is her friend."

"She can have Jenny," Daisy snapped. "I don't like her."

Rae held up a palm and sat down behind her desk. "I said we are going to be very quiet for a little bit, and then we'll talk."

Too bad she didn't have some of that virtual magic dust she had told Gunner about a couple of days before. Yesterday had gone so well that Rae had patted herself on the back at the end of the day. She and the girls had gone to the house, and she had helped them with their homework. Then she sent them out to the front yard to play while she rustled up enough ingredients to make a chicken enchilada casserole for supper. Gunner had come in weary to the bone from all the weekend festivities and the move and given her a long passionate and lingering kiss.

"I appreciate this so much, Rae," he had said.

"I'm selfish," she had told him. "I wanted to see your face when the girls told you all about their first day at the new school."

"No problems?" he'd asked as he washed up at the kitchen sink.

She shook the memory from her head and said, "Daisy, why don't you like Jenny?"

"Because she's saying bad things to Millie because her boyfriend quit her to be Millie's boyfriend," Daisy said. "And Heather played with Jenny at recess, so I'm mad at her. I told her not to play with Jenny, and Heather is my sister, so she's supposed to listen to me."

Holy smokin' hell! Rae thought. These were first graders. They were not supposed to be thinking about boyfriends at this age.

"Well." Heather crossed her arms over her chest. "Johnny only likes Millie because she's rich and brings him candy every day."

This was beginning to sound like some of the domestic disputes that Rae and her partner had to break up during her time on the police force—and this was seven-year-old little girls, not grown adults fighting over a guy that wasn't worth a grain of wet salt.

"Do either of you have a boyfriend?" Rae asked.

"Yuck!" Heather's nose wrinkled in a snarl. "Boys are stinky."

"They are not," Daisy countered.

Heather threw a dose of stink eye across the room. "You should have to sit beside Johnny after recess. He smells like a wet dog. I don't know why Jenny or Millie wants to hold his old sweaty hand on the bus."

"Do you have a boyfriend, Daisy?" Rae asked.

Daisy shook her head.

"I'm glad," Rae said.

"Why?" Heather asked. "Don't girls grow up to have boyfriends so they can have babies?"

Rae had never appreciated her mother more than she did at that moment. "*Grow up* is the key term," she said in the most authoritative voice she could muster. "You should enjoy being little girls because once you are grown-ups, you can't go back and be a little kid anymore. You'll have all kinds of responsibilities, like working all day and paying bills and mowing the lawn and cooking and doing the laundry."

"Then I don't want a boyfriend," Daisy declared. "I don't like to do the dishes, and I hate dusting."

"Me neither," Heather said. "Jenny and Millie are both crazy if that's what having a boyfriend means."

"What Millie and Jenny do is their business, and if you

can't be friends with both of them, then don't be friends with either," Rae suggested. "Friends will come and go in your lifetime, but you'll always have your sister. So, don't let anyone come between you. Are y'all ready to go home now?"

"Yes, but I'm going to my room," Heather said. "I'm not over being mad at Daisy."

"That's fine," Rae said. "You can love someone and still be mad at them for a little while. Do either of you have homework?"

"No," Daisy answered. "Are you going to make supper again tonight? We liked it when we were all around the table and got to talk about our day."

"I can, but we don't bring arguments or fights to the supper table," Rae said as she ushered them both out of her classroom and locked the door behind them.

On Wednesday morning, Aunt Bernie actually came up to the office that Bo had set up in one of the vacant bedrooms and sat down in the rocking chair in the corner. "Those steps get steeper every time I climb them," she moaned in between bouts of catching her breath. "December is already nearly half-gone, and the party is just two days away. Gunner and the twins are planning to be here if he doesn't get called out for an emergency. But that's not why I punished my old knees by climbing those stairs."

"You better be careful, or you might not be up for line dancing at the party on Friday night," Bo teased and hoped that her aunt didn't ask anything about Maverick. "Do you want to talk about the party, or do you have some special instructions for the advice column?"

"No, and yes," Bernie said. "I saw how happy you were when you were singing on the float and then later at the festival. I'm holding you back, and I love you too much to do that. Vera has offered to help me with the advice column, so you are hereby as of this minute relieved of your job. Here is your severance package. I have asked Noah about renting the old store so that you can put in a place to give music lessons. He's agreeable if that's what you want to do. My passion was owning and running a bar, and I don't regret a minute of doing just that until my old knees got too bad to stand on my legs all that time every day. You need to find and follow your passion, and I know music is what you love."

Bo was both relieved and sad at the same time. "Aunt Bernie, that's a lovely idea, but who is going to come all the way to Spanish Fort to take piano, mandolin, or fiddle lessons?"

"With a little advertising and promotion, you might just be surprised," Bernie said. "Now, for the rest of this day, I want you to forward all the files over to Vera. I bought her a new laptop, and she's eager to get started. Besides, I can drive over to her house every morning, and we can take care of the advice column. Noah says you can pick up the keys anytime at the café. Go on down to the store building and see what you think. That little severance check should be enough to remodel it into a fine place."

She stood up and headed out of the room. "When you make your first million, put in one of those lift chairs so your mama and daddy won't have to climb up here when they have a houseful of grandbabies."

Bo hopped up from her desk and hugged Bernie. "I don't know what to say other than thank you."

"Thank you is good enough, but if you really want to put the icing on the cake, then stay away from Maverick unless he is willing to go into the music business with you right here in Spanish Fort. And honey, who would have thought people would drive all the way up here to eat at Tertia and Noah's café or get wine from Jake and Ophelia? Or for that matter, to stop in at Luna and Shane's little store for bait and picnic supplies? Spanish Fort is growing, and you can get in on the ground floor with your own business."

Bo gasped when she saw the check in the envelope. It wouldn't compare to Maverick's trust fund, but it was beyond enough to put some paint on walls and shelves to hold music books. She couldn't believe that Aunt Bernie had brought her the perfect idea that would help her to put down roots while she did something she truly loved.

She grabbed her phone from the desk and called Maverick. His voice sounded groggy when he said, "Hello."

"Did I wake you? I'm sorry. Go back to sleep," she said.

"No, I'm awake now. Have you changed your mind about going to Jackson Hole with me?" Maverick asked.

"No," she answered. "So, are you really going?"

"I told Dave to find another manager. I'm looking

forward to getting back into playing the piano even if it is part-time," Maverick answered. "I wish you'd come with me. Christmas in that part of the country is beautiful. We could be good together, Bo."

"Go out to the jukebox and play that old song 'My Elusive Dreams.' I'm afraid that following a nomad life would someday bring me nothing but regrets."

"I don't have to play the song, Bo. I've sung it in two-bit honky-tonks up in southern Oklahoma before," he said.

Bo understood the draw of following a dream to a place, but when would it end? When he was old and gray and too broken down to enjoy life anymore?

He is free to make his own choices, the voice in her head whispered. He would soon be the one with regrets if he tried to change to suit her.

"I understand," she said, "but I called you to see if you had time to drive up here and see where my next dream is taking me. I'd like to see what you think of what I have in mind."

"Anytime, darlin'. I'll be there in half an hour," he answered. "May I ask if this idea came to you in a dream?"

"Actually, Aunt Bernie came up with it, and it came in the form of a pink slip. See you in a little while. I'll be the one in the sweatshirt with Frosty the Snowman on the front, and I'll be waiting on the front porch," she said and ended the call.

She finished backing up all the files for Bernie's advice column and then sent them to Vera. A sense of relief and peace washed over her as she opened the balcony door and walked outside. She thought of the storm Endora mentioned when she looked up at the heavy gray skies that morning.

As if on cue, her sister came out of her room and stood beside her. "There's something in the air, like maybe snow," Endora said. "I hope that's what it is, and not this antsy feeling that the other shoe is about to drop."

"Everything is fine. You've got wedding jitters," Bo assured her. "Aunt Bernie fired me this morning. That could be the other shoe, but behind every dark cloud is a silver lining. She gave me some wonderful advice along with my pink slip and generous severance pay."

Endora rushed over to give Bo a hug. "I'm so sorry."

"Don't be. It's a blessing in disguise. My new job will take a while to get going, but I'm at peace with the idea. I'm going to rent the old store building from Noah and start giving music lessons."

Endora took a step back. "That is the perfect job for you, but I still see sadness in your eyes."

"Maverick is taking a job in Jackson Hole, Wyoming. He asked me to go with him. He'll be bartending some of the time and playing the piano when he's not doing that. I would wear an Old West type of costume and be a barmaid or else singing," Bo said with a sigh. "There is chemistry between us that I've never known before, and I would really enjoy that job."

"But?" Endora asked.

Bo focused on the cattle on Remy and Ursula's side of the barbed-wire fence. "But what happens when he gets antsy and wants to try something else? Will he ever settle down, or will I be constantly on the move? Mama told each of us to listen to our heart when we finished school and were ready to get away from Spanish Fort."

"And we did," Endora said with a nod. "Seems like sometimes our heart changes its mind, though, because look where we all are right now. You and Rae are the last of us to get your wandering days finished and come on home."

Bo turned toward Endora and forced a smile. "Who would have ever thought that an old brothel in a tiny little community could have such an impact on all of us?"

"Wouldn't you love to know what happened to the madam, Miz Raven, and those ladies of the night when the railroad went in? Mama wrote historical novels about the women, but that was when they lived here. Where did they go when the madam sent them away, and what did they do with the rest of their lives?" Endora wondered out loud.

"Maybe one of them married a preacher," Bo teased.

"And one taught piano lessons to little girls in another town," Endora said with half a giggle, and then shivered. "Maybe the spirits of those women are what has guided us."

"According to Mama, Miz Raven mentioned an upright piano being in the parlor. Maybe whichever woman played it is my muse," Bo said. "For now, let's get back inside. Maverick will be here any minute to go look at the old building with me."

"It's going to take some elbow grease and work, but it's the perfect size and layout," Maverick said as he followed Bo around the old store building. "In its prime, this front part was probably the actually general store, and the back was for storage."

"Do you really believe that people will drive all the way up here to take music lessons?" she asked.

The remodeling job looked formidable. Yet, with a little paint, clean windows, and a bright park bench on the front porch, it might all come together in time for a grand opening in the spring. For sure, the job would give her something to take her mind off Maverick Gibson.

"'If you build it, they will come,'" Maverick said.

"You stole that line from an old movie," Bo said.

He gathered her into his arms and held her tight against his chest. For a split second, she reconsidered his offer. The electricity between them dazzled, but regrets on either side would soon put out the fire like it was nothing but a flash in the pan.

"I'm going to miss you, Bo Simmons," he whispered.

"The memory of me will fade," she told him. "By the time you have two or three more adventures, you won't even remember my name."

"I will never, ever forget you."

"I will cherish the memories we've made." She smiled up at him.

"I will unpack them out of my virtual memory box every Christmas and think of you," he promised.

"And I'll be doing the same." She took a step back before she changed her mind and did something that wouldn't bring anything but more sadness in the years ahead.

Chapter 20

THE ANNUAL PARADISE CHRISTMAS party had everyone hopping for two whole days. The aroma of smoked ribs, brisket, and turkey permeated the whole area around the Paradise. Rae finished setting all the side dishes on the buffet tables at five thirty and raced upstairs to take a quick shower. She, Bo, and Endora passed each other in the hallway, but they barely had time to nod.

The shower finished, makeup applied, and a few curls put into her dark hair, Rae raced over to her bedroom and slipped into the long crimson-red dress lying on her bed. She picked up her shoes on the way out of the room and put them on when she reached the foyer at five after six. People were already milling about the living room with either a glass of sweet tea or a drink in their hands.

"Early birds," she muttered.

"What was that?" Luna asked as she came out of Mary Jane's office, which for that night would serve as a coatroom.

"As always, there are folks who get here early," Rae whispered.

"Country folks think you are late if you aren't fifteen minutes early," Tertia reminded her. "Not to worry, though.

Endora and Bo aren't down yet either. They've been whispering a lot lately. Do they have something up their sleeves? Are Bo and Maverick getting serious or something?"

"Don't get me to second-guessing what my twin sister or yours are up to," Rae said. "But last I heard Bo and Maverick want different things in life, so there's no hope there."

"That will make Aunt Bernie a happy woman," Luna said with a smile. "I hear car doors. Hey, before I take coats again, how are things with you and Gunner?"

"I'm going to find out tonight," Rae said. "I'm not sure if I'm a nanny, a cook, a tutor, or a girlfriend, but I'm going to figure it all out at this party and move on from there."

"What do you want to be?" Luna asked.

"I really, really like him," Rae answered.

"Good luck," Luna said on her way to answer the doorbell.

Daisy and Heather, dressed alike in cute little red-and-green-plaid dresses, stopped inside the foyer so quickly that Gunner almost ran over them.

"You look like a queen," Daisy said.

"Thank you, but don't tell Queen Bernie that." Rae bent down and whispered, "She's dressed up special for y'all tonight, and she's waiting in the living room, but first you give your coats to Luna."

They shucked out of their coats and handed them to Luna, then made a beeline to Bernie. Luna disappeared into the coatroom, and Gunner stood just inside the door without saying a word.

"Is something wrong?" Rae asked.

"Wow," he answered. "You look amazing. Will you wear that to the policemen's Christmas dinner we're having tomorrow evening?"

"Are you asking me on a date? If you are, who is going to keep the girls?" Rae asked.

He took a couple of steps toward her. "Yes, I am, and my folks have asked if they can have the girls this weekend. They have retired to a lake house up near Kingston, Oklahoma, and they're having all the grandkids come stay with them for a couple of days. Want to ride along with me? I'd love to have some time to talk to you alone, and it's only a little more than an hour's drive."

"Love to," Rae answered. "When do we need to leave?"

"Eight is soon enough," Gunner said, "but until then I want to steal glances at the most beautiful woman in the world."

Rae looped her arm into his. "Thank you, but I imagine a lot of guys in here would disagree with you."

"Then they need glasses," Gunner flirted.

Did a real date make her his girlfriend? Rae wondered. In all honesty, was she ready to have that label attached to whatever this was between them?

———

"It fits beautifully, but it does need to be hemmed," Bo said as she slowly walked around Endora, who was turning around to catch all the angles in the floor-length mirror of herself wearing her new dress.

"Can we shorten the front at ankle level and leave the back so that it makes a short train?" Endora asked.

Bo put the last straight pin in the front of the hem. "That sounds like a wonderful idea. But for right now, we had better get on down to the party or else they'll start sending people up here."

Endora ran a hand down the sides. "I love it so much that I hate to take it off."

Bo stood up and unzipped her sister's dress. "Still feel like there's a storm coming?"

"Not right now, but something is bugging me," Endora answered and stepped out of her dress. "It's that same feeling I got down deep in my gut when Kevin was cheating on me. Something isn't right yet, but this beautiful dress sure helps."

"One day at a time..." Bo said.

"Sweet Jesus," Endora finished the sentence.

"Amen," Bo said as she hung the dress in her closet. Later, maybe tomorrow afternoon, she would sneak upstairs and work on the hem. Maybe she wouldn't even wish that it was her dress like she was doing right then. "Your feeling shouldn't concern Maverick and me. That's not going to ever work out, so put your mind at ease."

Endora butted in before she could finish. "Maybe it's that I feel bad that you and Rae are having to jump over so many hurdles to find happiness when Parker just appeared on my doorstep."

Bo turned around and patted her sister on the shoulder.

"One of us has to be the old maid aunt, like Aunt Bernie. The one who looks out after the nieces and nephews and spoils them. Looks like I drew that straw."

Endora waved from the door and slipped out wearing nothing but underwear and a smile. "It ain't over until it's over," she whispered as she closed the door behind her.

Bo merely shook her head at the false hope her sister had for her and Maverick. Endora simply had a case of wedding fever. That happened when the prospective bride was so happy that she wanted everyone else to have the same emotion.

"Sorry, but this time it's really over," Bo said as she left her bedroom and headed to the party. She was halfway down the stairs when that prickly feeling on the back of her neck told her that Maverick was close. When she glanced down the stairs, his eyes locked on hers, and a smile broke out across his face. Her breath caught in her chest and her pulse jacked up several notches, but she couldn't blink. She could see the desire in his eyes as clearly as she had the night that they had spent together—when only the dim glow of the moon shined through the window and lit up the room.

His jeans were creased and stacked up just right over his boots. He wore a blue shirt under a western-cut sports coat. He held out a lovely bouquet of roses when she stepped off the bottom step. Their hands brushed when she took them from him, and she wondered if she would ever again feel such an acute attraction to another man.

"You are a picture for sore eyes," he whispered.

"Right back at you," she said. "Thank you for these. They are lovely. Come on out to the kitchen and we'll put them in water."

"I wanted to bring you a going-away present," he said as he followed her.

"I'm not going anywhere," she said and then realized what he had said. "When?"

"First thing tomorrow morning," Maverick answered. "Dave's old manager got laid off at the boot place, and he's ready to come back to the bar. He's taking over tonight. I'm packed and ready to roll at daylight. I figure if I drive hard and don't run into too much snow, I can be in Jackson Hole by Monday."

Bo swallowed both the lump in her throat and the disappointment as she filled a quart jar with water and put the roses in it. "If that's the case, let's enjoy this party. Can I get you a beer or would you rather have a shot of whiskey? Name your poison."

"Beer is good, and Bo, you can always show up on my doorstep tomorrow morning with a suitcase in your hand," he said with one of his mesmerizing smiles.

"And give up having my own business teaching music and voice lessons?" She tried to keep her tone flirty, but it sounded a bit flat in her own ears. "Thanks for the invitation, but I've got my heart set on remodeling the old store and helping the rest of my family bring Spanish Fort back to its former glory."

Maverick took another step forward and tipped up her

chin with his fist. "I've always said that love at first sight was something that only happened in those paperback romance books, but you almost made me change my mind."

His lips found hers in a string of kisses that left her knees feeling like rubber. She was panting and it was hard to breathe. She took a couple of steps back when she heard Bernie's voice over all the commotion of the party.

"Well, well, look what we found in here, girls," Bernie said when she saw Maverick and Bo.

"Pretty flowers!" Daisy squealed. "I love red roses."

Bo pasted on her best fake smile. "So, do I. They're a going-away gift from Maverick. He's going to Wyoming tomorrow."

"I thought he was your boyfriend," Heather said.

"Just a friend," Bo said.

"We came in here to find some more forks for the buffet table," Bernie said with the biggest smile Bo had seen on her in a long time.

"They're in the pantry," Bo answered and then turned her focus back to Maverick. "Are you ready for some of the best smoked brisket you've ever had?"

"Yes, ma'am." He slipped his hand in hers and let her lead him out to the dining room where the food was laid out.

He picked up a plate and loaded it. "Your aunt Bernie looked happy."

"Yes, she did."

Daisy hopped up into the back seat of Gunner's truck and fastened her seat belt. "Queen Bernie danced with both of us girls, but, Daddy, you forgot to dance with Rae."

Gunner held the truck door for Rae. "I promise I will dance with her at the policemen's party on Saturday."

"But we won't get to see you," Heather complained.

"Then sometime next week we will dance in the kitchen so you can see us," Gunner promised.

The whispers that started behind Rae sounded like a hive of bees buzzing. From past experience of back when she was a little girl, she figured that if she and Gunner started their important conversation, the little ears in the back seat would perk right up. Nothing got past Daisy and Heather.

To prove that the world might change—technology had definitely changed, but nosy little girls did not—she whispered, "I forgot to ask how things were going with Millie and Jenny at school."

"Johnny broke up with Millie because she didn't bring him any candy yesterday," Daisy said.

"He is Rita's boyfriend now," Heather added. "And Millie and Jenny are our friends."

Gunner raised an eyebrow.

Rae slid a sly wink his way. "Those are all kids in Heather and Daisy's class at school. There was a love triangle between Millie, Jenny, and Johnny, but it's all settled now that he is Rita's boyfriend."

Gunner rolled his eyes. "In the first grade?"

Rae nodded.

"Rita is in the second grade," Daisy announced loudly, "but she's real bossy. Johnny won't break up with her."

"Why?" Rae asked.

"She'll whoop him all over the playground if he does," Heather answered and whispered something to Daisy.

"Is this for real?" Gunner asked.

Rae nodded again. "And little corn has big ears."

"Corn don't have ears," Daisy giggled.

"I believe you just proved that point." Gunner turned east on Highway 82. "Are y'all excited to get to see your cousins?"

"Yes!" They chorused together.

"Are they all about your age?" Rae asked.

"Nope," Heather answered.

"They're all older than us," Daisy said.

"I'm the baby of the family. My older sisters are ten and twelve years older than I am. They each have two daughters whose ages range between twelve and sixteen," Gunner explained. "Daisy and Heather love to spend time with them."

"Everyone is already there but us." Daisy sighed. "We're going to make Christmas cookies and decorate Nanny and Poppa's tree for them."

"And put puzzles together," Heather said.

"Sounds like a fun weekend." Rae had been nervously thinking about the conversation she and Gunner would have and getting to spend a little while with him alone. That she would be meeting his parents and possibly part of his family didn't dawn on her until she saw a sign that said Kingston was only seven miles away.

She was definitely overdressed since she hadn't taken time to change after the party. The girls had begged to stay just "ten more minutes," and then another five, so they had gotten a late start. Hopefully, his folks wouldn't think she was putting on airs. She was still worrying when they crossed a very long bridge over Lake Texoma and made a hard right turn.

"We're almost there," Daisy squealed.

Heather pointed to a two-story split-log cabin with lights shining out the windows. "There's the house."

"That looks like a model for a Thomas Kinkade painting," Rae said.

"Thomas's last name is Dally, not Caid," Heather said.

"I'm proud of you for remembering your classmates' names," Rae told her. "But I was talking about a grown-up man who is a famous painter."

Gunner parked behind the last of three cars in front of the house. "Remember that calendar that you girls like? The pictures on it were painted by Thomas Kinkade."

"Yep, Nanny's house does look like one of them paintin's," Daisy agreed.

"Were you raised here?" Rae asked.

"Yes, I was. My folks sold their place in town and bought this house before I was born," Gunner explained as he got out of the truck.

The twins had already opened the door and were inside

by the time Gunner helped Rae out. "We'll only stay a few minutes. Our little corn won't be in the back seat to listen to every word we say on the way back home."

Two words stuck in her mind as Gunner escorted her into the cabin—*our* and *home*. In some respects, Daisy and Heather did belong to them both since Rae was basically their babysitter. But after only one week, Gunner felt comfortable enough in his new place to call it home, which meant that—unlike Maverick—he was content.

"Mama and Daddy, this is Rae Simmons. Rae, meet my folks, Glenda and James Watson." Gunner made introductions as soon as they were inside the house.

"Pleased to meet y'all," Rae said.

"I told you that she was as pretty as a princess," Heather said. "Can we go put our pajamas on now and have hot chocolate and doughnuts?"

"Yes, you did, and yes, you can," Glenda said. "These are the other four of our half-dozen granddaughters, Tally, Irina, Emily, and Mischa."

The girls all waved and headed upstairs with the twins.

"They don't get to see each other often. Emily and Mischa live in California, and Tally and Irina in Tennessee," Glenda explained. "Y'all come on in and sit a spell. Can I get you a glass of sweet tea?"

"No, Mama, we should get back home, but we'll have time to visit when you bring them home Sunday evening," Gunner answered.

"I understand," James said. "Y'all be careful."

Glenda crossed the room and hugged Gunner. "It's always good to see you, Son, even if it's only for a few minutes." Then she turned around and hugged Rae. "I'm so glad you came with him. The twins are right. You are beautiful, but even more than that, they love you."

Rae returned the hug. "Thank you. I love them too. But I'm not always dressed up like this. We came straight here after a Christmas party."

Gunner opened the door and stepped outside. "See you Sunday."

James followed them out onto the porch with his wife right behind him. "The girls were really excited about going to a big-people party."

"They FaceTimed with us last night and were bouncing off the walls," Glenda said and waved from the porch until Gunner had helped Rae into the truck.

"Now, we can talk," he said when he had made the first turn.

"About?" Rae asked.

"Us and where this is all headed," Gunner answered.

"You go first."

Gunner did not hesitate. "I've argued with myself since I first met you in Saint Jo. I've never felt such a strong attraction to a woman, and I felt guilty because I didn't have that for Stacey. Don't get me wrong. I loved my wife, and I was devastated when she died. But this chemistry I feel with you is something deeper. Maybe it's age. Maybe it's something else." He hesitated a few seconds before he went on. "I've been afraid that your patience with my daughters was what I was feeling, but…"

Rae laid her hand on his shoulder. "I know what you're trying to say, but there are no words to really describe it, are there?"

Gunner shook his head. "Stacey used to tell me that I was as romantic as a rock. I probably shouldn't be talking about her when I'm trying to explain things to you."

"Stacey is the girls' mother and was a major part of your life," Rae told him. "They need to remember her, and they can't do that if you don't ever mention the good times y'all had together."

"Do you know how amazing you are?"

She gave his shoulder a gentle pat and then moved her hand back into her lap. "That would depend on who you ask. Now it's my turn. I do not believe in all that love-at-first-sight stuff, but I do believe in Christmas miracles. What we have could very well be one of those."

"Then I'm glad that our paths didn't cross until now, right during the holidays," he said with a grin.

"Me too, because I've fought the same battles you have. Was what I felt for you because I loved your girls, or was it real? Did I really want to start a relationship with a cop after being on the force and seeing what kind of job it is?"

"What are the answers to those questions?" Gunner asked.

"This thing between us has nothing to do with the children, and yes, I do want to have a relationship with you. I understand what a stressful job you have, and I want to be there for you," she answered honestly. "And honey, I will never say a derogatory word about Stacey to the girls, but she was dead wrong about you not being romantic."

"Well, thank you."

Gunner stopped the truck on the side of the road, got out, and jogged around the front end. He opened the passenger door and held out a hand. Rae wasn't sure what was going on, but she unfastened her seat belt and put her hand in his. He drew her close to him, cupped her cheeks in his hands and kissed her.

Like always, she left the world behind when his lips met hers in a steamy hot, fiery kiss. One minute she was floating somewhere in a place where her only thoughts were on Gunner. The next, she was standing on solid ground with a police car's flashing lights behind her.

"Y'all having car trouble?" The policeman yelled as he walked toward them.

"No, sir," Gunner answered. "I just wanted to kiss my girlfriend and didn't think it was safe to do so when I was driving."

"Well, then." The older man laughed. "You've got that job done, so it would be best if you get on down the road."

"Yes, sir." Gunner chuckled.

Chapter 21

"Turn out the lights; the party's over," Bo muttered as she walked Maverick out to his truck after the party that evening.

"You sang that on the stage at Whiskey Bent," he said with a smile.

"And you played the piano. Our band was good while it lasted, but alas, all things must come to an end eventually." She hated that old adage, but it was the absolute truth that evening.

"They don't have to, but in some cases, they do," he argued. "You can still come with me, Bo, and our Whiskey Bent Band can live on and on throughout the ages and adventures."

"I could, and we might be happy for a while, but my heart tells me I would have regrets eventually." She looked up at the stars in the sky and blinked away the tears. "I hate goodbyes."

He opened his arms. "Me too. I don't want to leave you, but my heart tells me it's time to go."

She walked into them, closed her eyes, and laid her cheek against his chest. "Let's don't say goodbye. Let's just say, 'See you later, and if you ever get an itch to come back to this area, call me.'" She had a lump in her throat but knew fully well they were simply trying to avoid facing the end.

Maverick brushed a gentle kiss on her forehead. "See you later."

"Maybe." Bo turned and walked away before he could say anything more. She didn't look back but went straight to the barn and slipped inside through the side door. She sat down on an old ladder-back chair, buried her head in her hands, and let the tears flow freely. Saying goodbye or even *see you later* was tougher than admitting that her dream of being a big Nashville star was dead in the water. When there were no more tears, she scolded herself for acting like a lovestruck teenager who had just broken up with her boyfriend. Maverick had been a flirtation that ended in a one-night stand. He was gone, and it was time she moved on to the next phase in her life—whatever that might be.

She remembered a meme she had seen on TikTok that said: "When in doubt, look up." She raised her eyes and stared out a dirty window. The stars were nothing but smeary little things up in the dark sky. The waxing moon didn't give much light, but there was a tiny sliver around one edge.

The light represents the memories I made with him, she thought. *If I was still in Nashville and trying to write songs...*

Before she could finish that thought, the words to "Goodbye Time," a Conway Twitty song that Blake Shelton covered, came to her mind. The lyrics said that if being free was worth what a person left behind, then it was goodbye time.

"No sense in writing that song," she said. "It's already been written, and now I'm feeling what those words meant."

It ain't over 'til it's over. Endora's words came back to her mind.

She was still sitting there, still staring out the window and replaying every single moment—all the bantering, the flirting, and even the goodbyes that she and Maverick had shared. She slipped her phone out of her hip pocket and looked up the word *maverick*. One of the definitions described an independent person who did not go along with everyone else. Then she noticed the time: four thirty in the morning. She had sat in that chair for hours.

"His nana named him right," she said as she stood up and stretched the kinks out of her body. "But I've grabbed the bull by the horns, spit in his eye, and I'm still alive," she told herself.

The sun was nothing more than the promise of a nice day as it cast the first rays of light over north central Texas. Bo didn't really care early that morning if there was sun, snow, or even a thunderstorm. Life would go on, and she would get over the pain, just like she and Rae did the chicken pox when they were kids. She had made it to the back porch when she heard a vehicle coming down the lane. Her heart skipped a beat. The sound was definitely a truck, and for that solitary moment she thought perhaps Maverick had changed his mind.

Her hopes were dashed when Gunner and Rae got out of it. Rae was still wearing her party dress. It didn't take the intelligence of a rocket scientist to know that it didn't take all night to drive fifty miles and back, or to figure out that she and Gunner were most likely a couple now—especially when he walked her up to the door and kissed her good night.

"Hey," Bo called out when Rae reached the back porch. "Are you sneaking in?"

Rae stopped and smiled. "Looks like you are doing the same thing."

"Yes, but from that grin on your face, it looks like you didn't spend the time sitting in a straight-back chair, wallowing in memories and misery."

Rae sat down on the swing and patted the place next to her. "I'm sorry, Sister. What happened?"

"Maverick is probably on his way to Wyoming right now," Bo answered with a long sigh. "My mind says for me to pack a bag and go with him. My heart says that's the wrong thing to do."

"Which wolf are you feeding?" Rae asked.

Bo remembered Joe Clay telling them the story about the two wolves. One was mean and hateful and very ugly. The other one was a sweet wolf, kind to others and loved to romp and play. One had to die, but one could live. The one that a person fed was the one that would survive, and each sister had to choose which one they would feed.

"The one that controls my heart, but it wasn't easy," Bo answered.

"Gunner and I are officially in a relationship that goes beyond being a babysitter. I'm glad that I didn't have to make the decision that you did," Rae said.

"Do you know what life is?" Bo asked and went on before Rae could answer. "It's a four-letter word, and you know what happened when we used that kind of language when we were kids."

"Yes, I do, but, darlin', so is love, and I have fallen in love with Gunner," Rae told her.

"I'm glad for you, but I'm jealous as hell too," Bo said.

Rae shot a smile her way. "I understand, and I won't even tattle on you for saying that particular cuss word."

"I'm happy you had a good night with Gunner while I licked my wounds. Did I do the right thing, Rae?" Bo asked. "I've still got time to pack a bag and go with him."

"What does your heart tell you?" Rae asked.

"That I came home to put down roots. I gave up my dream to be here. I should not be gallivanting off to Wyoming with a man that I've only known a few weeks. But, Sister, I hate it when you are right, and even more so when Aunt Bernie is," Bo whined.

Rae nodded. "I understand, but rest assured, she won't be strutting around like a little banty rooster because she was right about Maverick. She is still going to pitch a fit over Gunner. I'm not even going to try to keep our relationship a secret. She can just deal with it."

"Maybe her winning the battle and being right with me and Maverick will help soothe her temper. Besides, she gets two little great nieces who love and adore her in *your* deal," Bo said. "Let's go inside, get out of these dresses, and make some breakfast. Life—even if it is a four-letter word—goes on. But I mean it when I say that I'm happy for you."

"Thank you. Will you take up for me when Aunt Bernie pitches her fit?"

"Always," Bo promised.

Chapter 22

"Is it time? Is my hair bow straight?" Daisy was almost trembling with excitement.

"My mama says that Santa is coming after the program." Calvin puffed out his chest and dared anyone to disagree.

"My mama said that we have to keep our hands by our sides and not pick our nose," Annie added.

"My mama said that if I pick my underbritches out of my butt, Santa won't bring me presents," Donnie declared.

"I wish I had a mama," Heather whispered.

"Me too," Daisy whispered.

Rae's heart went out to the twins, and she blinked back tears. "Okay," she said around the lump in her throat. "If you are very quiet, you can hear the little children singing about Rudolph right now. Every seat is full out there, and you don't want your parents, grannies, and grandpas to say those kiddos did a better job than you, do you?"

Because Daisy and Heather shook their heads, the others did the same.

"Okay, now, just like we practiced," Rae said. "Go to your places. Remember what your mamas all told you. Don't fidget or pick your nose or pick at your underwear. Sing loudly, and when you are done, hold hands and take a bow. Then you can go sit with your parents."

"Why can't we curtsy like we do with Queen Bernie?" Daisy asked.

Rae stopped at the door leading out onto the stage and straightened shiny halos on each child's headband. "Because for today, you have to do things differently. Now, go on out there and make me proud."

"Can we pretend that you are our mama for today?" Daisy whispered.

"Yes, you can," Rae answered and watched from a crack in the doorway until her little group each hung an ornament on the Christmas tree while they sang "Jingle Bells." Sometimes Bo carried the whole song, but every child came in loud and clear when it was time to sing the chorus about riding in a one-horse open sleigh.

After they'd sang "Frosty the Snowman," they did a perfect bow. Rae smiled when Heather wiped her hand on her skirt when she dropped Calvin's hand. That was a good sign—boys were still yucky. When they had all run off the stage and were seated next to their families, Rae made a beeline out a side door, around the church, and into the fellowship hall.

She cleared the chairs from around one of the long tables and then hurried out to her vehicle and brought in a box. In a few minutes, a red crystal punch bowl took its place on a snowy white tablecloth. The second trip out to her truck netted a chocolate groom's cake. On the third one, she brought in the three-tiered wedding cake decorated with edible poinsettias dipped in sugar on the top and held her breath until it safely took center place.

Rae stood back and studied the arrangement for a few minutes, then decided that it needed something. She dug around in the first box and brought out a set of red candle-sticks and a couple of matching flameless candles. "Thank goodness I brought some extra stuff," she muttered as she set them on either side of the bride's cake and took a moment to take a couple of pictures.

That done, she raced back to her Sunday school room. She was panting when she rushed into the room where Endora waited for Rae to help her get dressed.

"Sit down for a few seconds and catch your breath. We've got at least fifteen minutes, and I can get dressed in five. I can't thank you enough for all this," Endora told her.

Rae handed her phone to Endora. "Take a look at your table and tell me what you think. I hope I didn't overdo it with the candles."

"Oh. My. Goodness!" Endora gasped. "It's beautiful!"

Rae didn't realize she was holding her breath until she let it out in a loud whoosh. "Okay, then, we are ready to get you dressed and to the front of the church without getting a spot of dirt on this white velvet. I'll carry the bottom, and you will go slow. Daddy is already waiting in the foyer. I had to tell him what was going on and he's in shock."

"Not as much as Mama will be," Endora said with a nervous giggle.

Rae removed the plastic bag from over the dress and took it off the hanger. "We're about to pull off the best-kept secret in Spanish Fort. People are going to talk about this for years and years."

"Why?" Endora asked.

"'The Girl Raised in a Former Brothel Marries the Local Preacher in a Surprise Ceremony.'" Rae held the dress for Endora to slip into it.

"That's too long a headline," Endora said. "Maybe 'Brothel Child and Preacher Marry.'"

"Much better," Rae agreed. "Now be still while I zip you up."

Bo played "Away in a Manger" and sang along with the choir. She stole glances at Ursula and Remy kneeling beside a manger that Joe Clay had built for the program. She couldn't see baby Clayton lying on a straw bed but knew that he was wrapped in a blue blanket that she had hemmed especially for the occasion. She envied both her oldest and youngest sisters that day. One already had a family started. The other was getting married and, if all went well, would probably have her own child to pose as baby Jesus by next Christmas. She had wallowed in self-pity for a week—telling herself that her one chance at love had vanished. Maybe it had, but like her mother had told her years ago, jealousy is a terrible thing that can eat away any happiness.

When the song ended, Shane, Noah, and Jake—the

three kings—entered the stage, and she hit the first chords for "We Three Kings." After that one was finished, Bo would only have to play one more, and then there would be a wedding. She smiled, not because all the envy had left her—that would take a while longer to get rid of. But she took pride and happiness in the fact that she had gotten to be a big part of Endora's secret.

Maverick startled her when he sat down on the end of the piano bench and nudged her. At first she thought he was nothing more than an apparition, a figment of her imagination. She didn't miss a note, but her breath caught in her chest when she realized that his hands were poised and ready to play. She lifted her trembling fingers, turned the piano over to him and let the choir sing without her. A ghost would not have been able to play, and it absolutely wouldn't have the ability to heat up her entire body by merely brushing his shoulder against hers.

"What are you doing here?" she whispered.

"Playing for you," he said. "Why aren't you singing?"

"You *are not* forgiven," she snapped.

"You *are not* singing," he said. "Can we please talk later?"

Bo blinked several times, but Maverick still didn't vanish. He was right there beside her—nine days after the Paradise Christmas party and the same amount of time since he left Texas for Wyoming. Nine days and nights of misery, and finally coming to terms and making peace with the fact that he was gone, never to be seen again. Was he just passing through? Did the job in Jackson Hole not work out after all?

Why? What? How? No answers came floating down from the church rafters to the questions that bombarded her mind as she and the choir sang the last verse and chorus of "What Child Is This?"

Silence filled the church, and Parker took his place behind the lectern. "This has been a wonderful program and a great turnout, but it's not over yet. If you'll just keep your seats for a few more minutes, we have one more event today. Your former pastor has joined us, and he will take it from here." Parker stood to the side, and an older man with gray hair and wire-rimmed glasses left the front pew and slowly made his way to the lectern. He took the microphone from the stand and stood in the center of the stage.

"Since Parker and Endora's friends and family are here, they have decided to get married today, and they have asked me to perform the ceremony," he said and nodded toward Bo.

"I guess you want to do the honors on this one?" Maverick asked.

"Yes, I do," Bo answered with a nod, and hit the first chords of "Mama He's Crazy," an old Judds song that Endora asked to be played as she walked down the aisle. Bo leaned into the microphone and sang the words about being afraid to let the man in because she wasn't the trusting kind. The lyrics could have been written just for Endora and Parker, especially when they said that he was crazy over her and thought she hung the moon and stars.

Bo didn't only sing the words but felt them when she sang about leaping before she looked. Maverick was sitting right beside her, and *if* he had come back to stay, Bo needed to look before she made a leap for sure. Her poor heart wouldn't take another nine days like she had just spent.

Rae threw the double doors open at the back of the church and the preacher motioned for everyone to stand.

———

"You are going to give your mama and Aunt Bernie a heart attack," Joe Clay said out the corner of his mouth.

Endora took the first step down the aisle. "But I'll be married and won't have to worry about all that planning."

"Yes, you will," Joe Clay agreed.

"Now she can focus on a wedding for Rae and Gunner, and good grief! Is that Maverick up there beside Bo?" She gasped.

"Looks like it," Joe Clay answered and stopped at the pew where Mary Jane was seated. Endora took a rose from her bouquet, handed it to her mother, and gave her a hug. "Be happy for me, Mama. I didn't want to wait until spring."

"Be happy," Mary Jane said.

Endora crossed the aisle to the other side of the church and handed Parker's mother a rose. Arlene hugged her and whispered, "Welcome to the family."

"Thank you," Endora said and tucked her arm back into Joe Clay's.

When they reached the place where the preacher and Parker were standing, Joe Clay took Endora's bouquet from her and handed it to Bernie. Then he put Endora's hands in

Parker's. "I'm not giving you this woman to be your bride. Her mother and I are sharing her with you. Be good to her."

"I promise I will love and honor her," Parker said.

"Everyone can be seated," the preacher said. "I understand that Parker and Endora have already said their personal vows to each other, so this will be short. Do you, Parker Martin, take this woman, Endora Simmons, to be your lawfully wedded wife?"

"I do, and that song was perfect. I am crazy over you," Parker answered.

Endora's eyes didn't leave Parker's. "I love you now and for always."

"I love you," Parker said.

"Looks like the vows weren't quite finished." The preacher chuckled and went on with the rest of the ceremony, ending with, "You may kiss your bride."

Parker did justice to their first kiss of their married life together, and then the preacher said, "I'd like to introduce for the first time Mr. and Mrs. Parker Martin. They would like to invite all of you to their reception starting right now in the fellowship hall. After dinner, Santa Claus will make an appearance and will bring presents to all the boys and girls, and there will be goody bags for the children to take home."

Bo hit a few chords on the piano, but Endora and Parker didn't make it past the first pew when Mary Jane grabbed them both in a fierce hug. "How on earth did you pull this off?"

"Rae and Bo helped me," Endora answered. "I didn't care about a big wedding. I wanted to be married."

"Well, darlin', you got your wish," Mary Jane said.

Bernie stepped up for the second hug and put the bridal bouquet back in her hands. "Does this mean I was your maid of honor?"

"Yes, it does," Endora answered.

"Where are you going for your honeymoon? You will be back in time for Christmas morning at the Paradise, won't you?" Ursula asked when she finally made it to get in on the congratulatory hugs.

"Honeymoon is going to be at the parsonage right here in Spanish Fort," Parker answered. "And yes, ma'am, we'll be there bright and early on Christmas morning. Right now, we should be getting into the reception room, though. Rae says we have a cake to cut for the pictures."

"I'm so shocked that photographs didn't even cross my mind," Mary Jane said. "Follow me. I'll lead the way."

Parker slipped his hand around Endora's waist. "You look like an angel today. I can't believe that we are really married, and I get to spend the rest of my life with you."

Endora tiptoed and kissed him on the cheek. "Remember the feeling you have right now when we have our first fight."

"Honey, I'm looking forward to it." He grinned. "You realize what comes after an argument since we vowed we would never go to bed angry."

"I do, and why argue? We can sneak off to the bedroom anytime we want," she whispered. "Want to ditch the reception and go right now?"

"Yes, I do, but…"

"Parker, I can't believe you and Endora did this"—his mother grabbed them both in a hug—"but we are so glad you did. Now we don't have to worry until spring about Endora changing her mind."

"Never!" Endora snuggled in closer to Parker's side. "This is forever."

———————

Bo waited until everyone was out of the sanctuary before she stood up, popped her hands on her hips, and narrowed her eyes at Maverick. "Now, what are you doing here?"

He ran his hand through his thick hair and frowned. "I am miserable. I can't sleep. I can't eat. When I played the piano at the bar up north, I had to swallow lumps in my throat. I know! I know!" He held up his hands. "Grown men don't cry, but I did. Everywhere I turned, I would see you, Bo. Every song I played reminded me of you. I dreamed of you every night and would wake up heartbroken that you weren't there beside me in the bed. I made a colossal mistake leaving here, and it wasn't until I was back in Nocona this afternoon that I started to feel peace again. That sounds corny, doesn't it?"

"A little," she said, "but it's still pretty romantic."

He reached out and took her hands in his. "Would you like a partner in the music business and to see where this thing between us goes? I don't deserve a second chance, but here I am, begging for one. I've never known this feeling, and I don't ever want to let it go again."

"Can I trust you to stick around and not get bored?" she asked, still wondering if she was dreaming. "Don't say yes if you don't mean it, and don't say yes if there's a remote chance you'll walk away from me again. I don't often give second chances, so…" She paused.

"I can say yes to both issues without blinking an eye," Maverick said. "I don't want to be away from you ever again if I have to feel like I have for the past nine long, long days and nights."

"Then yes, I would love to have a partner." She finally smiled. "And we'll go slow on whatever this is between us."

Aunt Bernie is going to pitch a good old southern hissy, the voice in her head shouted. *She's going to remind you daily that he ran away once, and he'll do it again.*

He stood up but didn't offer to hug her. "I've had a lot of time to think about things on the two-day drive back down here. One of the jobs I've had was in construction. If I could park a travel trailer next to the old store, I could live there and work on the building. When you learn that you can trust me, maybe you'd even move in with me." He hurriedly said, "But no rush, and I'm not expecting anything soon, honest. I'm just asking for a chance."

"I can do that," Bo said, "and if you know how to hang drywall and make shelves, it will save us a lot of money, but this thing—this attraction between us—it has to go slow."

Maverick flashed a smile that threatened to make her underpants start crawling down around her ankles. Even though it was tough, she resisted. She looped her arm into his and led him into the fellowship hall.

"Is your Aunt Bernie in there?" he asked.

"Yep, but I'll protect you. That's what partners are for," she told him.

Chapter 23

THE MORNING AFTER THE wedding and Christmas program, Bernie came into the house like a tornado and plopped down on a kitchen chair. She crossed her arms over her chest like a child who didn't get her way on the school playground. "Get me a cup of coffee, and clean me off a space, Mary Jane, because I'm about to give your daughter a piece of my mind."

"Aunt Bernie," Bo started.

Bernie held up a palm. "What in the hell—I mean, devil—did Maverick think? Showing up like that, crashing Endora's wedding like he did."

"He was invited to the program a long time ago," Bo reminded her. "He had no idea there was going to be a wedding when he came to the program."

Bernie's finger shot up so fast that Bo was glad she was sitting across the table from her aunt. "But you invited him to the reception and the Christmas with Santa at the potluck dinner. That's on you, and I don't like this, not one bit."

"We are business partners," Bo explained. "He's buying the old store building from Noah, and maybe later, he'll build a house on the land behind it. For now, he's getting things arranged to park a travel trailer next to the store. Feel free to tell me that you told me so but remember this—he came back because he was miserable."

"You and Rae never did listen worth a damn," Bernie hissed.

Mary Jane pushed back her chair, filled a mug with coffee, and handed Bernie a spoon. "Aunt Bernie," she said in a soft voice, "I want to you to take a breath and a bite of this pie. You know how much you love chocolate. Now, think about the time when you won your bar in a poker game. What did your twin sister say about you moving into the ratty apartment in the back of the place or, for that matter, running what was a glorified beer joint on your own? Respectable women didn't do those things"—she paused—"or a lot of the stuff you did, but you didn't give two hoots and a holler what anyone thought."

"Your mama said I was a disgrace to the family," Bernie answered in a chilly tone.

"And?" Mary Jane asked.

"I told her that my life was mine, and I would live it however I wanted. I also told her that if I couldn't make a fair living in the bar, I would start charging for what I was giving away free in that ratty apartment," Bernie answered through clenched teeth. "That shut her up for a little while."

"That's right, and each of my daughters is going to listen to her heart and live her own life just like you did. If they make a mistake, we are going to be there to support them while they get over it. That's what families do." Mary Jane sat down and took a sip of her coffee.

Bo reached under the table and patted Mary Jane on the knee. "Thank you, Mama, and for the record, Aunt Bernie, I know that you just want the best for me and Rae. I love you for that and for all you've done for me personally since I came back to Spanish Fort. Most of all, I'm grateful that you have given me advice on my new career. I really believe I'm going to love teaching music, and…" She paused.

A smile tickled the corners of Bernie's mouth and her eyes twinkled. "And what?"

"My life is mine, and I'm going to live it the way I want to," Bo finished her sentence.

Bernie slapped the table. "That's my girl!"

The noise startled the cats that had been sleeping in the warm morning sunrays coming through the window and sent them running toward the foyer. Pepper jumped up from under the table and had trouble getting traction on the tile floor, but finally slid out of the kitchen on his belly.

Bernie pushed back her chair. "You are welcome, and when—not *if*—you need help on how to tame that wandering man you seem to have your heart set on, you know where to come. After all, I run a romance advice blog. Now, I've got to go make sure Pepper hasn't had a heart attack. Carry on with *your* life."

"Yes, ma'am. I will do that, and thank you again," Bo said.

"Anytime, darlin' girl, anytime." Bernie patted her on the shoulder on her way out of the room.

Bo swiped a hand over her forehead in a dramatic gesture. "Thank you, Mama!"

"Once a mother, always a mother, and nobody messes with a mama bear's cubs, even if they *are* grown," Mary Jane said.

Rae came into the kitchen, slumped down into a chair, and took a sip of the lukewarm coffee Bernie had left behind. "What was that noise? I bet Endora heard it all the way at the parsonage."

"Aunt Bernie and I had a come-to-Jesus talk," Bo answered.

Rae covered a yawn with the back of her hand, carried the coffee to the sink, and poured it out. "Who won?"

"With Mama's help, we came to an understanding that left her with her pride and me with my sanity," Bo answered.

Rae sniffed the edge of the coffee cup and chuckled. "She had some reinforcements before she left her trailer. I can smell weed a mile away, and she left a little residue on the edge of this mug," Rae said and changed the subject. "Can you believe our baby sister is waking up a married woman this morning? I'm more than a little jealous, which brings me to a question, Mama. If—and I'm not rushing anything—things were to work out for Gunner and me, how are you going to feel about step-grandchildren?"

"Rae, there is no such thing as 'step' anything. Joe Clay told me that the day we got married. You girls were his daughters as well as mine, and he was your dad. If things work out for you and Gunner, then Daisy and Heather will be my granddaughters. Some grandchildren you get with a birth certificate. Some you get with a marriage license. It's all just worthless paper. What's in the heart is what matters, and I already love those little girls."

"Can I grow up and be just like you?" Bo asked.

"No, but you can grow up and be better than me," Mary Jane answered.

"Impossible," Bo and Rae chorused together.

Chapter 24

"GOOD MORNING, HANDSOME HUSBAND. Please tell me that it's another week until Christmas day," Endora said as she opened her eyes to find Parker propped up on an elbow staring at her. "I want more time with just the two of us."

Parker strung kisses from her eyelids to her lips. "Me, too, but I sure don't want to get on your mama's bad side, or Aunt Bernie's either for that matter."

Endora said, "Then we'll go, but we're leaving before supper. And darlin', you don't have to worry about Aunt Bernie. She was pretty upset at Bo and Maverick, and Rae and Gunner weren't far behind them. We should be good for several months."

He slipped an arm under her and drew her close to his side. "That would be pushing it, sweetheart. I'll be officiating at their weddings in the spring, or maybe early summer. Rae might wait until after school is out, but Bo is a wild card. She will probably be the one who elopes."

"We've got a whole hour before we have to be at the Paradise to open presents and have breakfast with the family.

Got any ideas about what we might do with that time?" she teased.

"Maybe one or two." Parker grinned.

———

Bo slipped down the stairs before the sun came up on Christmas morning. She curled up on the sofa, stared at the tree with all the presents under it, and let the past twenty years play through her mind. From the first Christmas they had at the Paradise, Joe Clay would have moved heaven and earth to get each of the girls what they wanted. She was always, always the first one down that morning, and there would be one big present under the tree from Santa and nine wrapped gifts for each of them. Three from Joe Clay and Mary Jane, because baby Jesus had three presents—gold, frankincense, and myrrh—and one from each sister to the other six.

"Are you thinking about the ghosts of Christmas past?" Rae shoved Bo's feet off the sofa and sat down beside her.

"Yes, and maybe a little of the Christmas future," Bo admitted. "Where do you think we'll be on this very morning one year from now?"

"I hope that I'm living in the house with Gunner. I would move in this afternoon, but he's old-fashioned enough to want to be married before that happens, so we don't set a bad example for the twins. What about you?"

"I'm hoping that Maverick and I are together. I figure if we can survive remodeling the old store and staying in a small travel trailer together, then we should be ready to build a house," Bo said. "I would never, ever tell Aunt Bernie, but something Endora said has made me a little antsy."

"And that is?" Rae asked.

"She told me that she could feel a storm coming," Bo answered.

Rae tucked a strand of dark hair behind her ear. "I hope her prophecy doesn't mean the storm is between me and Gunner. Maybe she just had a dose of pre-wedding jitters."

Bo shook her head. "She was pretty adamant about it, so I don't think so."

"It has to be one of us," Rae said, "and thinking of us being the only two left living here, you do realize that no one else is going to come down the stairs?"

Bo shook her head again. "Every year we all came home for Christmas. Rain, snow, or the threat of a tornado couldn't keep us away from the Paradise on this holiday. Doesn't seem quite right that there's just two of us, does it?"

"Nope," Rae agreed. "But rest assured Aunt Bernie and the other five will be here before the cinnamon rolls are ready. Then it'll be noisy and chaotic like always."

"And sometime before dinner is served, Gunner and the girls and Maverick will join us to add to all the confusion," Bo said.

"Do you think that by next year, they'll be here at gift opening and breakfast, too?" Rae's tone had a wistful sound to it.

"We can hope," Bo answered. "I hear a car door. Want to bet which one it is?"

Rae leaned over to peek around the tree and out the window. "Five dollars on Tertia and Noah."

Bo slapped her on the shoulder. "You can't cheat. I've got five on Ursula and Remy. Baby Clayton gets them up very early."

Bernie came in from the kitchen and yelled, "Merry Christmas, Ophelia and Jake." Then she looked over into the living room and said, "And to Bo and Rae too."

"I guess we both get to keep our money," Bo said and then raised her voice. "Merry Christmas to everyone!"

The living room looked like a paper factory exploded. Most of the gifts were set aside in bags marked with each person's name written on the side. Bo and Maverick were the only ones in the living room when he pointed to the mistletoe still hanging above the archway leading out into the foyer.

"Are we still just partners?" he whispered.

She shrugged. "What do you think?"

"I want to be more, Bo, but..." He let the sentence dangle as he moved closer to her.

Paper crunched under his feet and Sassy ran out of a gift bag. He jumped back and gasped. "That could be a mood breaker."

"Depends on how hot the mood is," Bo flirted. She wanted a Christmas kiss, and even more, she wanted to be more than partners.

He looked down at his feet, apparently making sure there

were no more cats to startle him, and took another step. "A couple of degrees hotter than hell. How about you?"

"Warm enough to melt that snow that's coming down outside," she answered.

Maverick moved closer and cupped her face in his hands.

"Maybe now ten degrees hotter than the devil's pitchfork." She moistened her lips with the tip of her tongue and closed her eyes.

His mouth closed over hers and the next few steamy kisses testified that she had not exaggerated one bit. If the doorbell hadn't rung when it did, she might have dragged him to her bedroom. The rule had always been that no boys were allowed upstairs, but she would rather have faced the consequences than have to fan her face all afternoon.

"Do you need to answer that?" Maverick's warm breath turned loose another rush of raging hormones.

"Someone else can," she answered.

"They are all out in the backyard taking pictures of baby Clayton's reaction to his first snow," Maverick reminded her.

She took a few steps back, blew him a kiss, and went to the door. If this was one of the twins playing a trick, they were going to get a piece of her mind—and it would not have a bit of sweet Christmas spirit in it.

Bo slung open the door and gasped. Standing before her a man who was the image of Joe Clay—at least the pictures of him when he was in his late twenties or early thirties. The same blue eyes, and dark hair, and stance even when he was just standing there waiting.

"Is this the Paradise?" he asked, his inflection and voice the same as Joe Clay's.

"Yes, it is. I'm Bo Simmons, and you are?" she asked.

"My name is Brodie Callahan. Could I please speak to…"

"Hey," Endora yelled from the kitchen and her voice got louder with each word until she was standing beside Bo. "We need you and Maverick to come outside for pictures. We're getting a white Christmas after all. My first one since getting married, and it's so beautiful." She stopped in her tracks and stared at the guy still standing on the porch.

"I'm sorry," Bo said. "Who do you want to talk to?"

"Joe Clay Carter," Brodie said.

"Why?" Bo asked.

Brodie removed his black hat and ran his fingers through his thick dark hair. "I'd really rather just talk to him."

"Not until you tell me why you are so eager to see him," Bo insisted.

"I want to meet him because he is my father," Brodie answered.

"Did you get lost, Endora?" Joe Clay hollered as he walked up to the front porch. "And who is our new guest?"

"He says he is your son," Bo answered, but her voice sounded hollow and weak in her own ears.

Brodie turned around slowly. "She always said that I looked just like you. I guess she was right. My mama was Jolene Baker. Evidently, y'all spent a weekend together about thirty years ago in San Antonio. I wanted to meet you, that's all."

"I remember Jolene very well," Joe Clay said, "but I didn't know about you. I expect you better come on in the house and meet the rest of the family."

"Are you sure about that?" Brodie asked.

"I am," Joe Clay said. "I'm in shock, but that seems to be the first step we need to take." He opened the door and ushered Brodie through the house and out the back door.

Bo blinked several times and shook her head. "You know that storm you were talking about, Endora?"

Her sister didn't seem to be able to do anything but nod.

"Well, darlin', I think it just arrived."

"Do we really have a brother?" Endora whispered.

"Looks like we do, whether we like it or not. You were the one who always begged for a baby brother. Merry Christmas to you!" Bo said.

Acknowledgments

As always, there are many people who have worked on this story from the time it was just an idea in my head, and they all deserve recognition. So, thank you to my agent, Erin Niumata, for everything she and my agency, Folio Management, have done to help put this series on the market. A huge thank-you to my editor, Deb Werksman, and Sourcebooks, for allowing me to write the stories. To all the copy editors, proofreaders, cover designers and folks behind the scenes whose names I don't know, please know you are appreciated. Without all of y'all, this would never be on the shelves. Also, a big thank-you to my family for all their support. Sometimes birthday parties and ball games have to wait when I have a deadline, and the family understands. Thank you once again to my husband, Mr. B, who has always been my biggest supporter. We lost him at the end of 2023, but I like to think of him still looking on and encouraging me to keep writing my stories. And to all my readers—y'all are awesome, amazing, fantastic, and the list could go on for pages and pages.

About the Author

Carolyn Brown is a *New York Times, USA Today, Wall Street Journal, Publishers Weekly,* and #1 Amazon and #1 *Washington Post* bestselling author. She is the author of more than one hundred novels and several novellas. She's a recipient of the Bookseller's Best Award, Montlake Romance's prestigious Montlake Diamond Award, and a three-time recipient of the National Reader's Choice Award. Brown has been published for more than twenty-five years. Her books have been translated into twenty-one foreign languages and have sold more than ten million copies worldwide.

When she's not writing, she likes to take road trips with her family, and she plots out new stories as they travel.

Website: carolynbrownbooks.com
Facebook: CarolynBrownBooks
Instagram: @carolynbrownbooks

Also by Carolyn Brown